THE GARDEN PLOT

An utterly charming English garden murder mystery

MARTY WINGATE

The Potting Shed Mysteries Book 1

JOFFE BOOKS

Revised edition 2023
Joffe Books, London
www.joffebooks.com

First published by Alibi, Penguin Random House in 2014

This paperback edition was first published
in Great Britain in 2023

Cover art by Sasha Alsberg

ISBN: 978-1-83526-075-3

To Leighton

PROLOGUE

He couldn't stay away. The thought of what lay beneath the earthen floor had consumed him for months. He'd let it slip only once, and at first he thought it wouldn't be noticed, but no luck. He'd been asked and asked until he shared details. Details led to plans, and plans led to grandiose dreams of fame and fortune; these had temporarily taken over his more sensible side. Now he had acquired a "partner" — an unwanted partner, one he wished with all his heart he could shed.

He stepped past the pots of faded pelargoniums — they certainly did need a gardener, he thought to himself, but why now? — and down the stairs. He let himself in quietly and pulled the door to, not wanting to risk another sound that might set the dog off. First morning light wasn't what it used to be — the autumn sun rose later and later, and on this day, fog dimmed the sun even more. He dare not switch on a light, and so he stepped carefully through the basement.

Up and out into the back garden, he stopped for a moment to make sure no one watched. Moving along the wall, he walked to the shed. He had been surprised to see the ivy cleared away. It made his task easier, but it made it easier for others, too, and that worried him. The fewer people who knew the real secret, the better. He'd already made one enormous mistake — he didn't want to make any more.

He wanted only to look again, perhaps dig a bit, just to feel as if he were doing something. If he could find one of the markers, he could use it as evidence that he was no amateur, but a professional who could find and recover new — old — pieces of history. He reached over and pulled one of the spades off the wall. He uncovered the mosaic again and then dug deeper. Water seeped into the hole, and he smiled to himself. Yes, he thought, you stay safe down there.

He plunged the spade in one more time and heard a metallic sound. Reaching down into the muck, his hand grasped the small treasure he sought.

"Digging? Have you reconsidered?"

He turned abruptly, not realizing he'd been followed. A wisp of fog trailed behind the speaker, like a ghostly companion.

"No, not really digging," he said, clutching the treasure in his hand while he leaned the spade up against the wall. "I told you, we can't disturb the place. This is too important."

"Important? To whom? Will you really let this slip away while the others take the glory — and the money — away from you? From us?"

It was the same argument, but only a trace of temptation remained, and he brushed it aside for good. He was finished with those thoughts, and turned to get his coat. He had just put it on when the spade came down on his skull.

Damson Hill Manor Farm House Gardens

> *2 Tumbly Hill Road*
> *nr Quedgeley, Cheltenham*
> *Gloucestershire*
> *GL2 5DH*

> *25 September*

72 Grovehill Square
Chelsea
London SW3

Dear Ms. Parke,

Further to our conversation on 30 August, I write to regretfully inform you that you have not been selected for the post of head gardener for Damson Hill Manor Farm House Gardens. Thank you for sharing with us your knowledge of the Arts & Crafts movement and William Morris's influence on garden design in the Cotswold landscape.

We appreciate your interest in this post and wish you well in your future endeavors.

Yours sincerely,
Lionel F. Arbuthnott, director
Damson Hill Manor Farm House Gardens
Charitable Trust
LFA/sar

CHAPTER 1

The rain leaked down the outside of the window, caught on the sash, and dripped down onto the sill, each drop a counting down of the days remaining before the end of Pru Parke's life. Through the rivulets, she could see the London street outside and, across the road, the line of plane trees inside the wrought-iron railing that surrounded the private square. Inside the railing, a mixed border, flowering shrubs, and climbing roses surrounded a three-tiered fountain that splashed merrily.

"What a pretty garden," an American tourist had said to Pru one day last summer when they both stood looking through the rails.

"It was designed in 1845 by Rowland Mason Ordish," Pru said, "the engineer who designed the Albert Bridge and the dome of the St. Pancras rail station. The fountain was added at a later date. There's a giant sequoia, more than a hundred and fifty years old, in the far corner."

"Oh, you're American," the visitor replied. "How did you learn so much about the place?"

Bits of garden history stuck to Pru like cat hair on wool — a master's degree in garden history and lifelong love of learning made sure of that.

"I grew up in the States, but I live here now." As much as Pru loved saying it aloud, she knew it couldn't really be true until she found a permanent job, a job as head gardener at a small historic garden. Give her a couple of acres and a place to live; she didn't need the grounds of Windsor Castle.

She continued to look into the square after the tourist departed, taking Pru's directions to Sloane Square Underground station. The plants, the fountains, the roses all called out for Pru to enter the square and enjoy, but only residents of the houses around the square held keys. Real residents, not her, not an American subletting in such a tony neighborhood as Chelsea while she searched for acceptance and a job that would keep her in the only place that ever felt like home.

. . . Thirty-six days, thirty-five, thirty-four . . . Pru felt time slipping away and taking with it her dream of escaping her former life in Dallas to live in England. Not that she had a life to go back to. She knew that sounded overly dramatic and carried overtones of self-pity — perhaps not the most attractive qualities in a woman in her early fifties — but Pru felt it true to her very bones. She hadn't begun a new chapter of her life by moving to England, but rather an entirely new book — one that she'd prepared her whole life to write. Not only had she given up the physical pieces of her life in Texas — sold her little adobe-style house, quit her steady job at the Dallas Arboretum — she had also relinquished all ties; she had untied herself in order to follow a path that felt new and old at the same time. England was her home. The boldness of her move had both energized her and scared her half to death.

She glanced around at the sublet surroundings that she got for a song, at least until the owners returned from a year in Italy — comfy chintz sofa, overstuffed chair and ottoman, tea tables, requisite Constable print on the wall by the door to the hall, piles of magazines — her own more recent issues of British garden mags next to a stack of two-year-old *Country Life* issues left by the owners. They had left the bookshelves on either side of the fireplace full, but locked up the rest of their possessions in the basement. Pru carried out no gardening here; the small space behind the house had been completely paved over.

"You've got the place to yourself," Jo, the property manager who had become her good friend, had said. "And you won't have to worry about stumbling into a vase or ancient Greek urn." Pru got the idea that antiques filled the basement.

When she first arrived, she had toyed with the idea of becoming The American Gardener in Chelsea. Maybe she could acquire enough rich clients and become so well known that she'd be asked to design a garden for the Chelsea Flower Show, win a gold, and be interviewed by that cute Chris Beardshaw from BBC One or possibly Alan Titchmarsh, a famous garden personality who, just a few years ago, had been named Sexiest Man in Britain. Only in Britain would a gardener be at the top of that list.

In reality, this temporary lodging plus filling her days with garden work at many different London houses kept her going, but it could not be a permanent replacement for an actual job and home. And she desperately wanted something permanent. She wanted to fit into this new life she had chosen. Middle-aged American woman with no head-gardener experience seeks complete life change in the form of a position in a highly competitive field in a foreign country. What was she thinking?

Three piano chords in G major came from her phone. She pushed her hair out of her face, reached for it, and wondered where her hair clip had got to.

"Is this Pru Parke? Mrs. Wilson speaking. Vernona Wilson. Victoria Pegg-Wells gave me your name," said a rushed voice, "Said you're a wonderful gardener, and I do so need someone to tidy up the bottom of the garden. It's frightfully overgrown, and there's a shed down there I would be afraid to even put my nose in — if I could get close enough. Can you come and sort it out for me?"

Oh fine, Pru thought. *I've gone from gardener to rubbish removal.*

"I could stop by tomorrow to take a look," Pru replied. "May I email you a brief form to fill out? It'll help me get familiar with your garden before I even see it. You can jot down exactly what you'd like done."

"Oh, no, dear, tomorrow is too late a start. You'd better stop by this afternoon. You can take a look at what you're up against, and after you've sorted this out, I've a whole list of other jobs for you," Mrs. Wilson said. "I'm sure your form wouldn't have room for everything. It wasn't terribly tidy when we moved in here last year, and I have had so much to deal with in the house, well, I'm afraid I turned a blind eye to the garden. We had such a large place before and to fit the furniture and all our photos and art into such a small townhouse . . ."

Pru had stopped listening to Mrs. Wilson's description of her change of life when she heard the post drop through the slot in the door. Hoping that one of her clients had paid a bill, she headed into the front hall, offering sympathetic "mmmm's" occasionally as Mrs. Wilson explained that the only reason she'd decided it was time to attend to the garden was that she was afraid her little dog, Toffee Woof-Woof, would get lost in the chaos and what would her luncheon guests think at the sight of it.

Pru scanned the few letters that had landed on the front mat, among them a note from her best friend in Dallas, Lydia Morales. She glanced to the end and saw that Lydia had added: "Marcus says hello." Marcus — Lydia's brother and Pru's old . . . what, flame? — could say all the hellos he wanted, but he shouldn't expect one back. A photo slipped out of the envelope — a snapshot of Lydia and her husband Ray's three girls, Yolanda, Dora, and Lupe, in their school uniforms. On the back Lydia had written: "They'll never be this clean again."

When Pru had announced her move to England, Lydia had protested, "But the girls will miss you."

Pru had responded, "You'll bring them over to visit."

That had prompted Lydia to say, with a sly grin, "Yes, you can take them up in that Ferris wheel on the Thames."

Lydia knew that Pru had a fear of heights. Just the thought of the London Eye — dangling more than four hundred feet in the air in a see-through capsule — sent Pru's head reeling.

"We'll take them through the maze at Hampton Court Palace," she had replied. A gardener needs solid ground.

Pru saw one more piece of mail . . . a payment? With her phone tucked between her ear and shoulder and Mrs. Wilson expounding on Toffee Woof-Woof's penchant for weedy thickets, Pru ripped open the envelope with an SW3 post code and found one piece of folded stationery:

Dear Pru,

I'm sorry to tell you that I won't be needing your gardening services any longer. You've done such a wonderful job and I thank you so very much for all your weeding and planting and your suggestion to remove the cordyline that my late husband planted in the front garden, but as it turns out, my nephew has just finished his O levels and has some time on his hands, and so he's to become my new gardener.

All the best,

Sarah Richards

P.S. I'll send your cheque very soon.

"It's dead," shouted Pru to the piece of paper. "The cordyline is dead, and no amount of waiting for it to resprout will bring it back."

"I beg your pardon?"

"Oh, Mrs. Wilson, I'm very sorry, I was just trying to . . . I saw a . . . right, this afternoon. We won't worry about the form right now."

With a woof in the background, Mrs. Wilson gave Pru her particulars, which Pru, still standing at the front door, scribbled on the back of Sarah Richard's envelope. A second after the call ended, a knock at the door startled her.

"Pru?" Jo called out. "Are you on the phone or are you talking to yourself?"

"A bit of both," Pru said, opening the door. "I've lost Sarah Richards." She waved the note in the air.

Jo shook her umbrella and closed it before stepping in. "That one with the dead cordyline who wanted you to string the tea lights for her summer barbecue? With the nephew who weeded out the delphinium you planted?"

"I did string the lights, and she still hasn't paid her bill."

"She isn't worth it. You'll get someone better to replace her." Jo was Pru's biggest cheerleader. "What about Damson Hill?"

"No," was all Pru could bring herself to say.

"Bateman's is looking for an intern. Think of it — Rudyard Kipling's house and National Trust to boot."

"I can't be an intern, Jo, you know that. They don't make any money. How would I live? If only I was fourteen, I could become a bothy boy."

"If you were a boy. If there were bothies. If it were still the nineteenth century."

Pru told Jo about Mrs. Wilson, whose garden — and dog — she would be meeting soon. "Once I clean up the shed, I might be able to design a proper town garden for her — you never know. It sounds like nothing has been done for ages. Tea?"

"God, yes. Cordelia had to shift her piano lessons to my flat this week while the pavement is repaired outside theirs, and my head is pounding from the scales."

Jo's daughter taught piano at home — or out of her mother's home when necessary — while Cordelia's longtime partner, Lucy, an architect, worked with a firm in London's Docklands, once an abandoned industrial area along the Thames, but now teeming with expensive flats and high-end offices. Jo's tiny flat suited her perfectly — she was, as Pru's dad would've said, no bigger than a minute — but there was nowhere to escape the piano lessons. Pru thought Cordelia must have gotten her height from her father, Alan, who lived in Edinburgh.

Pru couldn't imagine how she would have survived these months without Jo's friendship, which had developed over her first few weeks in London. Jo, the property manager, acted as Pru's main contact for the sublet. The people who held the lease on the house, the Clarkes, were away. He was a history professor on sabbatical, Jo said. Jo's name had been passed to Pru through the usual means — a friend at the Dallas Arboretum knew someone who had spent a year in London, and that person asked a friend in the city who knew about Jo from her own rental.

"Here's my number," Jo said on the first day, when they met at 72 Grovehill Square. "You ring any time you need something."

Pru had plunged into her voluntary internship at the Royal Horticultural Society Garden Wisley almost immediately after she arrived, and so, although she needed a great deal of help figuring out a new city in a new country, she had no time to ask for it. Early each morning for a month, she had made her way to Waterloo station — picking up a coffee and a roll on the way — to get a train to Woking. One of the gardeners at Wisley had kindly offered to collect her from the small station and drop her off again at the end of the day; otherwise she would have been on her own for the four-mile walk — pleasant enough in summer, but not ideal in late autumn — or she would have been out the cost of a cab twice a day.

Arriving home each evening exhausted from a day working in the chill and rain, her dinners consisted of sandwiches she bought at the rail station. After three days and nights of that and one splurge at the Cat and Cask, her local pub, she phoned Jo.

"I know this sounds like a silly question, but I've had no time to explore," Pru explained. "Where's the nearest shop? I'm not looking for anything fancy." Living in Chelsea meant that the surrounding shopping areas were filled with lovely, expensive food, clothes, coffee — all out of Pru's price range as she had yet to make any money at all. The frenetic shopping energy of King's Road, which cut across Chelsea and Kensington, made her nervous and was too far a walk for a quick shopping trip.

"Not to worry," Jo said, taking things in hand. "Tomorrow I'll take you around and we'll find everything you need." She was better than her word, showing her not just where to shop — the nearest Waitrose was two streets away, although Pru was on more of a Tesco budget — but also introducing her at Gasparetti's, the Italian restaurant nearby. Pru fell in love with Gasparetti's on her first visit, and stopped by often, although her dinners consisted mostly of Riccardo's minestrone with an occasional small plate of pasta.

By the time she finished her internship at Wisley, Christmas loomed, but she took a philosophical attitude about being by herself in London for the holiday. She couldn't help but enjoy the sights and sounds — secretly pretending she lived in some version of Dickens's *A Christmas Carol* — and decided she wouldn't mind being alone on the day. She hadn't talked with Jo in a week or two, and so was disinclined to phone her and sound pitiful as the holiday approached.

"You'll spend Christmas with us," Jo said, ringing one day out of the blue. "Cordelia, Lucy, you, and me. Cordelia will play for us — oh, you'll need a party piece."

Pru arrived at Jo's on Christmas morning with a bottle of wine, flowers for the table, and a printed-out copy of "'Twas the Night Before Christmas," which she had tried to memorize, but she kept getting stuck on the bit about throwing up the sash.

Jo's tiny flat had a tiny tabletop tree decorated with tiny exquisitely carved and painted wooden birds. Pru thought Jo might be a bird-watcher, but as it turned out, she had bought the entire tree, already decorated, from Selfridge's in an after-Christmas sale a few years before, and only because it fit in her flat.

As the turkey roasted, the three women asked Pru to explain how Americans could eat a turkey for their Thanksgiving in November and then again just a few weeks later for Christmas. "But isn't it the same menu?" asked

Cordelia. Pru agreed that it did sound odd, but pointed out that Christmas dinners might be ham or beef, whereas Thanksgiving was always turkey.

Lucy and Cordelia supplied the Christmas crackers. Pru knew about crackers — they looked like toilet paper tubes covered in wrapping paper. The cracker was yanked apart by a person on either end, and with a *pop*, it broke apart to reveal tiny gifts and tissue-paper crowns inside. "You see," said Jo to Pru, "you even us out. I wouldn't have anyone to pull the cracker with if you weren't here."

They spent the rest of the evening wearing their crowns, drinking wine, playing with the toys, reading the jokes, singing carols accompanied by Cordelia, and presenting their party pieces. Lucy did a few magic tricks, during which the other three helped by paying no attention when the coin she was about to pull from behind Pru's ear fell on the floor. Pru got through her poem with no hitches, and Jo sang a lovely rendition of "Flower of Scotland." "There," she said, "that's for Alan."

Pru spared a thought for Christmas the year before, which she had spent with Lydia and family. She missed Lydia — she missed having a girlfriend. She cherished the occasional dinners she and Jo shared, meeting for drinks or coffee, and certainly being included in Christmas, but had to remind herself during the long stretches of empty evenings that Jo was a busy woman and new friends were sometimes hard to work in.

After Pru had finished at Wisley, she acquired her first few business contacts in the gardening world, and Jo introduced her to several potential clients in the general Chelsea/Kensington neighborhood. Jo had the enviable position of being distantly related to the Bennet-Smythe family, who owned Grenadine Hall, a Grade II-listed house in Upper Oddington near the town of Stow-on-the-Wold in the Cotswolds where, unfortunately, they had no openings for a gardener, head or otherwise.

* * *

After a quick cup of tea, Jo left and Pru packed up her preliminary-client kit into the large canvas bag that rarely left her side: a few colored-pencil garden renderings made to look as if they were dashed off in a moment, when in fact Pru had labored over them, drawing not being her strong suit; notepad, pencils, pens; hand pruners, because you never knew when someone wanted to try you out by having you clean up a misshapen boxwood on the spot; and two pairs of gloves. When she stepped out, a shaft of sunlight hit her, and so she stored her slicker in the bag, too. She headed out to the bus stop.

What seemed odd transportation for a jobbing gardener moving from client to client through the day actually suited her. Pru found a patchwork of journeys on the Underground and buses to be the best transportation. All of her clients lived in central London, and many kept the necessary tools already — spade, fork, rake — which Pru need only augment. For particularly dirty or large jobs, she could give Sammy a ring. He would haul anything around, although his little Mercedes truck looked as if it should be chucked in the tip along with whatever trash he was dumping.

* * *

Pru sized up the front entry at the Wilsons' when she arrived. Two stone pots flanked the door. They contained the remnants of a summer planting of pelargoniums, perilously hanging onto life in powdery dry soil by a few leaves and a couple of optimistic, but unopened, flower stalks. Knowing there would be just cause for the name "Toffee Woof-Woof," Pru took a second to wonder which would prompt the bigger outburst, the knocker or the bell.

She opted for the bell, and a barrage of barks greeted her from the other side of the door. Mrs. Wilson answered. Well-dressed in tweeds, she held back a caramel-colored terrier by the collar and said, "Oh, the bell always sets him off. He's so much better with the knocker." Good start, Pru.

The townhouses around Chartsworth Square had the usual two-up-two-down arrangement, including a hallway that led straight to the back door. Halfway down the hall, a door on the right opened to a combined front sitting and dining room, and at the end of the hall, the kitchen. Stairs led straight up from the hall to two bedrooms and a bath. It was the same arrangement in Pru's house, although flipped: the rooms were left of the stairs. As Mrs. Wilson led her through the entry hall, Pru thought the Wilsons could easily have spread into the next townhouse over.

She dodged a maze of half-moon display tables with spindly legs, each one covered in framed photos, enameled boxes, and monogrammed letter openers. She caught bits of wording as she passed: "In great appreciation to Harry Wilson from his friends at the AASL" engraved on a gold plaque and "To Harry Wilson on the occasion of his first successful dig . . ." on an unrolled parchment scroll. On a silver-framed certificate, there was a pen-and-ink sketch of what looked like a Roman bust, and scrawled underneath "To Harry — a prince of a . . ." Pru didn't have time to decipher the illegible last word or the equally illegible signature.

They went straight through to the back door. Mrs. Wilson opened it, and they stood at the top of the outside stairs that led down to the garden, as she waved her arm in presentation. "There! Isn't it just awful?"

The back garden, as narrow as the house, and deep in that typical London fashion, was framed by brick walls. Near to the house, at the bottom of the stairs, a small flagstone patio gave way to lawn that had seen better days. Against the walls grew creeper vines, just starting to color up for autumn.

The lawn grew weedy as it receded, until at the back — the "bottom" of the garden — rose a mountain of ivy. On the left, a couple of bare white branches emerged from off a dead birch and, on the right, just visible above the sea of green, was a small roof. The garden on the other side of the wall contrasted sharply: a tidy lawn with an oval island bed full of shrub roses and climbers lining the walls.

"We haven't had a moment to sort it out since we moved in last year, and I'm afraid it's got the better of us now. Mr. Wilson, you see, is so very busy with work, and he didn't want me to bother with this at all. 'Just leave it, Vernona,' he said, 'don't touch it,' but I want to give him a bit of a surprise and get a good start on a proper garden, just like we had in Hampshire."

"It's a lovely space, and with good sun. May I take some snapshots today?" Pru asked, reaching into her canvas bag. "Once it's cleaned up, I'd love to be able to make a garden for you. Would you like to see any of my designs?"

"No, certainly not. Victoria couldn't say enough about you, wonderful American gardener. She said you transformed her rose arbor." Yes, Pru remembered that rose arbor — a neglected climber with vicious thorns engulfing it, and Pru had spent days untangling and pruning it back; she still had the scars to prove it.

"Shall we get down to particulars, dear? Let me write you a cheque now for two hundred pounds, and we'll say that's for your visit today and a bonus, then we'll begin your hourly wage when you get going — plus expenses, of course. Will that be sufficient? You can take a look at what you're up against now, and get stuck in tomorrow." Mrs. Wilson grabbed a diary off the small desk just inside the door and flipped a page. "Yes, you'll need to do it tomorrow."

What a wonderful woman, this Mrs. Wilson, thought Pru. Although she knew that the job would call for Sammy and his truck, and she wasn't sure how quickly she could get him. Still, she wouldn't argue with a £200 deposit.

At the sound of the phone, Mrs. Wilson retreated into the house with an "off you go, dear, have a look round" to Pru who, accompanied by Toffee Woof-Woof, struck out across the lump lawn for the wilds of the back garden, wondering if the Wilsons might be interested in an architectural water feature, just a small one, with a weeping willow leaf pear behind to echo the flow of the water.

Near to the ivy forest, the dog slowed, then stopped and growled slightly. Pru stopped, too, and considered the green mass. Rats? Neighbor's cat? Nothing flew out of the green tangle at her, so she dropped her bag, put on gloves, got out her pruners, and began snipping away at some of the freshest ivy stems, the easiest to cut. That made no difference at all, but it seemed to cause a head topped with reddish, curly hair to pop up over the back wall.

"Hello, I'm Malcolm Crisp. I saw you out my window. Are you helping Vernona with the garden?" Malcolm appeared neither young nor old — probably about forty. He rested his arms on the top of the wall, which was at least six feet high. Pru wondered what he stood on.

"Yes, hello, I'm Pru Parke. Mrs. Wilson's asked me to clean up down here, and I hope to do some design and planting after that."

"Oh, an American. Did you train here?"

"I did a month at Wisley, and I've done a few study days at Great Dixter . . . but I did my coursework in the States and worked at a garden there," she finished feebly, and a little too defensively. The conviction that an American could never know as much as a Brit when it came to gardening was something of a given in Pru's London life, but she didn't mind, as she pretty much thought the same. Why else would so many American horticulture students want to study over here? Pru hoped her own voluntary internship at Wisley, the most prestigious of the Royal Horticultural Society Gardens, had added some credibility to her own curriculum vitae.

"Did you? Where?"

"Dallas . . . Texas."

"Texas?" Malcolm sounded delighted. "Did you grow lots of cactus?"

Yes, we all have cactus gardens in Texas, thought Pru. We all ride horses and most of us can lasso a steer. "We have a lot of color in the gardens there — crape myrtles, lantana, roses."

"You grow roses in Texas? Brilliant. Roses are something of a speciality for me," he said, warming to Pru and the topic. "I've fourteen climbers, twelve species, twenty-three .

. . twenty-one shrub, mostly English or old varieties — very few hybrid teas, though. They're all over the garden, except down here at the bottom. I've lost several I tried to grow up against this wall. I believe the soil is too wet for them in this spot."

"Is that Quatre Saisons I see blooming against the wall?" asked Pru.

This apparently upgraded Pru's credibility with Malcolm. "Well spotted. What sorts of roses do you grow in Texas?"

"All of them, but the old-fashioned ones are my favorite." After a pause she added, "We have rose rustlers, you know." She thought she might as well go with the Texas mystique.

"Rustlers? People steal roses in Texas?" Malcolm's eyes grew large.

"No, they save old roses on abandoned farms and in cemeteries. The rustlers take cuttings and grow them on, trying to ID them. And some have been reintroduced into the trade, so gardeners can grow them again." Pru began to lose her enthusiasm for the topic as she felt the ivy mountain needed more of her attention. "I'd love to talk to you about it sometime," she said as she made a move with her pruners.

"I'll just let you work then, shall I?" he asked. "I'm sure Vernona's a slave driver, and I wouldn't want to get you in trouble." Pru started to protest, not wanting to paint such a generous client in a bad light — at least not this early in the game — but Malcolm carried on. "First chance you get, pop round for a coffee and we'll talk roses." After a second's pause and a quick glance toward the buried shed in the corner, he added, "Will you be starting on all this today?"

"No, I'm mostly just having a look around. I'll dive in tomorrow."

"Right," he said. "Good. Yes. Well then . . . cheers, bye!" And with that, he disappeared.

Pru thought better of going farther into the ivy, and instead snapped photos of the entire back garden with her phone, turning around for a panoramic sequence. She held the phone over her head and concentrated on the ivy, the tree, and what could be seen of the shed, both to remind her of the space and help with inspiration for design. She looked at the last few shots on the screen and saw Malcolm looking at the camera from the steps leading down to his basement. She hoped he didn't think she wanted to rustle any of his roses.

Toffee Woof-Woof, who had retreated to a late-afternoon sunny spot in the kitchen next to a tin of dog treats, met her at the back door. She stepped in, but before she could call out her re-arrival, Mrs. Wilson's voice drifted in from another room.

"Are you back in London?" Mrs. Wilson said. "No? Well, Harry's at work, and he said nothing about a letter." A slight note of irritation crept into her voice. "I don't know what Jeremy said about it, and really, isn't this your husband's business?"

While she stood and waited, Pru glanced down at a small writing desk. A letter from Hodges & Hodges Appraisals to Mr. Harry Wilson caught her eye. She wondered how much the Wilsons downsized before they arrived at the townhouse; perhaps they auctioned off furniture that wouldn't fit. If so, they hadn't got rid of enough. A small seating area had been nestled into the kitchen, and through a door from the kitchen into the dining and sitting room, Pru saw a table set for eight with three sideboards lining the walls.

"Well," Mrs. Wilson said, "that's it, then. We'll see you when you return."

After a pause, Pru said, "Well, Mrs. Wilson, I'm finished for today, but I'll be back tomorrow morning. Is eight o'clock all right?"

Mrs. Wilson's head ducked around the dining room doorway, her eyes wide. "Pru? I didn't realize you were there." She dusted off the front of her skirt and touched her hair — which looked as if it hadn't moved for the past two decades — then stepped back into the kitchen.

"Oh, don't bother to arrive before nine, dear. Mr. Wilson prefers to be out of the house before any work begins, and besides, I hope to make this a little surprise for him — he'll be so pleased I've actually got to work on the garden.

You'll still be able to transform the place before Thursday, I'm sure. That's when I have a luncheon here, Thursday, so I know you'll do your best to have the back garden in proper order by then."

Thursday? In no way would the back garden be "in proper order" in two days' time, £200 bonus or no. And yet, she could feel that check already being nibbled at by various bills.

"Shall I start in now, then? I'm happy to work as long as it's light." She should justify the advance, she thought, and two full days didn't seem long enough for the job.

"Mr. Wilson prefers a quiet evening when he gets home, so we'll just leave it until tomorrow, shall we?" Right, enough work to do in the meantime.

Pru began to mentally rearrange her schedule as she started toward the front door. "I met your neighbor Malcolm while I was out there. He says he's a rose gardener."

"Malcolm? Did he now?" Mrs. Wilson said, with a slight edge to her voice. "Don't let him distract you from your work, dear. He's a bit of a chatterer, and he . . . had a spot of trouble last year, as well. Not that he isn't friendly, but really, you don't want to get mixed up with him."

"What does he do?" Pru asked. "I mean, does he have a job?"

"He's 'retired,' or so he says. He doesn't do anything, as far as we can tell."

"How did he retire so young?"

Mrs. Wilson shook her head, as if baffled by the whole idea. "Harry says he started some computer software company and then sold it and made a great deal of money. Now his sole occupation is other people's business."

* * *

Deep in thought as she rumbled along on the Tube, Pru felt good about the extra work, yet the rejection from Damson Hill weighed on her mind. She couldn't be a jobbing gardener forever, yet she couldn't go back to the States, either; that life was finished. Born and raised in a happy home in Texas, an only child of only children, she always had kept Texas life at arm's length; she felt more at home in her English mother's stories of life in Britain.

The year before her mother died, Pru, just shy of her half-century birthday, went on her own to England, her mother already too ill to travel. On her return, her mother seemed hungry to hear Pru's tales of the gardens and countryside.

Her mother always had seemed to float above the surface of Texas, tethered only by her husband and her daughter, and after her husband died, by Pru alone. Her mother's love of her native England had infused Pru's life and so, although they remained in Dallas after her father's death, in her mind, Pru spent her mother's last years living in stories of the past — gathering elderflowers in May and making damson jam in late summer. It left Pru with nowhere to call home, except for faraway England. She avoided permanence in anything except her job — she was too practical to give that up, until she made the big move — and when personal relationships appeared to be heading down the path to commitment, she abruptly made a U-turn.

If she examined that time closely, it seemed as if her mother, Jenny Parke Walker, had had a plan. She had drawn Pru into her girlhood and made the Parke family so real that it seemed natural for Pru to change her last name. "It's your mother who was the Parke?" Jo had asked — as did others. She did it, Pru told them, to "help me find my mother's people," although in truth, she didn't believe her mother had any people left to find. She meant no slight to her father, whom she had loved, but he had been a distant parent, not only emotionally, but physically, as his job with the highway department took him all over Texas for weeks at a time. She felt like a Parke, and so she became a Parke.

Pru found the experience of her trip abroad impossible to describe to friends in Dallas; in England, she truly felt as if she had returned home. With her move to London — her "sudden" move, as friends described it — at age fifty, just after her mother's death and the messy end of a long-term relationship, she felt both settled and slightly at sea with day-to-day British life.

She'd made only a few cultural mistakes. Vocabulary could be confusing — *we all speak English, but not really*, she thought. She called a long-sleeved sweater a pullover, when she should've called it a jumper; a pullover was really a sleeveless sweater vest, but she learned not to say vest, because that turned out to be underwear.

One day in the shops, Jo had saved her. When she wanted to point out a display of specialty cheeses made near where Jo's relatives lived in the Cotswolds, she said, "Look, Jo, over there by the fellow with the fanny pack."

A dozen pairs of eyes turned to her, but Jo came to her defense. "She's American," Jo said quickly. "She didn't know." The excuse worked, although Pru didn't know why at the time. Most of the people smiled or sniggered and turned away. Pru was mortified when, later, Jo explained that "fanny pack" wasn't the right term in the UK, as fanny referred to a certain part of the female anatomy — just not the part Pru thought it did. Bum bag, she learned to say.

Oh, there was the time she got confused on the Tube about which way the Circle line went — if it's called the Circle line, then, really, shouldn't all the trains keep going in a circle? She'd wanted to head to High Street Kensington and, daydreaming that she'd been invited to visit Highgrove, Prince Charles's garden, she'd got on a train headed to Hammersmith before she realized her error. Instead of retracing her journey and spending almost an hour on the Tube, she'd got out on the street and taken a cab home — not the cheapest mistake she'd ever made.

* * *

Pru phoned Sammy on her way home and begged help first thing in the morning, passing on some of her bonus to add to his fee. "I need ten large terra-cotta pots, enough soil and I'd say thirty or forty six-inch pots of pelargoniums, red or deep salmon, something to stop the eye — not that bubblegum pink. We'll put them in a semicircle around the edge of the patio — the terrace," she corrected herself. "And enough tarps." Even though they would have access through the basement service entrance, Sammy could be a tad too casual with his hauling, and Pru didn't know how many more tiny tea tables and piles of mementos might be in the way. "It's a quick fix — we'll do more later. I hope."

With Sammy sorted, Pru took time to make sure the rest of her week's schedule didn't show a conflict. She changed her appointment with the Hightowers, where she needed only to cut and edge the lawn, and decided to talk with Wilf, the owner of the Cat and Cask, about shifting her work to Friday. Or perhaps she could get a bit done every evening this week, adding it all up to her usual three hours.

Pru tended the window boxes and pots for Wilf's pub. She felt grateful he hired her instead of one of the large companies that serviced so many pubs in London, supplying each of them with huge hanging baskets and pots of flowers throughout the year. Wilf, she discovered, preferred to do business on a person-to-person basis and didn't mind bartering and negotiating, so her payment of a couple of dinners a week worked for both of them. It helped Pru keep her food budget within reason while giving her some time out in the community.

She led a solitary life. Her wide and shifting client base meant she didn't work many hours in each place but instead spent lots of time traveling among edging, deadheading, watering pots, and sweeping leaves off walkways — Jo said she spread herself too thin. Digging into a good deep job of designing and building a whole garden for the Wilsons would not only give Pru a sense of accomplishment, but also would look great on her resume and might help with finding a more permanent position.

* * *

The next morning, Pru stuck long-handled loppers and a folding pruning saw into her bag. Sammy collected her after he'd stopped at the wholesale landscaping supply for all she'd need today. "It almost had to be pale yellow osteospermums," he said as she crawled in the cab of the truck, "but I found a stash of pelargoniums in the last greenhouse."

He pulled up in front of the Wilsons' just before nine, and Pru jumped out. When she knocked and heard Toffee's answer, the door opened four inches, showing a narrow strip of Mrs. Wilson's face. "You're a little early, dear," Mrs. Wilson said in a stage whisper. "Mr. Wilson hasn't left yet. Why don't you" — she spied Sammy sitting in the truck — "and your friend pop round the corner for a coffee first, and come back in thirty minutes?"

"Could we unload now, just to get started?" Pru whispered back. She could feel time ticking away and the mountain of ivy growing.

"No, no, just pull the lorry round the corner, and park by the coffee place. It will be fine, don't worry. Oh, and here, dear" — Mrs. Wilson handed Pru a key — "you keep that now for all the work. It will let you in the door at the bottom of the stairs right there. You can go through the basement and come out into the back garden."

Either a lovely surprise or a sneak attack — Pru wondered if Mr. Wilson really wanted anything done to the garden.

"Okay, we'll see you soon," Pru whispered and returned to the truck.

"Coffee, Sammy, on me."

"I'm all yours, Pru," Sammy said, "but only till eleven." Pru looked ahead and saw in her mind's eye a sea of ivy waiting to drown her.

She sat across from Sammy at The Chelsea Cup, coffees on the table, and heard a voice say, "Pru, not hard at work yet?"

Malcolm, it turned out, certainly had been standing on a large box or a ladder in his garden to see over the wall, because he was only about five feet tall. He had a long waist and he stood with his hands sticking into his trouser pockets. He rocked slightly on his heels. "Hello Malcolm, this is Sammy, who'll be helping me at Mrs. Wilson's. Will you join us?"

When Malcolm returned with his coffee, Pru explained, "We've been given an early-morning break, because Mr. Wilson hasn't left for work yet."

"Work?" snorted Malcolm. "Is that what she told you? Well, just as well you don't have to deal with the old fellow. He'd probably bore you to death with talk of digging up tiny bits of Roman glass or arrowheads or something else. You know, Pru, people aren't always what they seem. The Wilsons may appear a generous old couple to you, but they can have an ungenerous side, too . . . well, you just be on your guard."

Pru squirmed in her seat at this unwarranted warning. She was, after all, just the gardener. What had the Wilsons done to Malcolm to deserve this?

Malcolm switched subjects. "Say, I looked up your rose rustlers last night, and I was fascinated with what they've discovered." The three of them chatted about lost roses and the toughness of the species, although Sammy's main contribution was how difficult they could be to remove, as that was his usual involvement.

They finished their coffees just as the conversation arrived at the difficulty of finding a disease-free red rose. Pru thought that surely Mr. Wilson would be gone from the house. "We'd best be off, Sammy. Malcolm, it was good to talk with you. Good luck with the rose black spot."

It was almost half past nine by the time they got back to the house, and Mrs. Wilson met them at the door. "Oh dear, I wondered where you'd got to. I know you want to get stuck in just as soon as possible."

* * *

Sammy worked up to the moment he needed to leave — hauling in, setting out, planting, and cleaning up the semicircle of pots on the terrace while Pru dug into the mountain of ivy. "You'll be back tomorrow to help with cleanup?" Pru asked.

"I will. About one, is that all right?" Pru knew to take Sammy when she could get him; although he appeared to lead a carefree life, he seemed to be booked constantly.

Pru took her clutch clip out, ran her hand through her hair, and reclipped, then began to unleash the birch. Digging out the ivy was out of the question — at least with so little time — so she did her best to whack back and cut off the stems at ground level, hoping no one would walk back this far and trip on the stumps. Pru wondered what the shed actually looked like. A fresh swipe of green paint could help it fade into the surroundings. If she cleared enough away, maybe Sammy could paint tomorrow afternoon.

Toffee Woof-Woof led the procession as Mrs. Wilson marched out with a small tray of sandwiches and tea. "Take a break any time you need to, dear, and come inside, but in the meantime I thought you could do with a little sustenance. I wasn't sure if you might not be vegetarian — so many Americans seem to be — so I brought one chicken and one salad."

* * *

It was close to five o'clock, and Pru had yet to make it halfway across the mountain when Mrs. Wilson and Toffee appeared with a woof. "What a good job, so much for one person to do. I'm sure you're delighted to finish for the day, and as Mr. Wilson will be home by six, you can certainly be off now. You will be able to finish tomorrow?"

Ah, the old fellow. "I'll be here first thing . . . at nine, and Sammy will work in the afternoon. I thought we'd haul everything away, cut the grass and give the little shed a coat of paint, if there's time." Pru tried to make the pile of cut vines as neat as possible. As she left, she turned around to view the pots on the terrace, squinting a little, trying to blur the scene at the back of the garden in favor of what was closer. Well, it was a start. She left through the basement service entrance.

Pru headed for the Cat and Cask after a shower at home. Just before she got to the door, her cell phone rang. *Mobile,* she corrected herself, *not cell phone.* She answered while still on the doorstep. Although Wilf didn't have any signs up banning mobiles in the pub, using one brought no end of the dirty looks from people who had stopped in just for the very reason of getting away from all that.

"Pru, listen," Jo began.

"Jo, I'm at the Cat. Come down."

"Yes," she said quietly, "yes, I'll come down. That will be better." Before Pru could ask, "Better than what?" Jo rang off.

Sitting in the corner, leaning against the back of the wooden settle with a pint of bitter in front of her and a bowl of curried pumpkin soup on its way, Pru contemplated the possibility that she could survive after the first year. With another client or two like the Wilsons, and a flat in a cheaper neighborhood, it just might work.

Maybe she could live in Crystal Palace. The actual Crystal Palace, designed by Joseph Paxton for the 1851 Great Exhibition in Hyde Park and moved to South London in 1854, burned to the ground in 1936, but the neighborhood still carried the name. She could fill her window boxes each summer with the pelargonium named in its honor, Crystal Palace Gem, and that could be her signature plant; she could include it in all her gardens.

Pru couldn't quite see herself living in Crystal Palace forever, though, and when her daydream began to unravel, she welcomed the sight of Jo sitting down across from her. Jo seemed to carry out her property-management duties without ever being observed doing business. Pru had seen her receive phone calls about a property to let, but she always seemed to take care of the matter in a sentence or two, and only three times — four counting today — had she seen Jo dressed in a smartly tailored business suit. More often than not, Jo wore black trousers and cardigans — elegant, and most likely pricey, but casual.

"I heard from the Clarkes today," Jo began carefully.

The news hit Pru hard and her heart sank. "They're on their way home," she said as unwanted tears filled her eyes. "I'll have to leave. I'll have to move out, back to the States." That was all it could be: the worst news — the real occupants of her house returning. Time to give up. Time to move out.

Jo took a breath as if she was about to speak, stopped, and then started again. "No, Pru — that's what I was afraid of, that you'd be upset. I believe they were just checking in."

"You know, I really thought I could do this," Pru said. "I thought I'd find a job — a proper job. I thought I had something to contribute."

"I'm sure you'll have buckets of time before you have to make any decision. I don't want to see you worry." Jo patted her hand on the table.

How sweet of Jo to make light of the call from the Clarkes, but Pru didn't believe it for a minute. Jo could try to soften the blow and bolster her with false hope, but Pru knew that her life in England held on by the slenderest of threads. Pru nodded. "Yes," she whispered, "buckets."

"Let the Clarkes enjoy themselves in Italy. And after all, you've another new client now," Jo said encouragingly, "and Damson Hill wasn't the only CV you've sent out recently — there are others. What about that garden in Suffolk?"

"You're right." Pru tried to look on the bright side Jo offered. "I'm still waiting to hear from Halstead House. They asked for my references, so I've got that far. And I've got letters out to Boxgrove Manor and Boars Hall and . . . a few others. And here in town, with Mrs. Wilson, that makes twelve clients . . ."

"Too many," said Jo. "You're pushing yourself too hard."

"I have to take what I can get, even if it means cutting lawns or stringing lights. Mrs. Wilson seems interested, and the whole back garden certainly needs doing."

"Is there a Mr. Wilson?"

"Rumor has it, but she's steered him clear of the project so far. He's into archaeology — there are piles of mementos and awards everywhere. It looks like he's quite active with some group — they dig up ancient British history. I don't think that's his job, though. Maybe he fancies himself as an amateur like . . . what's that fellow's name who discovered King Tut's tomb?"

"There were never any Egyptians in Britain, Pru."

* * *

The next morning, on her own, Pru made sure she didn't arrive at the Wilsons' until five minutes after nine. She walked down the steps next to the front door and let herself into the basement.

Not burdened with flowerpots and free of Sammy, Pru took stock of the basement for the first time. The Wilsons had not filled it with the overflow of furniture that Pru expected. Instead, four stacks of boxes lined one wall, and it looked as if Mr. Wilson had made himself a study and workspace for his archaeology efforts: bits of pottery and some flint arrowheads lined the ground-level windowsill, and several page-worn reference books, stacked up carelessly, teetered on the edge of a plywood-topped desk.

An overhead light switched on and she jumped. In the doorway to upstairs was a man, standing on the bottom step and head and shoulders above Pru. He had rimless glasses and thick hair that was more gray than brown.

Pru's throat closed up when she tried to speak. This must be Mr. Wilson — would he think her an intruder?

"Pru?" he asked, his eyebrows lifting as he took the last step. "Are you Pru?"

She nodded, coughed, and said, "Yes, I'm Pru Parke," She said and put out her hand. "Hello."

His handshake was solid. "Harry Wilson, Pru. Not to worry — Vernona told me you would be coming through this morning. I'm just gathering up a few things and I'm away."

"Mrs. Wilson told you about the garden? Is it all right?" Pru steeled herself for the dismissal.

He moved to his makeshift desk and shuffled through the tower of papers until he came across a small ledger, which he dropped in a pocket, "Jeremy told us not to bother with the garden, and so Vernona was worried that I'd mention this to him and that he wouldn't like it." He caught Pru's blank expression. "Jeremy is the fellow we let this house from."

"A nice landscape increases the value of a house," Pru said. "Gardens are always a wise decision — even tidying up the back will make a difference. You might want to reconsider." A last-ditch effort couldn't hurt, could it?

Mr. Wilson smiled. "No, you don't understand — I'm not calling it off." He glanced up the stairs, a small frown furrowing his brow. "Vernona is still sad about leaving Greenoak, our house in Hampshire — we both miss it. And we did have a lovely garden there. She's been at sixes and sevens since we had to move out and up to London. And so I'm quite happy that you will make a garden for us here." He chose a book from the precarious stack, opened the door to the back, and looked out. "You will let the shed be, though, won't you?"

"Yes, certainly," Pru said, as they walked up the steps to the terrace.

"I look forward to seeing the results. It'll be nice having a young person around," he said, "liven the place up a bit."

Pru laughed at the joke and she caught his smile just as Mrs. Wilson threw open the back door.

"Good morning, Pru," she said in a rush. "You would've been welcome to start early, as you can see, Harry is in full knowledge of my little scheme. He rang me up after you'd left yesterday and we met for a meal at a little Moroccan place near Piccadilly, and I confessed all. Harry, are you off? Your bag is by the door, and the taxi may be waiting."

Mr. Wilson cocked his head toward Pru. "They've found a Roman road marker near Bishop's Cleeve. We're off for a long weekend — my amateur archaeology group — to help out with the dig. There are indications of a settlement nearby."

Toffee Woof-Woof and the phone went off at the same time, drawing Mrs. Wilson back inside. Pru deposited her bag on the table, and said, "Good luck on the dig — hope you find something amazing."

"I'll leave the garden in your hands, then," Mr. Wilson said and departed.

Pru made her way to the back and began again with the ivy. It wasn't long before Malcolm's head popped up over the wall.

"Morning, Pru. No time for coffee?" he asked.

"I'd better not, Malcolm. This has all got to be cleaned out today."

Malcolm didn't move, but watched her cut, cut, cut, and then pull out and wind up long pieces of ivy. "Pru, do you know the rose called Highway 290?" he asked. "I read about it online when I looked up your rose rustlers."

"I do," Pru replied, as a strand of the vine whipped her in the face. "It's found all across Texas, at least from the central area south. It's named for the road that runs east-west from Austin to Houston. Little, double pink flowers. It's called Highway 290 Pink Buttons." Pru gave an extra hard yank to one thick stem and almost toppled backward.

"You're doing an admirable job there, Pru," Malcolm said. "The place has been overgrown for ages. I don't suppose you've found anything interesting as you clean up."

Pru assumed he meant some choice plant under the ivy canopy. "I don't think anything could survive under all this."

"Well, you never know what's hiding in someone's back garden, do you?" he asked.

You'd know, thought Pru, *because you're always watching*.

"I'll just leave you to it then, shall I, Pru? Cheers, bye!"

* * *

Sammy arrived in time for lunch — a plate of Mrs. Wilson's sandwiches — and to collect green rubbish to haul away. Pru had already cut most of the vines off at ground level and had discovered a curious thing. It looked as if the shed might have been in use after all. The rest of the mountain of ivy had been a tangled thicket, but against the shed — although it looked impenetrable — the vines had been stretched over the door loosely. Step back, and it appeared as if nothing had been bothered for ages, but it took little effort to sweep the growth away from the entrance. Did Mr. Wilson have a special getaway in the shed — far from little Toffee Woof-Woof's intrusions? *Well, now he'd find the access even easier,* Pru thought.

With Sammy off to the green waste collection site, his truck piled high with ivy and well secured with his own style of crisscrossed bungee cords, Pru stayed past the five o'clock bell. She stripped off her gloves and ended the day by snapping more pictures of the now-cleaned-up back garden, including the shed with its peeling green paint.

Mr. Wilson had told her not to bother about the shed — just as well as they hadn't the time — but no harm in peeking inside. She picked her way carefully across what had been the ivy forest and now resembled the site of some terrible catastrophe. Stumps of ivy, as thick as her wrist, stuck up just above ground level. In many places the vine had risen and fallen as it grew, like a sea serpent gliding through the ocean. Each time a stem fell to earth, it had rooted, forming secure loops just waiting to catch a foot unawares. Pru had cut off most of those, but not all; she hoped the lunch ladies wouldn't venture this far out.

The metal latch on the unlocked shed door worked easily and the hinges were quiet. She pulled open the door.

Inside, the shed did indeed look disused, not Mr. Wilson's hideaway at all. A dampish smell pervaded; the floor was packed dirt. All the tools — three rusted spades, one long-handled and two short, a rake, a circle hoe and fork — still hung neatly from wooden pegs on the wall; some equally rusted hand tools lay in a line on the bench. Under the bench sat four large, rusted tins.

Two high windows, coated in grime, offered little light. When her eyes adjusted, Pru could see that the dirt floor showed scratchings of some kind — she thought of Toffee's growl that first day and stood quite still as she glanced around to see if any rodents were looking back at her. Pru didn't mind a little mouse or two, but drew the line at rats. Nothing moved, so she took a few more steps toward the back wall, where it looked as if a bag of leaves had been left. She looked round.

If they let her, it could be cleaned up and used as is, she thought, or it could be taken down and the whole back corner turned into a separate seating area, enclosed with a short clipped hedge, it would be apart, yet still within the garden. Pru wondered if there was a foundation below the dirt and took down one of the spades to test a tiny area that no one would notice.

Plunging it into the dirt floor took less effort than she thought — the soil was loose. When she stepped down on the spade a second time, she heard a *plunk*. She dug away at the spot and saw something whitish below. Widening the hole, she saw more bits of white, then bits of black and some bits of red.

It was a design — like a mosaic. *There's a tile floor under the garden shed,* Pru thought; that's sort of a fancy piece to cover up. Why put a sunken tile floor out in the farthest part of the garden? She continued to dig and widen the hole to get a better idea of what lay beneath and then sat back on her heels to take it in. It looked like the rounded hind end and part of the tail of . . . a horse. The hind end of a horse, designed in a fancy, curlicue style. *What fun*, she thought. *I wonder if Mrs. Wilson knows this is back here.*

The light was just beginning to fade, and Pru couldn't see well enough to dig any longer. She heard Mrs. Wilson call, "Pru, Pru dear — cup of tea?" Pru walked out of the shed and approached the back door, but when Mrs. Wilson saw the state of her, she offered to bring the tea out to the little table on the terrace.

Mrs. Wilson poured and Pru took a piece of shortbread off the tray. Toffee Woof-Woof sat expectantly at her feet.

"He does love just a tiny treat, dear," Mrs. Wilson said, nodding toward Pru's shortbread.

"Oh, of course." She broke off a small piece. "Here you go, Toffee." The dog took the shortbread out of Pru's fingers carefully before crunching it down.

"Mrs. Wilson, I'm sorry I couldn't get more finished before your luncheon," Pru said, looking past the pots of pelargoniums. The cleared ground resembled a moonscape, full of craters and pits.

"Just getting that mess out helped a great deal, Pru. No one will look beyond these lovely flowers. Harry will be very pleased."

How lovely that Mr. Wilson wanted his wife to be happy, and she wanted to please him. Pru held her teacup up to her face and let the steam rise as she basked in the glory of the day's work, the fine weather, and the companionable ambience of taking tea with someone. She had made only one strong connection since moving to London, Jo, who could spare only random bits of time for her. Transience filled the rest of her life; Mrs. Wilson made her feel at home.

"Mrs. Wilson, did you know you have a tile mosaic under the dirt floor of the garden shed?" Pru asked as they sat with the tea steaming into the air.

"A what, dear?" Mrs. Wilson stirred her tea.

"It looks like part of a picture of a horse, done in mosaic."

"A horse? In the shed? Are you sure it isn't an old calendar illustration or something? Who knows what was kept back there."

"Come see," said Pru. "Do you have a flashlight — a torch, I mean?"

Mrs. Wilson fetched a large torch and out they went to the shed, Pru cautioning her about the uneven ground. In the shed and under the broad bright beam, the back end of the horse showed up even better. Mrs. Wilson stared at it without speaking, squinting her eyes just a bit.

"Well, Pru, I believe you're right — it does look like part of a horse. What a funny place to put a garden decoration, way out here and inside the work shed. You know," she said thoughtfully, "this looks quite old. I believe we should show this to Harry — I did want to surprise him with the garden. I never worked in the garden at our house in Hampshire, although we did have a lovely gardener, Simon Parke, and he . . . oh, Pru dear, that's your surname, isn't it? Is he a relative? Well, I don't know what Harry will say when he sees this." She looked back at the mosaic. "You know, it looks just like some of the photos he brings back from the country when he goes off with his group. It looks like something Roman."

Pru had lost track of Mrs. Wilson again, getting caught on her former gardener's name — Pru's name, too. Then the last part filtered through. "Roman? You mean, ancient Romans from two thousand years ago?"

"Yes, yes, that might be it," Mrs. Wilson said. "We might have Roman ruins right under our very feet."

* * *

"Just think, Jo" — they sat across the table at Pru's house, an almost-empty bottle of wine between them and dinner plates pushed aside — "there could be an entire Roman villa beneath our feet there. Maybe it extends into other gardens, too. And the remnants of the Roman garden could be there . . ."

Jo interrupted Pru's dreaming. "Pru, you don't think that two-thousand-year-old plants would just be petrified under all that soil, waiting for you to find them?"

"The outlines of the garden could be there, indications in the soil, the difference in paths and planting areas, seeds, you never know. There's that Georgian garden in Bath that they've been able to recreate because when they dug down, they could see how the chalk from the walkway outlined the garden."

"That's just two hundred years ago."

"And," Pru continued, "the garden at Fishbourne was uncovered and re-created after almost two thousand years

34

— that's real Roman. We know what plants they grew. We know they had ornamental gardens. I wonder if the Wilsons would like a Roman garden," she mused more to herself than Jo. "It would suit Mr. Wilson's hobby, and he could have all his digger friends over for meetings or whatever they do."

"Maybe Fishbourne should hire you as its head gardener."

"Maybe I should recreate my own Fishbourne." Pru thought she might be underestimating her chances at the Wilsons'. What if the mosaic were part of a larger floor, and the floor led to finding a villa buried since A.D. 400 and that villa — perhaps covering the entire Chartsworth Square area — could be reestablished and she would be the lead designer on planting the first new, very old, Roman garden in London. Talk about a permanent position.

* * *

Pru thought fondly of Mrs. Wilson all the next day — the day of her special luncheon, which turned out to be a group of women she'd been in school with at Newnham College, Cambridge — and, although Pru had come closer to her senses, realizing the whole Roman garden thing might be a bit of a stretch, she kept hold to part of the dream, to make a garden for the Wilsons, just as soon as Mr. Wilson dug up the Roman tiles.

Work from the Wilsons could more than replace Sarah Richards and so prolong the time when a decision would be forced on her — stay or leave. And any day she should hear from Halstead House in Long Melford.

It didn't even matter that she would spend the day grooming the beds at Mrs. Barrie's and weeding the Connors' tiny front garden, because tomorrow, Friday, she'd be back at the Wilsons'. She'd downloaded photos onto her laptop and sat staring at them with her cup of coffee in hand, beginning with shots of the first day when the ivy still held control. She could see Malcolm, of course, in a couple of photos — one standing in his own back garden standing next to a short ladder leaned up against the side of his house. Another caught him at his back door, hands on his hips, looking down his own basement steps as if he were talking with someone.

Then the ivy disappeared; the removal really did make the garden look bigger. With the ivy out of the way, it was easier to envision the potential of the space available. A water feature — a rill? Yes, a brick rill running down the middle from the house to the bottom of the garden, where it would spill into a pool of marsh marigolds accentuating the narrow depth of the space. Pru realized she borrowed that directly from Sir Edwin Lutyens and Gertrude Jeykll garden in Somerset. Hestercombe. Hestercombe had no openings for a gardener at present.

Halstead House

12 The Vicarage
Long Melford, Sudbury
Suffolk
CO10 9JL

27 September

72 Grovehill Square
Chelsea
London SW3

Dear Ms. Parke,

On behalf of the garden committee, let me thank you for your application of 5 September for the position of head gardener of Halstead House and sharing with us your ideas for incorporating both Saxon and Viking elements to echo Suffolk's ancient history. I write to regretfully inform you that you have not been selected for the post, but I am confident that you will find a position suitable to your qualifications and ideas.

We appreciate your interest in this post and wish you well in your future endeavors.

Yours sincerely,
Marietta Woods-Russell, Chair
Halstead House
MWR/lmw

CHAPTER 2

Lydia's email from Texas arrived hot on the heels of the rejection letter from Halstead House, the most incredibly bad timing. Pru's old job at the arboretum was opening up — vacated after only a year by someone from San Francisco who couldn't take the Dallas weather — and Marcus said they could hold it open for her, but not for long. Wasn't it time for her to come back? Lydia asked. Pru deleted the email and a second later, guilt washed over her. Lydia was a dear friend and only trying to help. She didn't understand that Pru saw the offer of comfortable employment back in the States as quicksand — put one toe in and she'd never get out again.

* * *

Thoughts of the Wilsons' new back garden design — rill, perhaps borders running along the walls, and a seating area where the shed now stood — carried her through to Friday morning, banishing all thoughts of failure from her mind, at least for a while. She wondered how it would compare with their Hampshire garden.

Thinking of the Wilsons' Hampshire garden reminded her of the name of their gardener: Simon Parke. Here was someone with Pru's mother's surname, now her own. Her mother, Jenny Parke, although an only child, must have had a few distant cousins somewhere that she'd never researched. She made one trip with her parents to England; only eight years old at the time, she couldn't recall if the people they'd stayed with had been family or old friends. Here's another reason to stay in England — follow the trail of breadcrumbs leading to what might be her only family. *Just don't send me back*, Pru pleaded silently.

* * *

Fog filled the Friday morning London landscape. Not an impenetrable Dickensian fog, but certainly thick enough to disguise buildings and people, creating small moments of astonishment every time a figure emerged from the mist.

The fog had mostly lifted by the time Pru arrived at the Wilsons', only stray scraps lingering, which the sun seemed bent on dispatching. Pru — ready to take measurements, do some rough sketches, and talk with Mrs. Wilson, who'd promised to give her the time — knew she wouldn't be able to create the same garden the Wilsons had in Hampshire, but she could leave her own mark.

Pru decided to take a few shots of the front of the townhouse, too. She could suggest to Mrs. Wilson that she replace those tired pelargoniums and add window and railing planters she could change out seasonally. It would create a more welcoming scene at the front door. She walked across the street away from the house and turned back to get a wider view, inadvertently snapping a few passers-by, too.

Typical of London townhouses, a wrought-iron railing ran along the front with a gate that opened onto steps leading down from the sidewalk, instead of up to the front door. The below-ground access had been used for tradesmen, those in service, or coal deliveries, but now Pru opened the gate and walked down to let herself in through the basement.

She walked past Mr. Wilson's desk in the dim morning light, out the back door, and up onto the flagstone terrace, plopping her sketchbook and bag on the table. She dug around inside for her clip, secured her hair, and surveyed the landscape. Her line of sight led directly over the back wall to Malcolm's house, where a slight movement of the upstairs curtains caught her eye. The best entertainment is what's going on at the neighbors'; that's universal. Standing on the terrace gave her the overall vantage point she needed, so she snapped a few more photos with her phone and then, checking them on the phone's screen, saw what she had not noticed before — the door of the shed stood partially open.

Hadn't she latched it when she left on Wednesday evening? Surely a tour of the old shed hadn't been part of the luncheon activities yesterday. If she had left it unlatched, she supposed an animal could easily get in, pushing open the door for better access. What if it were a badger — or were there even badgers in London? Pru knew they were a protected species in Britain, and she seemed to remember they were large and could be fierce, but she didn't think any lived in Chelsea. In Dallas, she would've suspected an armadillo or a possum.

She walked down to the shed, but her steps slowed the closer she got. A few feet from the door she stopped and listened. Morning sounds drifted in from the roads nearby on the early-autumn air: traffic, the occasional car horn, a dog barking a few houses away. Quiet all round her, and no movements from the shed, but Pru still felt nervous. She stepped up to the door, took hold of the latch, and pulled the door open farther. As it lightly scraped on the ground, something scurried toward her and she let out a shout before she saw the mouse, just as startled as she, hightail it out and into a pocket of grass near the wall.

Hand to her chest to help calm herself, Pru laughed. *Good gardener*, she thought, *frightened by a little mouse.* "Any more of you in there?" she asked as she stepped in. The light poured in from the door behind her, casting the rest of the interior in deeper shadow. She heard no more scurrying. Silly Pru.

Her eyes adjusted to the light and she could see more clearly, although the corners of the shed remained dim. The long-handled spade lay on the ground. *Had Mrs. Wilson let the ladies in here after a couple of gin and tonics?* Pru wondered, picking it up and hanging it back on its wooden pegs. She pulled out her phone to take a few interior shots, but then stuck it back in her pocket; it still seemed too dark to get a good shot of the far corners. It looked as if someone had done more digging around the mosaic; she walked further back into the shed to look. She turned toward the door when she heard a loud male voice outside, getting rapidly nearer. "Who's that? Who is in there?"

The voice cut through the quiet morning, and, startled, Pru took a few steps back. Was that Mr. Wilson's voice? Her heel hit something, she lost her balance, and fell backward into the corner, plopping down on something lumpy. She put her hands down on the cushion, turned around to see what had broken her fall, and froze. She had fallen onto the body of a man that lay slumped like a rag doll thrown in the corner. She couldn't see his face, because it was covered in blood — Pru could see it glistening even in the poor light — blood matted his hair, ran down his neck, and soaked into his shirt.

Pru flew up, screamed, turned, and ran straight into Mr. Wilson. He grabbed her upraised arms by the wrists and shouted, "Who are you?" as he peered closer at her. "Oh Pru, I'm sorry, it's just that . . ." and then he looked past Pru. "Good God, what's happened?" He dropped Pru's wrists and bent over the still figure. "Jeremy? Jeremy? Are you all right?" He whirled around. "What happened?" he asked Pru.

"Harry? What is it? That's just Pru you saw — I'm sure of it."

Pru heard Mrs. Wilson and yet couldn't react to her or to Mr. Wilson, who lifted an arm of the body and checked for a pulse. At last, Mrs. Wilson's voice seemed to sink into his consciousness, however, and he jumped up, brushing past Pru and getting to the door just as his wife arrived.

"No, Vernona, don't come in here. It's Jeremy — it's dreadful, you can't. We must . . . phone an ambulance. And the police."

"What's wrong?" Mrs. Wilson stepped in past Mr. Wilson's weak attempt to stop her. "Harry, what's wrong? Who is that? What's happened, who is hurt? Pru, dear, were you attacked?"

Mr. Wilson turned back to Pru. "I'm sorry, Pru, I didn't mean to come at you like that. Are you all right?" Mr. Wilson's voice and hands shook. He towered over Pru and Mrs. Wilson both. He blinked rapidly, his rimless glasses fogging slightly in the emotional atmosphere.

"I'm fine," Pru reassured him, although her voice shook. "Well, I mean, I'm . . . okay. No, Mrs. Wilson, I just arrived and walked in here and found . . ." *Jeremy* — she'd heard that name.

"Harry, is he . . . ?" Mrs. Wilson's question faded away.

"Yes, no pulse and his head . . . there's blood everywhere."

For a second, the Wilsons and Pru stood close to one other in the small space. Pru felt the presence of the lifeless body behind her; a cold clamminess came over her. "Can we . . . get out of here?"

"Yes," said Mr. Wilson grimly. "We should go inside. I'll ring the police."

* * *

It took only a few minutes after the call was made — Pru had heard Mr. Wilson on the phone in another room, talking in a low voice — before several uniformed policemen and women arrived. Pru couldn't quite tell how many because they moved in and out of the house and garden. Following them, a woman and two men in plainclothes appeared. Mr. Wilson met them all at the door and came back to the small sitting area in the kitchen to report that the three of them needed to stay indoors for now. *You don't have to tell me twice,* thought Pru.

Mrs. Wilson made tea, and Pru tried to make small talk with Mr. Wilson, who sat on the sofa facing the window that looked onto the back garden where the police were getting down to business. His eyes had a hollow appearance, and

Pru noticed that although he faced the window, he looked everywhere but out it.

"Is he . . . was he a friend of yours, Mr. Wilson?"

"Jeremy," Mr. Wilson named him. "Jeremy Pendergast. I'm sorry I startled you, Pru. Are you sure you're all right?"

"Oh, the both of you," Mrs. Wilson said. "Such a shock finding him like that. Pru, do you take sugar in your tea?" Milk, of course, goes without saying.

"No, thank you." The cold clamminess she felt in the shed had been joined by a slight nausea. Is this shock? "Yes, please, one spoonful."

It's true that a cup of tea fills many needs. Not only does a hot drink soothe the nerves and warm the hands, but also the whole process — beginning with "I'll put the kettle on" — speaks of order and calm and just a touch of tenderness.

The police and other workers — Pru thought one of them had to be the medical examiner — continued to come and go through the hall. Eventually Pru realized that one person had stopped in the doorway. They all looked up to see a tall man, dark hair flecked with gray — as short as it was, it was still neatly parted as if it wouldn't dare do anything else. He wore a navy suit, light overcoat, and a grim expression. He had well-defined features that accentuated permanent lines between his brows. He waited on the threshold holding his identification for them to see. "Detective Chief Inspector Pearse. May I come in?"

As DCI Pearse entered, Mr. Wilson stood up and introduced himself and his wife. "And this is Pru," he said. Mrs. Wilson bustled around with the teapot, pouring another cup. Pru wasn't sure of the protocol, so she stood, too, and said, "I'm Pru Parke."

"Please, everyone sit down. Thank you." Pearse took his cup and sat on a kitchen chair with his back to the window. It cast his face in shadow, but he seemed to realize that, and scooted the chair ninety degrees. Pru glanced at his face, which was all business, although she thought she detected a few smile lines around his eyes — brown eyes that caught her looking at him. She glanced away.

43

"Mr. Wilson, you knew the deceased?" Pearse asked.

"Jeremy Pendergast," said Mr. Wilson. "We work at the same firm. He's a friend. He's let this house to us."

"And he's in your group," Mrs. Wilson added. "Your group." She turned to Pearse. "It's the Amateur Archaeology Society of London. Harry's been a member for years, and so has Jeremy. That's how they became friends, and that's why they were so interested in the mosaic that Pru found in the shed. Harry's group goes off all over the country digging around and looking for flint arrowheads and Saxon jars and Norman whatevers. They're very good at it, and Harry has received many awards and notices about his work. County museums love to display their finds."

"It's just a hobby," Mr. Wilson said weakly. "A bit of history, a bit of the outdoors."

Pearse looked at Pru. "And why are you here?"

"Oh, Pru is our gardener," said Mrs. Wilson. "Well, barely our gardener — she's only just started, clearing out the bottom of the garden, planting flowers, but she's going to do the whole back for us, tear down the shed and build a little barbecue or something out there. Aren't you, Pru?" Mrs. Wilson glanced out the window and away again. "Not today, of course."

"Ms. Parke," Pearse said. "Pru is short for . . . Prudence?

"No, it's Prunella." *Wait for it*, thought Pru.

Pearse paused a moment, then looked down and wrote in his notebook without comment. "You're American? Canadian?"

"American."

"Are you in Britain visiting?" Pearse asked.

"No, I live here and work here. I moved to London from Texas. I'm here legally — do you need to see my passport? I have a British passport, because my mother was British. I have dual citizenship. I work as a gardener. I'm legal. I have gardening clients. It . . . it's legal for me to be here." *Could I be more defensive*, she thought?

"Of course she's allowed to be here," Mrs. Wilson said. "She's American. How legal can she be?"

"Yes, fine, thank you," Pearse cut in before the Pru legalfest could reach another level. "I would like to see your passport when you have the chance to bring it by the station, Ms. Parke. There is no question about your . . . legality, just for identification purposes. How long have you lived in London?"

Like a poorly edited film, short scenes leading up to her London move flickered through Pru's mind: her mother's funeral, October at the Dallas Arboretum with hundreds of pumpkins floating in the fountains, Marcus standing at her front door shouting that she was unable to make a commitment.

"Almost a year," she said quietly.

Pearse turned his attention. "Now, Mr. Wilson, can you tell me what happened?"

"Well, I put the kettle on, then I looked out the back window, and I saw someone go in the shed. I didn't realize it was Pru . . ."

"Ms. Parke, you arrived on the scene first? What time was that?"

"It was just about nine, maybe quarter past," Pru said. "I noticed the shed door slightly open, and I went in. I was inside and I heard someone shouting — Mr. Wilson was calling as he came out — and it surprised me. I stumbled backward over the . . . Mr . . . the body." Jeremy something — what was his last name? "And then both Mr. and Mrs. Wilson were there . . ."

"I heard Harry shouting," Mrs. Wilson filled in, "and I knew it must be Pru that he saw and perhaps he'd forgotten she was coming round again. I didn't want him to frighten her," she said. "Harry was off for a long weekend with the society down in Gloucestershire. When I told him on the phone yesterday morning about finding the mosaic in the shed he was so surprised he came straight home to see it. I didn't want Pru to think there was a problem."

"I wasn't going to attack, Vernona. I just didn't realize it was her. It startled me, that's all." Mr. Wilson's nervousness, gone for a few minutes when the policeman first arrived, returned.

"When did you arrive back in town, Mr. Wilson?"

"Late yesterday afternoon."

"Was Mr. Pendergast in Gloucestershire with you?"

"Of course he was, yes. Jeremy organizes most of our digs."

"Mrs. Wilson, who has access to your back garden?" asked Pearse.

"Oh, no one, no one at all," rushed Mrs. Wilson. "Jeremy told us we needed to be careful about who we let in, and so no one goes through the house without one of us knowing, and no one has a key to the basement door, no one at all." A thick silence filled the room. "Except for Pru, of course."

Pru cut her eyes at Pearse and saw him looking at her.

"You came through alone this morning?" he asked.

"Yes."

"Was the basement door locked when you arrived?"

"Yes."

"Did you see anything unusual?"

"No, I'm afraid I was thinking about the garden. I wasn't looking for . . ."

"Sir?" Someone in a disposable blue coverall came to the door, relieving Pru of finishing her sentence.

Pearse went into the hall and spoke for a moment. He returned with two clear plastic bags. One contained a wallet and some keys; the other, what looked like a coin.

"It appears that Mr. Pendergast was hit at least once on the back of the head. There's a good deal of blood. His body may have been pushed into the corner. He certainly didn't fall there. He could've been dragged. It's probable he was hit with one of the spades in the shed, but if that's the case, the murderer took care to replace the spade on its rack."

Pru remembered the spade on the ground. "Oh, I did that. When I went in, the spade was on the ground, and it hadn't been there the other day, and so I thought I would just . . . straighten up."

"Thank you for tidying the murder scene, Ms. Parke," Pearse said.

"I didn't know it was a murder scene at the time," Pru pointed out.

Pearse's eyes lingered on Pru for two seconds — penetrating brown eyes. She dropped her gaze and he turned away and patted the pockets of his jacket and shirt until he pulled out reading glasses. He examined the contents of one of the bags for a moment, before handing it to Mr. Wilson. "Do you know what this is?"

Mr. Wilson stepped to the window for more light and held the bag in the palm of his hand, turning it over to see the reverse side of the coin. His hand began to tremble.

Pru stood up and insinuated herself between Pearse and Mr. Wilson to get a better view. "Mr. Wilson, what is it?"

He held his palm out for her to see. "It appears to be a Roman coin, a sestertius, a brass coin. Look." He pointed at the raised image in profile, a man with curly hair. "That's Hadrian. You can see his name along the edge, 'Hadrianus.' And on the reverse" — he turned the bag and coin over — "it's an image of Britannia." He could have been giving a college lecture.

"Excuse me, Ms. Parke." Pearse leaned over and took the bag out of Mr. Wilson's hand. "Is this authentic?"

"I'm unable to verify that," Mr. Wilson's manner became businesslike, although Pru saw that his hand, now at his side, still shook. "Where did it come from?"

"Mr. Pendergast had it clutched in his hand," Pearse said as he put the bag in his pocket. Pru sat down again, feeling lightheaded at the thought. "When was the last time you saw him?"

"Well, I . . . he . . ." Mr. Wilson stumbled over the straightforward question, but Mrs. Wilson cut in.

"You were out at the dig together until yesterday." She turned to Pearse. "They were out at the dig until yesterday, near Bishop's Cleeve in Gloucestershire, and they were supposed to stay until Sunday but Harry decided to come back and take a look at the tiles." She turned to Pru. "You didn't do anything wrong, dear. How could you know something so dreadful would happen? I really thought we should do something about the garden even if Jeremy said to leave it be — well, the state of it — and it's a good start, really it is." She reached over and patted Pru on the knee.

Pru felt quite breathless after that explanation, which seemed to leave more questions in the air.

"Why didn't Mr. Pendergast want the garden done up?" asked Pearse. He glanced out the window. "And what exactly did you do to it?"

Pru raised an eyebrow. She'd had only two days, after all. "I cleared out the entire back of ivy and planted all the pots on the terrace in two days — to get it ready for Mrs. Wilson's luncheon yesterday."

"An entire garden renovation in two days?" Pearse asked.

Pru's eyes narrowed. Was he making fun of her? "I don't do instant makeovers," she said. "It's a start on a larger project."

Mrs. Wilson brought their attention back to the murder victim. "Harry, you showed Jeremy the mosaic Pru found in the shed, didn't you?" She said to Pearse, "When I told Harry on the phone about the Roman tiles, he was very excited, and that's why he and Jeremy wanted to come back. I hope that Jeremy got a good look at them before . . ."

Mr. Wilson set his cup down with a clatter. "Yes, Vernona, he did get to see them. You see, Inspector, Jeremy would have been very interested in any Roman ruins found here, as that was one of our main interests. We've been down to Fishbourne many times, studying what they've found, and we go off on amateur digs, helping out the professionals from time to time."

"Would he have wanted to dig up the back garden? Excavate the whole area?" asked Pru. She had a fleeting thought of her garden design. "Or maybe he would've sold the house?"

"Oh no, dear," Mrs. Wilson said, "Jeremy doesn't own this house. No one owns anything around here except the earl."

Outside the window, movement caught their attention, and they all turned to see the body, zipped up in a bag and laid out on a stretcher, being carried out of the shed and up to the terrace. They paused and a PC came in.

"Sorry, sir," he said to Pearse, "it would be easier this way."

"Mrs. Wilson," the DCI said, "would you mind if they came through the house?"

"No, no," Mrs. Wilson said. "Not at all."

They watched as the procession came and passed along the corridor to the front door.

"Now, Ms. Parke," Pearse said, "would you take me out and show me these tiles?" asked Pearse. Pru felt sure he'd already been out to see the mosaic and hoped he wouldn't take this opportunity to accuse her of jeopardizing artifacts from ancient Rome, too.

As they walked out, Pearse exchanged bits of information with some of his workers. Then he said to Pru quietly, "The earl Mrs. Wilson mentioned is the Earl of Cadogan. He owns much of Chelsea and Kensington. Most people just let from him." *That's a lot of rent to collect*, thought Pru as Pearse continued. "Fishbourne is down in Sussex, a Roman palace . . ."

"With a garden," Pru interrupted him. "Parts of Fishbourne were discovered in about 1830, but nothing much was done until the 1930s. When they excavated, they discovered not just the palace, but the garden, too. The Romans brought ornamental gardening to England, and at Fishbourne they found the outlines of the original garden, then planted it up with boxwood hedges and fruit trees modeled on Pliny's description of his own first-century garden and the way Fishbourne might have looked."

Pru realized she'd started to lecture, but she felt as if she needed to show Pearse that she knew something about the country. He had stopped and listened to her without interrupting. She shrugged. "I've been to see it. It's amazing."

She stopped at the door of the shed; Pearse stepped in and turned back to her. "If you could just be careful where you step." She had trampled much of the crime scene already, so she picked her way in delicately.

Inside, battery-powered lights had been clipped up so that everyone could see everything, including the large, dark bloodstain on the ground, just next to where Pru had uncovered the tiles. She looked away and brushed off her bottom, praying she didn't have any spots of blood on her trousers from Jeremy's body.

"The soil was loose there" — she gestured without looking — "and I dug down about a foot and hit something hard. I wanted to find out if there was a foundation for the shed, in case the Wilsons wanted a barbecue out here. It was easy to dig a wide enough hole, and I saw the mosaic, little black-and-white tiles, and some red ones, too. I kept brushing away the soil and it looked like a swirly picture of the back end of a horse. I showed Mrs. Wilson." Pru took a breath and looked over at the area. "But I didn't uncover this much. And it looks as if someone has dug out more under the edge of the mosaic."

"And which spade did you find on the ground?"

"That one. Have I destroyed evidence? You'll find my fingerprints on the handle. Do you think I covered up the murderer's prints?" She thought for a moment. "You'll find my fingerprints on the door latch, too, won't you?"

"And your footprints on the ground outside and in here," Pearse said, as if taking account of all the ways Pru had disturbed the scene. "You won't be out here again any-time soon, will you?"

Yes, Pru thought, *I live to compromise murder scenes*. "Not until I'm allowed." She drew herself up. There went the big account, the big garden project, the big paycheck. "How long will that be?"

"A few days, at least. You can ring me to be sure, before you start making your own Sissinghurst here." He handed Pru a business card as he spotted the pile of leaves in the far corner.

Pru followed his gaze. "Is that more evidence? I didn't go in that corner." At least she had left one corner undisturbed.

Pearse stepped around the bloodstained soil and bent down to look more closely. "Look at that, a hedgehog nest. Now, there's a reason to leave an untidy corner of the gar-den — give them some space of their own. Looks like last winter's nest, it's empty now." Pru observed Pearse observing the hedgehog nest: he looked nothing like an inspector now, rather more like a naturalist in the country. Now she could see where those smile lines came from.

"Is there still a scent?" Pru asked. "Toffee growled a little the first day I was out here. Maybe that's what he growled about."

"Toffee?"

"Toffee Woof-Woof," Pru said, trying not to smile, "the Wilsons' dog. He must be upstairs in a bedroom right now." She gestured back to the house.

Pru swore she could see a ghost of a smile on Pearse's face.

"It's possible, if the hedgehogs have been back round here," he said. "Toffee might have picked up the scent."

"At first, I thought it might be a badger," Pru said.

"Badger? In Chelsea? Might as well look for a unicorn, too." He stood up and was once again a police officer.

Overcoming her reluctance to look at the bloody stain on the soil, Pru peered over at the dug-out area around the mosaic. "Hmmm," she said.

Pearse looked at the ground, too, and then up at her. "What do you see?"

"The soil looks quite damp there in the hole." She started to step closer and stopped. "Is it all right if I check?"

"Go ahead."

Pru knelt down and saw on closer inspection that the soil wasn't just damp, it was wet, and looked as if it got wetter the farther down it went. She reached down, gathered up a handful of soil and squeezed. Dirty water dripped out.

"Malcolm, the neighbor in back, said he tried to grow roses against his wall down here, and they died. He thought it was too wet. I wonder, could there be a stream running underground here?"

"I don't know, Ms. Parke. Perhaps that's something you'll discover when you make your garden here." Pru sensed an approaching dismissal. "You can go for now, but please take your passport by the station."

She walked back into the kitchen, where the Wilsons had remained on the sofa.

"Mrs. Wilson, I'll be going now," Pru said. "Would you like the key to the basement back?"

"Not at all, dear, we still want a garden — although I suppose we'll need to sort that out with Xanthe, Jeremy's widow. Ex. Well, never mind. We'll just wait until all this is finished. Would you like another cup of tea?"

"No, thanks. Mr. Wilson, I'm sorry about your friend."

"Thank you, Pru. And I'm sorry I frightened you."

Pearse stepped back into the room, his attention on the Wilsons. Pru tried to blend into the scenery, staying near the door, hoping to hear more that would help her understand what had happened.

"Mr. Wilson, what time did Mr. Pendergast leave yesterday evening?" Pearse asked.

"It was just before seven, I believe. We were getting ready for dinner."

"More of a tea than dinner," Mrs. Wilson cut in. "Really, after getting ready for my luncheon yesterday, I didn't have a moment to cook. And Mary had left some cold chicken for us."

"Who is Mary?" Pearse asked.

"Mary comes in a few mornings a week to help out, but I'm always here. She doesn't have a key," Mrs. Wilson explained.

Pearse turned back to Mr. Wilson. "Did you know Mr. Pendergast was coming back to the house? Did you have any contact with him later yesterday evening or early this morning?"

"I didn't see him again." Mr. Wilson looked out at the shed, not at Pearse. "He saw the mosaic yesterday, and then we covered it back up. He left in the early evening."

"There's no sign of a forced entry, and the basement door to the street was locked."

"Jeremy had his own keys to the house and basement, of course," Mrs. Wilson said. "But he always rang before he came. He was very considerate that way."

Pearse looked into the hall, handed the plastic bag to a policeman, and noticed Pru. "Did you need something else, Ms. Parke?"

Pru had no answer, but escaped eviction when one of the police workers came to the door. "Sir? There's a neighbor here. He wants to talk with you."

"Yes, ask him to come in here, if that's all right." Pearse turned to the Wilsons and ignored Pru. Malcolm walked in.

"Harry, Vernona, how terrible this is about Jeremy. Oh, is there tea, Vernona?" Without a word or greeting, Mrs. Wilson turned to put the kettle back on for a fresh pot.

"Are you the inspector? I'm Malcolm Crisp — I live just to the back. I'm sure you've got every bit of information already. Do you have any idea who did this?"

Pearse turned to the new arrival. "Mr. Crisp, we've just started the investigation. Did you see or hear anything unusual during the night or early this morning?" he asked.

"I don't really keep a constant eye out the window," Malcolm said, and Pru noticed the Wilsons glance at each other. "Of course, I'm sure Harry already told you about the argument he had with Jeremy last evening out in the shed."

"Did you and Mr. Pendergast argue, Mr. Wilson?" Pearse asked.

"Oh, I'm sure it was nothing." Malcolm's voice contained just a trace of delight. "Just some loud voices, that's all. I couldn't really hear what was said, just snatches of phrases — 'Not yet' and 'I won't let you jeopardize . . .' and something about 'what it's worth.'"

"Jeremy and I discussed how to go about examining what might be there." Mr. Wilson's face colored up, and Pru noticed he avoided using the words "Roman" and "mosaic." "There's no question that it needs to be looked at, and we discussed . . . how best to go about that. We talked — perhaps we were loud. That's . . . that's all."

The policeman with the plastic bag stepped in the doorway and spoke quietly with Pearse, who turned to the Wilsons. "Mr. Pendergast's door key was still with him, and the basement door was locked. You say no one else could've come through?"

Silence filled the room, until Pearse noticed Pru still standing near the door. "Ms. Parke?" he said sharply.

"Yes, Inspector, goodbye. Mrs. Wilson . . ."

"Pru, dear, I'll see you tomorrow morning for coffee, shall I?"

Pru accepted graciously and then left before Pearse had her removed forcibly.

CHAPTER 3

Just as well, she thought. The Nethercotts' topiary awaited her — seven geometric shapes, from balls to pyramids — dotted around their back garden. The Nethercotts had great hopes of turning the shapes into something more fanciful. First they had requested the center plant to be turned into a crown — they were proud monarchists — and next they thought that the two on either side of the crown could be quickly changed into lyres. After that, they hoped she could transform the balls into peacocks. *Everyone wants a peacock*, Pru thought.

They'd also asked if she could secure a window shutter; many clients assumed that if the chore took place outdoors, the gardener could do it. She needed to sift through the events of the morning, but garden tasks had piled up in the few days since she'd taken the Wilsons on, and if she wasn't going to be raking in the money on their new garden, she'd better continue her other gigs. Standing at the bus stop, she pulled out her phone. She had to tell someone.

"Jo, you won't believe what I've got to tell you." Pru gave a quick rundown of the morning's events.

"No one would be murdered over a Roman mosaic, surely," Jo said.

"It's more than a mosaic. This could be huge," Pru replied, envisioning the garden she could create around the ruins of a Roman villa.

"But the Wilsons will have to tell the earl before they can dig," Jo said.

"Yes, the inspector told me about the earl. I suppose it'll all belong to him, no matter how amazing the discovery." Despite the murder, Pru couldn't get out of her head the possibility of taking on a project bigger than anything she'd ever dreamed up. "Look, do you have time to meet me at the Cat at three?"

She had just ended her call when Malcolm spoke behind her.

"Pru?"

Pru jumped.

"Are you all right?" he asked, standing with his hands shoved in his pockets and bouncing on the balls of his feet. "It's a terrible business, isn't it? So, you found the body?"

She didn't know if she was supposed to talk about the murder, but on the other hand, Pearse hadn't given her a silence order. "Did you know Jeremy Pendergast, Malcolm?"

"Oh yes," Malcolm said, "we all knew Jeremy. What was it like? Was he alive when you found him? Where was Harry? In the shed with you?"

This seemed too gruesome a subject, and thinking about the details made Pru slightly queasy again.

"Had anyone . . . disturbed anything? Did you see anything else in the shed?" Malcolm persisted.

Besides a dead body, Pru thought. "No, I didn't really have time to look around."

"What about this mosaic — I couldn't help but hear what you said on the phone" — *yes*, Pru thought, *you couldn't help but hear when you were eavesdropping* — "is that what Jeremy and Harry argued about?"

Malcolm's manner pushed Pru too far; she wouldn't be the one to reveal the possibility of Roman ruins — she'd be stealing Mr. Wilson's thunder. At least, she didn't want to reveal the news to Malcolm.

"I don't know, really. You should talk with the Wilsons or with the inspector. Maybe you saw someone in the garden? I don't even know when he was killed."

"Oh, someone was in the garden all right," said Malcolm, sounding sure of himself. "Did you have any evidence for them? Anything to . . . show them?"

"I didn't have anything to show them. All I could do was say that I found the body. Sorry, here's my bus. I've got to run. I'll see you soon, though."

Pru stepped on the bus, tapped her Oyster card to pay, and took out her phone. She found a seat and, as the bus pulled away, saw Malcolm staring at her through the window.

* * *

Pru began the crown topiary transformation at the Nethercotts' and took a stab at a light shearing for the lyres and peacocks. She had encouraged Helen and Gordon Nethercott to let her whack away at the yew, explaining that it was one of the few conifers that would grow from old wood. "I can cut right into these shapes now, and the new growth will pop out before you know it. It'll be a fast start to the new look," she said.

But they were hesitant to commit to such a drastic move. "We don't really like the look of the bare wood," Helen had explained as she and her husband stood there anxiously watching Pru, who held hedge clippers in her hand.

"Of course, of course," Pru had said. "We'll go slow." She had turned away from them and rolled her eyes. *Yew wood was a gorgeous dark red-brown that flaked off dramatically. Who could object to that? Perhaps I could wave my magic wand, she thought, and the yew would instantly transform into a crown, lyres, and peacocks and make them dance around the garden.*

She had to admit, the slow clipping created a sense of calm after the morning's drama and settled her queasy stomach. By the time she arrived at the Cat, she was more than ready for lunch; Mrs. Wilson's sugary cup of tea being the last thing she'd had.

She gave Wilf a wave — he stood in a corner instructing a new barmaid on food composting. Pru had suggested the Cat and Cask sign up with a local company that collected kitchen scraps from restaurants and pubs, and Wilf had jumped at the chance to do his part to reduce the amount of waste heading to the tip — he also liked to use his newfound eco-consciousness as a bit of a marketing tool. It helped Pru, too. When she finished tidying the pots and window boxes, she could dump the spent flowers and wilted leaves in the bin along with the scrapings from plates.

When Jo arrived, Pru ordered a chicken salad plate and they each drank a half pint of bitter while she went through her morning again, this time in detail. Freshly shocked at the event, Jo fumed about a member of the Metropolitan Police treating Pru in such a fashion. Pru followed up with telling her about Malcolm at the bus stop; he obviously had been listening to her side of the conversation. They speculated on the murder, motives and method, and wished they knew more about everyone involved.

"You really don't think it was because there might be Roman ruins in the shed?" asked Pru.

"Roman ruins?" Jo snorted. "Roman ruins are as common as dirt in London. You can't move without tripping over a pile of pottery or a bit of a statue. They found Hadrian's head in the Thames, for God's sake." She thought for a moment. "I'd say a fair number of Roman leftovers in London get discovered and then get undiscovered — covered back up again, lest the find hold up some building project. And if there is a villa under there, it didn't belong to this Jeremy Pendergast." Jo sat upright. "Pru, what if it was a random act? It could've been you — what if you had disturbed someone about to break into the house . . ."

"The person was already in the back garden, and the only way there is through the house or the basement," Pru said. "And I would like to know what Jeremy Pendergast was doing back there again. I wonder if he and Mr. Wilson really did have an argument. But then he could have just ended their lease, couldn't he, and then the Wilsons would have had to move." Silently, Pru wondered if the Wilsons had money problems, as she did. The letter she'd seen in their house from appraisers — they could be selling off their belongings for quick cash. Perhaps Jeremy had given them a deal on rent, as the Clarkes gave her, and they couldn't afford to move. Pru's line of thought was leading her down a path she didn't like.

"I see all sorts of disputes over lets and sublets," Jo said. "People may get turfed out, but the disputes don't end up in murder." She glanced at the time on her phone. "I'm supposed to go to Cordelia and Lucy's for a meal — do you want to come? I'd hate to leave you alone tonight, thinking about all this."

"No, I'll be fine. I didn't remember until I was leaving the Wilsons' about all the photos I've taken — during the work and this morning when I got there. I'm going to download them and take a look. Maybe I have a photo of something that will help the investigation. You never know."

She thought back to the murder scene and her discovery of the wet soil beneath the mosaic. Murder she couldn't fathom, but wet soil, that's something she understood.

"Jo," she said, "could there be an underground stream or seepage or something at the bottom of the garden? Without anyone knowing about it?"

Jo looked thoughtful. "Well, they covered over the Fleet," she said.

"You mean Fleet Street?" asked Pru.

"The river Fleet," said Jo. "It was a sewer, I mean really a sewer, flowing to the Thames. It was covered over ages ago."

"But this couldn't be the Fleet, that's over" — Pru waved her hand vaguely — "by Ludgate, isn't it?"

"Yes, but there could be others." She shrugged. "Oh, I don't know, Pru, you'd be better off asking some historian."

"I might just look into it," Pru said. "It will affect whatever I do with the garden." She took a breath. "Jo, anything from the Clarkes?"

Jo studied Pru's face for a moment — *gauging my tolerance level for bad news, no doubt*, Pru thought. "No," Jo said, "There is no need to add something else to your list of worries — you just put them out of your mind." She stood up, gathering her bag and phone to leave. "Pru, next weekend — come to the country with us. The Bennet-Smythes invite us all every year. The village has an autumn fête on Saturday, and there's loads of room at the house. It'll be good for you to get away . . . and we can go to Chedworth. You can become an expert in Roman villas."

* * *

Pru made her way home and spent the early evening filling out more applications for jobs, one for Stanborough Castle, a small private estate in Yorkshire and one for a large ravine garden in Cornwall. She had hoped to hear by now from a small garden near Royal Tunbridge Wells, Primrose House, just four acres. She had applied several weeks ago. It had sounded the perfect size — just four acres. It sounded like somewhere she could design, dig, plant, tend, and avoid small-engine repair. The advert for Primrose House offered what most did for a full-time head-gardener post: regular hours, holidays, and — she loved the idea of this — a cottage of her own.

Pru's dreams of cottage living, born of her mother's stories of growing up in England in the 1930s and '40s, had a vintage look. In Pru's vintage cottage vision, someone sat across the table from her, drinking tea. She could never quite make out the other person's face, but she felt sure they both drank out of her mother's Spode china — the blue-and-pink Queen Mary pattern, the last few pieces of which had been packed away carefully and stored at Lydia's.

Memories of sitting and drinking tea with her mother in their kitchen in Dallas always comforted Pru. No matter what the temperature, their afternoons had been marked with this small ceremony. "There's nothing cools you off better than a hot cup of tea," her mother would say.

Pru's dad had taken a decidedly different view. "In America," he would say with a twinkle in his eye, and a quick glance at his wife, "we drink our tea with ice." His proclamation notwithstanding, Pru kept close to her heart the sight of her dad, every afternoon after his retirement, sitting down in the kitchen for a nice, hot cup of tea.

* * *

Late in the evening and almost too tired to care, she remembered about the extra photos on her phone. She downloaded them onto her computer and then put the entire set on a flash drive. As an afterthought, she did the same again and dropped both flash drives into her bag. She would take one to the police station and keep the other for Mrs. Wilson. But first she would take a look; she didn't want to waste the inspector's time.

She'd fallen into the easy digital trap — snapping way too many photos for her needs. She clicked through quickly — overgrown and forlorn back garden slowly evolving to less overgrown and nearly barren back garden — until she got to that morning, the morning of the murder. A few shots of the front included a woman holding the hand of a young girl in a school uniform — the girl stood on a small scooter and glided along, pulled by the woman; another with the postman pushing his cart; and another with a large man in his sock feet — *there's a sight you don't often see in Chelsea*, she thought. She hadn't been able to get a clear shot of the front at all.

Her eyes began to glaze over. She didn't see any big clues jumping out at her, no murderer slinking along the wall or attempting to hide in a corner. Malcolm had moved his ladder, and she could tell in a couple of shots that he had been watching her from an upstairs window, but that was no surprise. The garden played a role in the murder, but perhaps only as a stage.

Before she shut the computer down, she searched for "Hodges & Hodges Appraisals," just out of curiosity. She remembered seeing the letter at the Wilsons' and wondered just what the company appraised.

Antiques, artifacts, and antiquities, as it turned out. Hodges & Hodges specialized in Greek and Roman statuary, artwork, intricate jewelry, and objects of beauty — all quite old, incredibly expensive, and passing from private owner to private owner for what, Pru could only imagine, amounted to vast sums, although the actual amounts were deemed too crass to mention online. The sleek and subtle website didn't shout the company's importance so much as whispered it. Right smack in the middle of the home page a notice read: "A rare and exceptional opportunity to own a piece of ancient Rome: please contact one of our associates to enquire on an upcoming private auction of this most incredible find. We will be accepting bids for the item in the near future."

* * *

The next morning, Pru stopped by the Cat to freshen the window boxes on her way to coffee at the Wilsons'. She wondered if she'd have the chance to replant for winter. Or will I be tending cactuses, as Malcolm thinks we all do in Texas? The thought of leaving England gave her a desolate knot in her stomach. Sure, she could stay in London and spend every penny of her savings, but if she'd found nothing by the time she got to the bottom, what then?

Wilf came out to her as she worked. "Pru, you aren't leaving us, are you? Only, I saw Archie Clarke the other day."

Pru stood stock-still with a broken branch of petunias in her hand. "What? No, they aren't back, Wilf — they can't be back. You saw him?" The Cat was the Clarkes' local as much as hers, and they were known to Wilf.

Her forceful denial seemed to throw Wilf off base. "I don't want you to go, Pru. Maybe they were only back checking on things."

"No, Wilf." Pru felt defeat sneaking up on her. "How could that be? They haven't told me anything. Jo hasn't told me anything." Her breathing was shallow. "Are you sure it was him?"

"He wasn't in the pub — I just saw him on the street. But maybe I was wrong," Wilf shrugged.

* * *

Tragedy will bring people together, and this, she thought, must be why Mrs. Wilson had asked her round for coffee. She set aside Wilf's sighting of Archie Clarke — maybe Wilf needed new glasses — and knocked at the Wilsons' door. She waited what seemed a long time for an answer, until Mrs. Wilson, slightly breathless, opened the door a few inches. Oh no, Pru thought, had she got it wrong? Or had Mrs. Wilson had second thoughts about her invitation yesterday?

"Oh, it's you." Mrs. Wilson opened the door wide when she saw Pru's face. "We've had the most annoying visitors since this all happened. I didn't want to answer any more questions." She headed back to the kitchen and said over her shoulder, "Come through, dear. Harry is downstairs with his bits and bobs."

Pru saw that the shed and its immediate surroundings were taped off, although no police moved about on the job as yesterday. "Are they finished with the investigation?"

"I don't know, but we were told to stay out of the garden as much as possible and under no circumstances go into the shed." Mrs. Wilson poured boiling water over the ground coffee in the cafetière. "Apparently, the inspector was concerned about how much you had walked round in there. He seems a stern sort."

Stern, brusque, irritating — Pru could fill in a few more descriptive words. "Will you still be able to live here?" asked Pru, unsure of how English subletting worked. Her own agreement was cut and dried; it would last only one year. And the end of that year was breathing down her neck.

"I suppose it all depends on Xanthe, Jeremy's ex-wife. They still had all their business together, and I would think she'd see to the property." She held the milk jug in her hand and stared off into space. "I'd hate to have to look for another place in a hurry again."

"Did you . . . sell your house in the country?" Pru asked carefully, not sure if that was a safe question.

"No, dear, we didn't sell it. It was a family home — my family. A great-uncle had left it to my brother Alf, and we let it from him. Alf's life is always a bit uncertain, and I felt that — apart from the fact we were able to live in a lovely country house — it was like an insurance policy for him, that he would have the money when he needed it." Mrs. Wilson paused. "It's just that he needed it without giving us much warning."

"Where is it?"

"In Hampshire, near Romsey, a manor farm, nineteenth century." Mrs. Wilson got a faraway look in her eyes. "Such a lovely setting, and I told you about the garden. Alf decided to sell. He wrote all the particulars up about Greenoak — a description for the estate agent to work from — even asking Simon, our gardener, about a boggy place on the property, but it's far enough from the house there would be no difficulty with the foundations. Still, I suppose it's the kind of thing you need to know when selling." She poured their coffee. "Greenoak is just about the perfect place — I'm sure it attracted a great deal of attention. Alf said he was going to sell it to a couple of lads from the village who want to turn it into a boutique hotel, and so we had to move out."

"Did Mr. Wilson work in London while you lived in Hampshire?"

"Harry worked out of the firm's office in Winchester, although he came up to London often."

"Vernona?" Mr. Wilson stood in the doorway.

"Oh Harry, it's just Pru."

She sank into the comfort of being "just Pru" to the Wilsons.

"Hello, Pru, I'm sorry, but Vernona does have the ability to spread all our private news around the city." Mr. Wilson looked a little rough around the edges — his eyes were hollow and marked with dark circles underneath.

"I understand what it's like renting," Pru said, thinking back to the Wilsons' Hampshire arrangements. "I'm subletting my place from a couple who have spent the last year in Italy. They'll be coming home soon, and then I'll . . ." *Then you'll what, Pru?*

She changed the subject. "Mr. Wilson, were you able to examine the mosaic at all?"

"Just that evening with Jeremy. You had uncovered only about two feet of surface" — he measured it out with his hands — "and we really don't know what else is in there. And when will we be able to find out?" He seemed to ask himself.

Pru had seen the mosaic again that morning when she had found Jeremy's body — someone had been digging much more than she had. "Will you ask your society to help excavate — whenever you're allowed?"

"I'd say the professionals will be called in — depending on what the earl wants to do. We've got a contact in the archaeology department at University College — one of the professors is an adviser to our group." Mr. Wilson paused for a moment and squinted his eyes at nothing. "I know he'd love to take a look. Some of the tiles were loose — a few were missing. The Romans set the tesserae, little cube-shaped tiles and pieces of stone, in a cementlike base. It's inevitable that some would come off during the last two thousand years."

"Two thousand years," Pru said. "It's hard to believe that something could last that long in London without anyone knowing."

"Happens all the time." Mr. Wilson warmed to his subject. "In general, cities get built on top of the past, layer after layer, but it could have started with the Romans themselves, when they left. They had a practice of covering up the places they were leaving, as a way of keeping the spirits in. We're always running into something. Why, just a couple of years ago, the Duke of Northumberland found remains of a Roman settlement in west London."

"So, this is no big deal? Do you know how large the mosaic might be?"

"It could be an important find. We don't know. And it could be part of a larger floor, or it could be just a contained square for decoration. No way to tell now — at least not until the police are finished. 'It's a crime scene first, Mr. Wilson, and a dig after that,' the inspector said. I'd love to get back there and take a look." He gazed out the window at the shed wrapped in blue-and-white tape. He spoke again, thoughtfully. "Jeremy didn't seem very surprised at the find. Perhaps he'd known for a while."

"Mr. Wilson," Pru began, "when I went out there with the inspector, it looked as if someone had dug down behind the mosaic." The snapshot appeared in her head of Jeremy Pendergast's bloody body slumped in the corner; she blinked it away. "The soil was wet, really soggy the deeper the hole went. When you were with Mr. Pendergast, the night before . . . he died, did you notice that?"

"No," he said with mild surprise. "We didn't dig down, we didn't disturb the . . . scene while I was there." His voice faded, and Pru had to listen carefully. "On Thursday evening when we talked Jeremy wanted to dig the whole thing up without telling anyone, as if he'd thought it all through. The last few weeks, he'd started talking about how much these things we find are worth, and I tried to stop him . . ."

He looked down at the floor. Pru felt a cold creep over her skin. Harry had tried to stop him — how?

"That's what we argued about," he continued in a stronger voice, "but I know he wouldn't have done that. He had too much honor. I wonder if someone was trying to push him into it. But Malcolm heard us arguing. Malcolm always hears what's going on. I truly believe that Jeremy thought better of it by the time he left — we parted on a good note. We weren't angry. But then, he came back. Maybe just to look at it again."

"One misleading word can send the police off in the wrong direction," Mrs. Wilson said. "Malcolm's got that way about him. It wasn't long before the inspector was treating Harry like a suspect, if you can believe that."

Pru wondered if had they had found more evidence? Did Mr. Wilson say something to implicate himself? But she couldn't pry without sounding like Malcolm.

"What was the trouble that Malcolm was in last year?" she ventured to ask, knowing that, too, was really none of her business.

Mr. Wilson looked at the floor, then out the back window, at the floor again, then at Pru. "Malcolm tried to blackmail Jeremy. He said that Jeremy was hiding something, an artifact he dug up at a site in Sussex. Misinformation and courtesy of Vernona's brother, Alf, as usual."

"Alf," Pru spoke up. "The one who owns Greenoak?"

Mr. Wilson gave a single nod. "Yes, that's him. It wasn't true, of course — what Malcolm had said — and when Jeremy confronted him, Malcolm backed down. Courage isn't one of Malcolm's strong points," Mr. Wilson said darkly.

"Did you tell . . . is that something the police know?"

"We didn't mention it," Mrs. Wilson said. "It seemed petty after Malcolm waltzed over here to practically accuse Harry of murder. But perhaps we should tell them. Harry?"

"Yes, perhaps," Mr. Wilson said, although with little conviction in his voice. "You would think that Malcolm would have enough to occupy his time with his obligations at home."

Pru wondered how a rose garden could be considered an obligation. Then, a thought struck her. "How does Malcolm know Alf?"

"Alf helped us with the move here," Mrs. Wilson explained, and Mr. Wilson muttered, "The least he could do" before his wife continued. "And you know how Malcolm is. One glimpse of something going on and his head pops up over the back wall."

"Does Alf . . . work in Hampshire?" Pru asked, although from even the brief description of Mrs. Wilson's brother she could almost answer that herself.

"Alf doesn't work at all, if he can help it," Mr. Wilson said. "Instead, he spends his time thinking up ways to keep from working."

"He's always had difficulty with authority . . ." Mrs. Wilson began.

"Vernona excuses him," Mr. Wilson said, "but the truth is he's been in jail a couple of times. Once for breaking and entering — it was unfortunate for him that the house he chose to break into belonged to the local constable, who was home watching telly at the time. Alf tried to explain himself away by saying he was investigating a local crime ring, and he'd been hired by the police."

Pru thought that sounded like a comedy routine.

Mr. Wilson continued, "And then there was the time . . ."

"Harry," Mrs. Wilson's voice held a mild reproach.

"Hmmm?" Mr. Wilson looked at her, eyes wide and a smile playing around his mouth.

Mrs. Wilson seemed to consider his unspoken question. "Oh, go on then," she said.

"Alf thought he'd found the perfect crime," Mr. Wilson said, picking up the story, "when he decided to imperson-ate a Scottish businessman looking to open a branch of his Glasgow manufacturing company, which he said made sci-entific instruments that detect radon."

"He'd just seen a program on BBC Two about it," Mrs. Wilson interjected.

"He talked it up and said he might consider taking on a few investors. He set up a meeting where he thought he would collect all their cheques and be off with the money before anyone was the wiser. The trouble started when one of his potential marks brought an actual one of these radon-de-tecting instruments to the meeting — Alf had no idea what it was. And he had trouble remembering that Glasgow is west of Edinburgh. Then, he was recognized by one of the potential investors — someone he'd been in school with." Mr. Wilson tried to cover up a laugh, which turned into a snort. "He might've thought of taking his scheme outside his own county."

Pru tried not to smile, but Mrs. Wilson took it in stride. "He's always had quite an imagination, Alf, but a poor head for geography."

"A couple of years ago," Mr. Wilson said, "he lurked around a dig we had down in Hampshire. Do you remember, Vernona, the time we found the remains of a Roman garrison near Thorny Hill?"

"The place you found the knives and spoons?"

Mr. Wilson turned back to Pru. "It was a great cache of everyday implements, utensils, shoes. But we also found several parts of shields, the center part, the metal boss." He looked thoughtful. "Alf was quite taken with the idea of a Roman shield. I thought for sure we'd see a load of fake ones turn up somewhere that he had manufactured and tried to sell off." His face clouded over and he glanced up at his wife, who had moved to the kitchen sink and had her back to them. "And now this."

* * *

By the time she left at midday, the Wilsons had fielded several calls and not answered the door three times. Pru couldn't see how Inspector Pearse would ever suspect Mr. Wilson of murder. He seemed a kind and gentle man, concerned about his wife and enjoying his archaeology hobby. Yes, he was uneasy when talking about Jeremy Pendergast, but who wouldn't be when a friend had been murdered in your garden and there were no other suspects and no way for anyone else to get in?

As she stood on the Wilsons' front step, Pru saw out of the corner of her eye a man lingering across the road, watching her. She didn't make eye contact, but kept her eyes on the ground, worried that he was a reporter who would then add her name to the big murder story. She wondered if she could be asked to leave the country even if she did have a British passport.

Reaching the sidewalk, Pru looped her bag over her shoulder and pulled out her phone to call Jo. A strong jerk on the strap from behind pulled her off balance and she fell back into someone, turned, and saw a scrawny, rough-looking fellow no taller than she, jerking the strap to her bag, making it cut into her neck.

She began shouting, "Stop it, let go, stop it" over and over as loud as she could as she flailed at him. He cowered slightly, and so she kept up her resistance, but then he seemed to recover and batted her away. He looked at the phone in her hand and caught hold of her right wrist. That one action triggered in her mind the many practice sessions she'd had with her female crew members after taking a short self-defense class offered to employees at the arboretum.

She swung her arm in a wide circle, which broke his grip, but she lost hold of her phone, and it flew through the air and landed on the pavement with a *crack*. Her second move, just as practiced, took him by surprise while he looked down at her phone — the heel of her other hand came up from below and struck him under his chin.

He screamed, fell on his backside, then scrambled up again as Pru heard someone yell "Oi!" from across the street. Before she could get her bearings, her attacker ran off, empty-handed, around the corner. The whole incident couldn't have taken more than a minute — too quick to even get scared — but it left her disoriented, rattled, and breathing hard.

"Are you all right?" said the man she'd thought was a reporter, as he ran up and looked into Pru's face. "You gave him a wallop, I must say. I dialed 999 when I saw him grab you — the police should be here."

"Pru, Pru, what happened?" Malcolm came rushing up, and cautiously touched her arm. "I saw that fellow running off. Did he hurt you?"

She stood, clutching her bag to her chest and rubbing the place on her neck where the strap had cut in. "Malcolm, where did you come from?"

"I live just round the corner, Pru, and I was walking back from the shops." He did have a canvas bag in his hands with something leafy inside and a baguette sticking out the top.

A patrol car pulled up to the curb and an officer got out. After explanations all round, and Pru saying, "Where's my phone?" the officer suggested she come into the station to make a report. The reporter and Malcolm both said they would follow and give their accounts and possibly offer a better description of the man than she could give.

The reporter — kind enough not to press her when she ignored his questions about why she had been at the Wilsons' — handed her the phone. She looked down at its shattered screen. "I think it's broken," he said. She switched it on with no luck, so it wasn't only the screen that broke.

At the front desk of the police station several streets away, the desk sergeant handed Pru a form to fill out when he heard the story. That seemed to be all there was to it. As she finished, a door behind the desk swung open and out came DCI Pearse. Pru noted that even on a Saturday he wore a suit. "Ms. Parke," he said with surprise. "You're quick with your passport."

"I was attacked," Pru said, not in the mood for his attitude, "just now, just outside the Wilsons' house. Someone tried to grab my bag. And he knocked my phone out of my hand before he ran off."

Pearse's policeman's concern took over. "Were you hurt? Was he caught? Did you get a good look at him?"

"I'm fine," she said, although she felt as if she'd just come out of a cocktail shaker. "I got a quick look, but the reporter and Malcolm might remember more — they're here now giving their statements."

"We have reporters covering bag-snatchings now?"

Pru knew that it wasn't the biggest crime in London, but it was a crime committed against her, and she thought it warranted a little more concern and a little less sarcasm.

"No, the reporter was outside the Wilsons'. He said he saw this guy lurking at the corner, as if he was waiting for me."

"And Mr. Crisp? What was he doing there?" Pearse glanced around the lobby, and then back at Pru. "Why would someone be waiting for you outside the Wilsons'?"

"I don't know. He broke my phone." *A little sympathy here, please*, she thought.

"Why did he run off?"

"I hit him, like this," Pru demonstrated her successful defensive move.

"Excellent," Pearse said, and Pru blushed. "Now we can narrow down our search to someone with a broken jaw."

She didn't smile.

"Ms. Parke, have you thought of anything else you want to tell us about what happened at the Wilsons'?"

Pru thought about her photos and the flash drive in her bag, but she didn't want to waste anyone's time. "No, not yet. But I'll let you know."

"Right. Now, do you have a way home?"

"I can get a bus."

"I'm leaving now, just stopped in for some paperwork. Let me give you a lift."

Pru wasn't sure she wanted to be cooped up in a car with Pearse, however short the journey. "No, thanks, I'm sure I'll be fine."

"Nonsense, I'll just get my coat."

Pearse combined his good deed with a few further questions for Pru once they settled in his car and Pru gave him her address. He asked if anyone saw her arrive at the Wilsons'. No one that she had noticed. Did anything in the basement look disturbed? No.

"How long have you known the Wilsons?" he asked.

"I met Mrs. Wilson on Monday," Pru said. "It was a referral from another client. She hired me to clean up the garden, and I was there Monday, Tuesday, and Wednesday — I met Mr. Wilson that day — before her big luncheon on Thursday. Then I was back yesterday morning."

"And Mrs. Wilson asked you round to coffee this morning?"

"Yes," said Pru, then caught herself. "You think that they lured me there and set someone up to accost me? They wouldn't do that. They were concerned about how I was getting on, and I am going to build a garden for them . . ."

"Yes," Pearse said, "your Sissinghurst."

"It could be my Hidcote. Or my Kiftsgate. Or my Great Dixter." Silence. "On a smaller scale, of course."

"Quite a nice square you live on, Ms. Parke," Pearse said as he turned the final corner and pulled up in front of Pru's townhouse.

"I've sublet the place for a year at a very low rate, and my year's almost up, so I'll have to be moving . . . along soon. The owners are in Italy for a year. He's a history professor, but I think they're also in antiques — Clarke. Archie and Pippa Clarke. I've never actually met them." Pru offered as much information as possible, thinking that this might be part of the investigation.

"Did you go through a service to find it?"

"No, it was a friend of a friend of a . . . friend. In Dallas." Pearse had stopped the car, but she didn't get out. "So, he died when someone hit him with the spade . . . Mr. Pendergast?"

"He was struck hard three times. It smashed his skull and left hair, blood, and tissue on one of the spades in the shed," Pearse said, as if rattling off a shopping list. "You must not have noticed that when you replaced it on the wall. He died instantly. Time of death was probably not long before you arrived on the scene."

Pru made an embarrassing squeak. She'd meant to be studied and detached and say, "Oh, I see," but as the brutal act played itself out graphically in her mind, she was afraid what would happen if she opened her mouth. She swallowed hard.

Pearse changed his tone, as if remembering that he wasn't speaking to one of his officers. "I'm sorry, Ms. Parke. I'm sorry. Murder is never pleasant, but it's easy for me to forget how terrible it really is." He put his hand on her arm. "Are you all right? Do you need some assistance?"

Pru blinked away the image left on the screen in her mind, wishing she didn't have such a vivid imagination. "No, thanks, no, I'm okay." She got out of the car and turned. "Thanks for the lift." She hesitated. "Inspector, Mr. Wilson is genuinely upset about what happened to his friend, you know. He wouldn't have done anything to hurt him."

Pearse held her gaze for a moment. "Keep an eye on your bag, Ms. Parke," he said.

Stonechat Gardens

The Old Rectory
Tolpuddle
Dorset
TD2 7EX

29 September

72 Grovehill Square
Chelsea
London SW3

Dear Ms. Parke,

Thank you for your enquiry of 30 August regarding the post of head gardener at Stonechat Gardens. We regret to inform you that the post has been filled. We appreciate your interest in and enthusiasm for the Dorset landscape, and we know that you will put your knowledge and experience to good use.

We appreciate your interest in this post and wish you well in your future endeavors.

Yours very sincerely,
Arthur F. Mortimer
Stonechat Gardens at The Old Rectory
AFM/ssc

CHAPTER 4

It rained Sunday. Pru wouldn't mind if the rain always confined itself to Sundays, in order to keep her workweek dry. She considered staying in, but she'd had another email from Lydia, and she needed to avoid her computer for a while.

"Marcus says that if you call him and tell him you want the job, he'll keep it open. Please do it soon, *mija*. You know we only want the best for you," she had written. Marcus being Lydia's brother had made for a sticky exit from Dallas, leaving her friend, ending a relationship, and escaping her former life all in one fell swoop.

She'd distract herself with Romans, she decided. Although she had visited before, Pru thought a rainy Sunday perfect for a return to the Roman rooms at the Museum of London. The museum occupied the center of what seemed like an enormous roundabout. Its front entrance was not at ground level, and was accessible only by covered raised walkways that looked like spokes of a wheel radiating from the building and extending over the busy street below. *Better than dashing through traffic*, Pru thought.

She wandered through rooms of ceramic amphorae, soldiers' shoes, reddish Samian pottery. What had been part of the original Roman city wall could be seen through a glass display, although it had been altered so much over the centuries that only the foundation remained Roman. Mosaic floors helped to recreate the Londinium of the few centuries of Roman Britain. *Layers and layers of civilization just below all our feet.*

But the mosaics brought to mind Jeremy's bloody body crumpled in a corner of the shed. She shook her head to get rid of the picture and tried instead to imagine what she could do with the townhouse garden space. Maybe a collection of representative Roman plants, Pru thought. And something to replace that dead birch. A bay laurel would work — it could take the London climate. Boxwoods to line the rill, slicing the garden into three sections, accentuating the narrow, deep shape even more. Her mind wandered back through the centuries as she considered the possible plantings.

Pru stopped short at the end of the Roman display and, instead of continuing into the Saxon era, left for home. Walking back from the Tube station, she arrived at five o'clock to find Jo standing on her front step rapping on the door. "Pru? Are you in there?"

"I'm here," she said, and Jo whirled around, her face full of worry.

"Where've you been? I tried to phone you, and I've been round twice today. What's happened to you?"

"My phone got broken yesterday when I was . . . Come in. I'll open a bottle of wine and explain."

They settled in the sitting room with their glasses, but when Jo heard about the attempted bag-snatching, she jumped up and paced the room. She worried that Pru acted too flippantly about her chances of being accosted again. "What if it had something to do with the murder? There you were right out in front of the Wilsons' house — he was obviously waiting for you. And then you walk off today all alone."

"I was around loads of people. I was in no danger. And what do I know about the murder? Why would anyone want to hurt me? I can't tell them anything because I don't know anything."

"You may know more than you realize," Jo said mysteriously, then immediately lightened up. "Isn't that what they always say in those novels?" She sat back on the sofa next to Pru, and gasped. "I forgot my news — Cordelia's pregnant!"

"Pregnant? Ah, Jo, you'll be a granny."

"Dele and Lucy have been planning it for ages — I wasn't allowed to breathe a word until they knew for sure. They even picked out the sperm donor together."

Pru heard a small, muffled crash from behind a closed door somewhere. "What's that?" She turned her head around, trying to locate where the sound came from.

Jo didn't move her head but blinked. "What?"

"Did you hear that? Didn't it sound like it was close?"

"I didn't hear anything," Jo said.

Pru stood up and walked into the hall and listened. "Did it come from the basement? It sounded like something fell."

Jo became engrossed in her phone. "I didn't hear it. Are you sure it wasn't something outside?"

"No, I . . . I don't know. Maybe." Pru stayed in the hall.

"Pru," Jo said, looking up brightly, "maybe it's a mouse. There might be a mouse in the basement."

"A mouse?"

"You aren't afraid of mice, are you?" Jo asked with a concerned look on her face.

"No," Pru said in a faint voice, picturing the mouse running out of the Wilsons' garden shed just before she found Jeremy's body. "I don't mind a mouse. Do you think it will stay down there?"

"It would never come up here, Pru," Jo said, putting a hand on Pru's arm. "I'm sure of it. It'll probably just go back to wherever it came from." She was at the door in a flash for as quick an exit as Pru had ever seen. "I'll see you at the weekend. Bye now."

Sir Frank Chesterton Victorian Gardens and Grottos

The Bank
Much Wenlock
Shropshire
TF13 6AA

30 September

72 Grovehill Square
Chelsea
London SW3

Dear Ms. Parke,

Thank you for your application of 27 August for the post of head gardener at the Sir Frank Chesterton Victorian Gardens and Grottos. I write to regretfully inform you that you have not been selected for the post. We appreciate your enthusiasm for and knowledge of Victorian gardens, ferneries, and stumperies, which we are sure will be valuable to you in securing a post of your choosing.

We appreciate your interest and wish you well in your future endeavors.

Yours sincerely,
Albert Pymm-Scott, director
Sir Frank Chesterton Victorian Gardens and Grottos
APS/scw

Primrose House

Bells Yew Green
Royal Tunbridge Wells
East Sussex TN3 9 BJ

30 September

72 Grovehill Square
Chelsea
London SW3

Dear Ms. Parke,

Thank you for your application for the post of head gardener at Primrose House. We would be happy to speak with you in person about the post at your earliest convenience. Please ring us on 0871 951 9177 so that we can set up a time for your visit and interview.

We've included a brief leaflet about Primrose House for a little background reading.

Kind regards,
Davina and Bryan Templeton

First stop Monday: a new phone. *How did we live before we had phones in our pockets and bags?* After getting the lowest-cost phone possible and letting the phone experts transfer her contact list — the only bits of information that survived the crash — Pru thought she had time to stop off at home and check the post.

She opened the bad news first and got it over with. Pru didn't know how much more she could take of this. Well, she did know how much more — one look at the calendar and it was all too evident that she would need to find a position in less than a month or she would be on the first boat back to the States, so to speak.

Her application to Sir Frank Chesterton and his Victorian Gardens and Grottos had slipped her mind — ferneries and stumperies had never been her strong suit. But Primrose House, that felt different. Her hopes instantly swelled, and buoyant, happy images filled her mind. She wished it were as easy to steel herself for disappointment.

She phoned Primrose House in the afternoon, set up an interview for Thursday, and then checked the rail schedule. She'd take the train to Frant, just past Tunbridge Wells — only an hour's journey — and get a cab from the station to the garden. A pleasant day in the country.

In the meantime, she needed to get some real work done, something she could get paid for, but even before that she must take her passport in to the police station, as DCI Pearse had requested. Stepping out and pulling the door closed behind her, she glanced around and thought she saw someone ducking around the corner, but when she looked again, she realized it was a young mother bending down to her child in a pram. *Don't get carried away*, Pru, she told herself. *No one is after you.*

* * *

She had phoned Jo that morning, thinking that they could meet later in the day for a glass of wine. Pru wished it could be a more common occurrence, because it was one of the only social engagements she had, and it meant a great deal to her. But Jo had — Pru could think of no other way to describe it — brushed her off. Meetings, showing potential clients their potential office space, must finish the contract on so-and-so's house let. Deserted, Pru walked up toward Fulham Road and the police station.

Preoccupied with her personal woes, she barely noticed the woman waving at her from across the road, until the second or third time she called. "Hello! Sorry, hello?"

Pru came out of her daze to see a woman dressed in tight jeans, spike heels, a purple cardigan, and stylish, small glasses with heavy black frames; she sported cherry-red lipstick on a kewpie-doll mouth.

She walked across to Pru. "Sorry to bother you, but I'm completely lost. Can you tell me where" — she looked down at a crumpled scrap of paper in her hand — "Lecky Street is?" She looked up at Pru with a hopeful expression.

"No, I'm sorry. I don't know where that would be. Is it a business?"

"No, I'm trying to find a flat, and I was supposed to view one there." Her whole manner slumped. "God, this is a disaster. I don't know anyone in London, and you're the first person that's stopped to talk to me."

The woman didn't move and continued to look at Pru, who didn't have a remedy for her problem, although it seemed as if one were expected. "The police station isn't far. I'm headed that way. Maybe you could ask there."

"Police?" The woman looked left and right, and her shiny blond hair swirled around her face like a little girl twirling in a full skirt. "No, no, I don't need that." She smiled at Pru. "I have a map in my bag. I'll just sit down somewhere and give it a look, shall I?" She hesitated and then said, "If you had just a moment, maybe you could look, too? I'd be ever so grateful. Could I buy you a coffee?"

Her plight struck a chord with Pru, who had known no one in London herself not long ago. "Sure, I've got a few minutes."

They headed to the next corner and walked into a tiny coffee shop. Her new friend headed for a table in the corner by a large potted palm as she said over her shoulder, "I'll have a cappuccino." Pru wondered how the invitation got reversed.

With coffees in front of them, the blonde said, "I'm Romilda. I'm very pleased to meet you." Romilda stuck out her hand, and Pru saw long, elegant cherry-red nails on the ends of stubby fingers.

"I'm Pru. It's nice to meet you. You're just moving to London?" That set Romilda off on a long tale of moving from Birmingham and finding a job inputting data at a local social-services agency. Pru got a little lost with Romilda's detailed description of just what data she would be inputting — although she had some funny bits to tell about her interview — and she couldn't quite follow Romilda's story of looking for a flat. She talked fast and seemed to backtrack a great deal. She's quite chatty, Pru thought.

Romilda segued from her new job into telling Pru a story about some fellow she dated once or twice when she was a teenager because she thought he looked like James Bond and how he seemed to have a great talent for getting "in" places — Romilda waved two fingers of each hand in air quotes — especially the time he pulled the car over and was about to get "in my knickers when a copper stopped, and when I looked up, there was my dad looking in the window." They both laughed, Romilda sounding like a machine gun — ha-ha-ha-ha-ha — and then she sighed and said, "I never saw the fellow again, as you can well imagine. He went straight back to Birmingham."

Pru thought for a moment. "I thought you were from Birmingham," she said.

Romilda's eyes got big, and then she said, "No, no, Pru, I didn't say that. I'm from Cronton, up near Liverpool."

Pru didn't think she could confuse Birmingham with Cronton, but Romilda interrupted her thoughts.

"And what kind of work are you in?" Romilda asked, giving Pru her full attention.

Pru explained her gardening. Romilda seemed to find it fascinating and asked all sorts of questions — what kind of flowers could she grow in London, what are those big trees out there, what kind of clients did Pru have, did she ever make a whole new garden for someone? Somehow, she asked so many questions that before she knew it, Pru was explaining about the murder at the Wilsons'.

She was brought up short when Romilda asked, "What kind of evidence do they have against this Wilson character? Did they find his fingerprints? What about a letter? Was there a letter from the victim, or was he able to scratch someone's initials in the dirt?"

"I . . . I'm sorry, Romilda," she stammered. "I really don't know much about what's going on there." As entertaining as Romilda had been, this felt intrusive, and Pru thought she needed to get back to her life. "Look, I'll have to be going. It was lovely to meet you. Good luck with the flat search."

"Thanks, Pru, you've been such a help — cheers, bye!" Romilda smiled and wiggled her cherry-red fingernails at Pru.

Pru got out on the sidewalk and shook her head to clear it of Romilda's nattering. It was only as she walked that she realized they hadn't looked at her map at all.

* * *

In the station, after getting her passport details on file, Pru looked up to see Mr. Wilson come in the door. "Mr. Wilson, is everything all right?"

"Pru, Malcolm told us someone tried to take your bag right outside our house on Saturday. You should've told us."

"Oh no, it was fine, I'm okay, and we've filed a description, although they haven't caught him. That's not why you're here?"

"No, the inspector asked if I would come down so that they could take my fingerprints." Mr. Wilson said in a quiet voice. "Just routine, of course."

"Your fingerprints? They had no right to ask you that." Of course, they did have that right. "I mean, it seems unnecessary."

"My fingerprints are on the tools in the shed, of course," he explained. "I must've gone in there at some point after we moved in, probably mucked about, thinking that I'd start on the garden. Although Jeremy had advised against it." Pru was quiet. She didn't think anyone had gone in the shed before she cleared away the ivy — unless that person knew the mass of vines could be peeled away so easily. Perhaps a year ago the ivy hadn't been such a forest. Perhaps. "And good thing, too," Mr. Wilson continued cheerfully, "because that's your job to make us a garden."

"Yes." They hit on a pleasant subject at last. "I'm going over this afternoon. I won't disturb the shed, but I want to get a feel for the walls and the sun exposure. Will you be at home?"

"No, I'm back at work this afternoon, and Vernona is spending the day with her old aunt Libby in Wandsworth. But you have your key," he said encouragingly, "and so you go right ahead and get started. We'll see you when we arrive home."

Pru started for the door, then turned and walked to the desk just as Mr. Wilson said to the sergeant, "Harry Wilson, DCI Pearse wanted my fingerprints taken in regard to the . . . crime at our house."

"And you need to take my fingerprints, too," Pru said in solidarity. She wouldn't let him go through such an ordeal alone.

"Pru, that isn't necessary, surely," Mr. Wilson said to her.

"Yes, it is, Mr. Wilson. I'm just as much . . . I mean, I'm just as involved as you are. I was there in the shed. They need my fingerprints, too."

"Right," said the desk sergeant. "Let's not all crowd up to the front. We've plenty of ink."

* * *

Pru cut the grass and edged for the Hightowers as quickly as possible, swept up, put everything away in the tiny tool cupboard at the bottom of their basement stairs — she was grateful it wasn't a shed — and headed for the Wilsons', carrying a borrowed short-handled spade. She had left a message for Sammy, hoping he could get over there and help her measure and mark some beds out in chalk lines. Through the basement and up into the back, the first thing she saw was the shed, wrapped in blue-and-white tape. It held a repulsive attraction. She wanted to go in and look around — the body, after all, had been cleared away — but knew that she'd already compromised the scene enough.

Her gaze drifted from the shed to the brick wall at the bottom of the garden. It was at least six feet high, and when she had stood directly in front of it, it was impossible for her to see over. What did Malcolm perch on so that he could look in anytime he pleased?

She saw no sign of movement from his house — no curtain twitching — and so she slowly walked down to the wall and looked at it closely. There were no footholds or spaces from missing bricks that would make for an easy escape from the Wilsons' garden. *I wonder what's on Malcolm's side.*

Pru looked back at the terrace to the small table and two bistro chairs. Just the thing. She fetched one of the chairs and set it against the wall, the ground underneath held firm enough so that the legs didn't sink in too far when she stood on it. On her toes, it added just enough height to her five-foot-seven-inch frame.

Keeping a lookout on Malcolm's curtains and readying her excuse — "Malcolm, didn't you say that the soil down here was dampish?" — she leaned as far over the top of the wall as she could and peered into his trim, rose-filled garden. The ladder, which she had seen in the photos, did not rest upon the wall. No, that would be too easy. But on the wall, right at the spot where his head had popped up for a chat, were four wrought-iron rungs, painted black and secured like steps up a ladder. That would give Malcolm plenty of boost not only to see, but also to climb over.

But if he had climbed into the Wilsons' garden and killed Jeremy, how did he get out again? Perhaps his ladder

— lightweight aluminum — functioned as the stairway down into the Wilsons' garden and then back over to his own. He could have hoisted it over from his side and dragged it back when he finished. She looked at the ground on the Wilsons' side, right where she thought Malcolm might set the ladder, but she saw no indentations in the soil. She did see some of her own footprints, though. *Good move, Pru.* When she picked up the chair, she smoothed over the shallow holes in the soil with the toe of her shoe.

This entirely plausible theory of how Malcolm made his way into and out of the Wilsons' back garden kept Pru's mind chugging along as she replaced the bistro chair and began walking out the beds, spade in hand. As she paced off four feet away from the side wall and turned to walk down to the back wall, she heard a sharp voice behind her.

"Ms. Parke?" She whipped around to face DCI Pearse. She put the spade behind her.

"You weren't thinking of disturbing the garden yet, were you? We have not given the Wilsons the all-clear. Surely they told you that."

There are no Wilsons at home, she thought. "I'm not digging. I'm just marking out some new beds with chalk." She looked past him to a blank house. "How did you get in?"

"When there's been a murder, and the murderer is still at large, and you yourself have been attacked on the street outside, and the person who did it has yet to be apprehended, then it's probably not wise to leave the basement door unlocked when you're all on your own back here, now is it?"

What had seemed like a convenience to her sounded dangerously foolish when he described it. "I was waiting for Sammy to arrive — he helps me with big jobs in the garden. I didn't think it would be a problem. He's supposed to be here by now."

He cocked his head, as if to look behind her back. "Does chalk come out the end of your spade?"

"Look, I need this job or I'm going to have to move back to the States. I realize that doesn't make any difference to you. Yes, I have a spade — not from this shed, by the way — but I'm not digging." *Not yet.* "And Sammy was only going to help me with my lines . . ."

Her phone rang. Pru pulled it out of her pocket and looked down. The action reminded her of that odd moment when Malcolm watched her with keen interest as she pulled out her phone on the bus, the day of the murder. She looked up at Pearse, who looked at her.

"Is there a problem?" he asked.

Irritation drove out of her mind what she was going to say to him, and she answered the phone instead. Sammy couldn't make it, he was sorry, but he still had a load to take to the green waste and would never make it back before the end of the day. She ended the call annoyed and disappointed.

"Ms. Parke, did you take your passport by the station?" Pearse asked.

"Yes. Today." Indignation rose up. "And I saw Mr. Wilson there — why did he have his fingerprints taken? He didn't do anything, and I can't imagine you believe for a minute that . . ."

"Did you have your fingerprints taken while you were there?"

Defiant in the face of what she thought sounded like an accusation, she stuck her chin out. "I did. So, am I a suspect now?"

"Ms. Parke, you did pick up the murder weapon, didn't you? We need to identify your fingerprints on the handle in order to eliminate them."

"Oh."

"Pru, dear," Mrs. Wilson called from the back door. "Oh, Inspector, how lovely to see you. Is there something I can do? Pru, why don't you both come in for a cup of tea?"

Pearse and Pru glanced at each other then back at Mrs. Wilson and at the same time replied, "No, thank you, I can't stay." They looked at each other again, and Pru stifled a laugh. Even Pearse smiled.

They walked to the house. "Mrs. Wilson, I'll be back in the morning with Sammy to mark off some beds — I won't be digging." She made a point of looking at Pearse. "And I'll lock the basement on my way out," Pru said as she walked through the house.

"Mrs. Wilson, could you ask your husband to give us a list of the members of his society?" Pearse asked.

"Oh, I can get that for you right now, Inspector," Mrs. Wilson said. "Harry printed one out for you, it's just in the dining room, I won't be a moment. Toffee will keep you company. Pru, dear, I won't be in tomorrow morning, but you come straight through and get to work."

As she left, Pru glanced back to see Pearse. At his feet, Toffee Woof-Woof looked up expecting a treat.

The inside door to the basement was closed, and so she walked out the front door, opened the gate and went down the outside basement steps. Pearse had left the door to the basement slightly ajar, just as she had. "When there's been a murder and the murderer is still at large," Pru mumbled to an imaginary Pearse, "then it's probably not wise to . . ."

She walked through the basement, leaning her spade up against the wall, locked the door to the garden and turned to head out, but something on Mr. Wilson's makeshift desk caught her eye. Near the edge, away from his papers and copies of *Archaeology Today*, was a coin. Pru thought it must be a £2 coin, but one that had darkened so that the bronze color of the outer ring had overtaken the silver-gray center. She hadn't noticed it on her way in, yet her eyes were drawn to it now. She bent over the desk to look closer. It was not a £2 coin. On the face of the coin was not an engraving of the queen, but a picture in relief of a man with curly hair; surrounding the head was the word "Hadrianus."

Pru froze. This was the coin found in the dead man's hand — but that couldn't be, because the police took that coin with them. But then, whose coin was this sitting on Mr. Wilson's desk? It couldn't be his, not Mr. Wilson's coin, because that might mean that he had something to do with

. . .

"Ms. Parke?"

Pru whirled around. Pearse stood at the door to the outside steps.

"What's wrong?" he asked, coming toward her.

She didn't speak, but only looked down at the desk. He looked, too, and as he did, Pru's hand made an involuntary movement.

Pearse caught her wrist, and she pulled it away from him. "I wasn't going to touch it," she said, embarrassed, because she realized that very thought had crossed her mind. She put her hands stiffly at her sides.

He reached into his jacket pocket and pulled out a small plastic bag.

"Do you always carry plastic bags in your pocket?" asked Pru.

Pearse had to lean over in front of her, because, in a small act of defiance, she would not budge from the spot. He turned to her, entirely too close. "Yes," he said, "I do."

Using the bag to cover his fingers, he secured the coin and, with his other hand, patted his various pockets until he found his reading glasses. "This is the same kind of coin we found in Mr. Pendergast's hand. Was this here when you came through earlier today?" he asked.

"No, it wasn't. At least, I don't think so." She didn't care for the ambiguity of her reply. "No, I know it wasn't. I saw it just now. It wasn't here earlier. I came through to lock the door, and there it was." A happy thought came to her. "It wasn't here when I arrived," she said, "so someone must've come in while we were in the garden." Pearse was quiet. "Did you see it when you came through?" Pru asked.

"Are you sure it wasn't here when you arrived?" Pearse asked. "Or perhaps you might not have noticed. Isn't that possible?"

"Did you see it?" Pru demanded.

"No," he admitted, "I did not."

"Then someone must have come in and planted it here. Planted evidence to try to make Mr. Wilson look bad." Pearse didn't speak. "Don't you think that's what happened?"

"It's possible," he said as he pressed the bag closed. "But it is also possible that Harry Wilson took this coin from the murder scene and kept it."

"And left it out in plain view for anyone to see?" Pru hoped he could hear how ridiculous that sounded. "Are you going to ask Mrs. Wilson about it?"

"Harry Wilson is the person to ask about it."

"He's at work," Pru interjected.

"But as he is not here," Pearse continued, "I will ask Mrs. Wilson a few questions."

Pru backed away from the table slightly as a concession. "May I come along? Please?"

"Are you worried I'm about to use harsh interrogation tactics on her?" Pru thought she detected just a bit of humor in his dry tone. "Yes, you may come along."

They went out the basement door. Pru locked it behind them and they walked up to the front step. Pearse knocked on the door, and Mrs. Wilson showed surprise when she answered.

When asked about the coin, she said she knew nothing about it but did think it looked a great deal like the one the police had found with Jeremy. She said Mr. Wilson never kept any coins from digs, they were usually presumed to be of some value, and, at any rate, the group's finds mostly ended up in museums. Although no harsh interrogation tactics were involved, Pru still thought Pearse could have been less confrontational with Mrs. Wilson, especially when it came to requesting that Mr. Wilson go down to the station again for further questioning.

Mrs. Wilson showed them to the door. "I'll talk to you soon," Pru said to her. "I'm sure the inspector will find out who sneaked into the basement and left that coin." She looked at Pearse, waiting for a response, but he gave none.

When Mrs. Wilson closed the door on them, Pearse asked Pru if she would like a lift home. She was in no mood. She crossed her arms, and said "No," after which her manners got the better of her. "Thank you, no, I can make my own way."

"I am not singling out the Wilsons without reason," Pearse said, sounding slightly weary.

"Someone planted that coin," Pru insisted. "You've got to admit that. Mr. Wilson wasn't home. The coin wasn't there when I arrived — or when you arrived," she pointed out.

"And we will take all that into consideration during the investigation," Pearse said. "Are you sure I can't give you a lift home?"

Pru thought perhaps she'd have more time to make her case in the car. "Thank you," she said, "I would like a lift."

On their way to 72 Grovehill Square — Pru tried to give Pearse her address, but he said, "Yes, I remember where you live" — she began to speak in a casual way about the Wilsons.

"Mr. Wilson's archaeology group has a university sponsor, you know," she said. "It's an educational endeavor, really. They do it because they love learning." She glanced out of the corner of her eye at Pearse, who made no comment. "You probably saw all the awards and commendations he's received, from people and places thanking him for what he's done."

As Pearse turned a corner, he asked, "Did you accept a lift from me just to give a testimonial on Harry Wilson's behalf?"

Pru didn't answer, and they were quiet for the last few minutes of the journey. Pearse pulled up in front of her house, stopped and turned to her. "We are not in the habit of arresting and prosecuting innocent people," he said. "Harry Wilson is part of this investigation, and so questions must be asked."

"I don't believe that Mr. Wilson murdered Jeremy Pendergast."

"Yes, I understand that. I hope you understand that I must do my job." As Pru reached for the door handle, he added, "Please take care."

He took her by surprise with a kind and gentle admonition instead of an officious warning. She flashed him a smile. "I will."

* * *

Pru arrived before Sammy the next morning. She picked up the spade she'd left just inside the basement door and took it with her to the bottom of the garden, where the sun already had warmed the brick wall. She sat down with her back against the wall, surveying the view that the Wilsons would have from this end of their new garden. She closed her eyes, enjoying the sun on her face. Perhaps she did miss the Texas sunshine just a bit, but not the summer heat. With less intense sun exposure, her hair was turning from blond to its original medium brown, and she was surprised to find a dash of silvery gray at each temple.

She opened her eyes again and looked at the blue-and-white tape surrounding the shed. The forensics team had attached the tape to the brick wall, so that the small space — about two feet wide — between the shed and the wall shared with Malcolm's garden was marked as off-limits. Still, Pru reasoned that small piece of ground couldn't really be part of the murder scene. She thought that if she did a bit of work behind the shed, it wouldn't be noticed.

She would need to do this to find how far this damp-ish patch of soil went. She might also discover how far the mosaic extended, but she told herself that that would be secondary to researching the conditions for the new garden. With a cursory glance around, she ducked under the tape and behind the shed when she heard voices.

"Listen, Saxsby." It was Malcolm's voice quite close on the other side of the wall. "You can't go over there now. It's broad daylight." Malcolm's voice bounced as if he were hurrying along.

"Calm down, Crisp," said another man's voice. "I won't be caught breaking and entering, if that's what you're worried about. Look, I want this business finished up — my latest deal didn't go through, and I'm a bit hard up right now."

"The house? What happened?" Malcolm asked.

"Never you mind," the man said. "Did you get in to look?"

"No, no there's no way in now. We'll just have to wait until the police are finished," Malcolm said. "Although after that, Pru will probably start on the garden."

"Pru? Who is Pru?" Saxsby said.

"She's the American gardener Harry and Vernona hired. It's all right. I can handle her — she won't be a problem."

"What's Vernona doing hiring a bloody American gardener? Didn't Pendergast tell them to leave off the garden?"

Alarmed that her name would come up in such a conversation — and annoyed to be called a "bloody American gardener" — Pru tried to breathe as quietly as possible so that they wouldn't discover her eavesdropping.

"I said I'd take care of it."

"Does she know something?" Saxsby asked. "Haven't you told her she might be in danger herself hanging about Harry?"

"I've tried to warn her," Malcolm said, "but she thinks he's harmless."

"You just remember what I told you, Crisp," said Saxsby. "He's no harmless old git." He paused for a moment, and Pru wondered if they'd left. Then Saxsby said, "Did she see what was there?"

"She might have," Malcolm replied. "But I'm taking care of it," he said with emphasis.

Pru had lost track of the spade in her hand as she listened in, and it slipped out of her loosened grip, hit against the wall, and landed with a *plunk* on the ground.

She heard muffled exclamations and footsteps in the gravelly soil at the base of the wall. Malcolm must be heading to his brick-wall ladder. She grabbed the spade and looked for an escape. The shed was almost flush with the wall adjoining the next garden, and so she had to slip under the tape the way she came and then into the shed. When she turned around to pull it to, she looked up to see Malcolm peering over the wall. Their eyes met, and she waited for him to call her out, but instead he turned back to Saxsby and said, "No, I don't see anyone. Now, do you want to be out here when they come back? We'd better go."

Pru stuck her head out the door in time to hear the two voices retreating. She thought she heard Saxsby say, "Did you

. . ." but she couldn't catch the rest. After that, she heard a door close.

"Pru?" Sammy asked as he came up from the Wilsons' basement entrance. "You aren't supposed to be in there, are you?" She had left the basement door open again and felt a little guilty about it. She hoped Pearse wouldn't stop by and discover her misbehavior. "Who was that with the nosy parker?"

She couldn't quite figure out what had happened. Malcolm saw her — she was sure of that — but she didn't know if he protected her by not revealing her presence or if he would tell Saxsby all about her eavesdropping when they were well and truly out of earshot. And she didn't know if she would be in more or less danger either way.

"Sammy, did you see Malcolm? Could you see the other fellow? What did he look like?" She stepped out of the shed quickly, but with a backward glance toward the mosaic, still partially uncovered, and the hole behind it, still open. The blood-soaked soil looked disturbed, as if a sample had been taken.

"I saw them go up the steps to the door, but they didn't go in. Then they went back down again. I suppose they went down the basement steps. Yeah, I caught a quick look at him . . . I don't know — he looked sort of normal." Sammy's powers of observation were kept for estimating the size of a load he could get into the back of his truck. "Stringy black hair, thinning. Were you hiding from them?"

"Well, I just didn't want to be caught up in another discussion about roses," Pru said. That was enough for Sammy, who had sat through one of those with Malcolm already. "Let's mark off some beds."

As they measured, Sammy had to keep reminding her what they were doing. "Pru, we've done that side already, haven't we?"

"Sorry, Sammy, yes." The questions in her mind pushed everything else out. Several times she found she'd stopped moving and stood thinking. How much more had Malcolm learned about the Roman mosaic, and how was Saxsby involved?

Saxsby seemed to be pressuring Malcolm into thinking the worst of Mr. Wilson — Pru felt sure that explained the business about warning her. Pru thought Malcolm was full of himself if he thought he could "take care of her." As she and Sammy worked, the conversation she'd overheard, along with her own feelings and opinions, were getting tossed around in her head like clothes in a dryer.

When they'd finished and Sammy had gone, she phoned Pearse.

"Detective Chief Inspector Christopher Pearse, please leave a message," said the recording. She believed this information needed to be delivered live, not on tape, so she didn't leave any message and decided she'd phone again later. She considered looking into it herself in the meantime — maybe she could clarify a few things they'd said and so the evidence would be more helpful to the police.

Her initial scare faded over the next couple of days in the rush to stuff four days of work into two, and although she kept meaning to phone Pearse again, she didn't get round to it. She focused on her interview at Primrose House on Thursday and spending the weekend in the Cotswolds with Jo and family, and pushed aside the murder and its investigation.

CHAPTER 5

On Thursday, Pru took the train from Charing Cross station to Frant, the small rail station nearest Primrose House. It took only the short train journey for her to begin thinking about life in Bells Yew Green. With the town of Tunbridge Wells only four miles away, loads of services and shops would be near at hand, and the area was chock-full of fine gardens to visit for inspiration.

Pru rang for a cab from the station and took down the driver's phone number so she could ring him for the return trip. She had barely settled back into the seat, when they arrived.

Good clay soils led to an abundance of brickworks in Kent and Sussex, and so brick buildings were a common sight in towns and villages — along with those made from local ironstone. Brick-built Primrose House sat slightly back from the road with an oval gravel drive leading to it and back to the road again.

Although good-sized, it was certainly not enormous; it was the smallest of the manor farms on what had been a grand estate. The castle — owned by the Earl of Lamerton — came with a Grade-II listing, noting its historical status, but none of the manor farms had a listing and had been sold off individually over the past hundred years. They had been built in the late eighteenth century. It was reputed — or rumored, Pru couldn't remember which — that the landscape around the estate, including Primrose House, had been designed, or perhaps influenced, by Humphry Repton, renowned landscape gardener, in the early nineteenth century. That's all she had learned from the slip of a leaflet included in the letter from the Templetons.

Pru glanced around the landscape. Away to the back, a tall row of yews ran parallel to the house. At the end of the row to the right, and behind what could only be the walled garden, she could see the looming figure of a mature cedar of Lebanon — at least two hundred years old, she thought — characteristically flat-topped with horizontal branches stretched out like a hen covering her chicks. Nothing grew up against the house — that wasn't unusual, although it may have been that vines or roses had been cut down.

Two columnar yews flanked the front door — she peeked inside the wall of foliage to see if they were sheared or one of the narrow-growing selections. Sheared, she thought, and by the looks of things, the only bit of gardening that had been done in a while.

She arranged herself before knocking — she could see no bell. The knocker, an enormous brass piece fashioned in the shape of a badger's head, made a marvelously deep sound on the wood and echoed inside. She heard footsteps, and the door opened.

A short woman with bobbed white hair answered, offered her hand, and said, "Hello, Pru, I'm Davina Templeton. Please come in."

They shook hands and Davina led her down the hall, saying "We're in the kitchen, I hope that's all right with you." Pru nodded and followed, glancing around as they went. It looked as if Primrose House had been "sympathetically restored," as the saying goes. The exterior remained late eighteenth century, and the furnishings were traditional but with quirky twists throughout. She saw an enormous modern painting with splotches of bright color above a fireplace, with a leather Chesterfield sofa in front of it, and on a nearby wall, a large, gilded mirror with fat cherubs decorating the top. Flanking the mirror were two avant-garde wooden chairs, the kind you weren't sure if you should sit in. In the corner of the room, Pru thought she saw a tall cactus in a pot.

Davina and Bryan, gracious and just as eclectic as their décor, were a delight, and Pru felt a great burden lifted from her just talking with them; for a time she was able to forget her money problems, her life decisions, and anything associated with murder.

Over coffee at the large farm table, Pru told them her background and they expressed understanding at her decisions. They in turn told her about how they'd moved from Manchester to live in Sussex and had spent five years restoring Primrose House. It sounded as if they threw themselves wholeheartedly into the project, living only for its completion. Pru thought that if the kitchen, which included a new British-racing-green Aga cooker, farm sink, tile backing everywhere and one of those waterspouts right over the stove for tall pots, was any indication of the care they took, the rest of the house must be amazing.

"We care too much about our English heritage to completely wipe away the past," Bryan said. "But we know it's possible to respect the past and celebrate the present, too." Although Bryan worked in international investments, he had gotten a second in history at Cambridge.

Pru talked about the vernacular landscape as it tied into architecture and how the genius of English garden design lay in its ability to absorb international influences and reflect them in its own style. She included a bit on Humphry Repton's contribution to English garden history and how she so much preferred his ideas of formality near the house that slowly changed to a more naturalistic landscape over those of Capability Brown's projects that moved heaven and earth to make the landscape look as if nothing had happened. She hoped it sounded good. They asked questions about her experience and how she enjoyed working in London and what her hopes were. She answered everything except her diminishing window of opportunity.

Pru felt good about how it was all going, and when Bryan said, "You and Davina have a look around the garden, and I'll get busy on lunch. You'll stay, won't you, Pru?" she had a fleeting urge to ask if they would adopt her.

They walked out the front door, and Pru asked about the badger knocker. "It's our nod to the country," Davina said, "and made by a local artist. You know, I think we have a badger sett near the woods, but we haven't really investigated yet."

* * *

Primrose House, as it turned out, had no primroses. "At least we've never seen any," Davina said. "We don't know where the name came from — were there primroses in the past, or was it just wishful thinking on someone's part? Still, it's such a charming name, we'd never want to change it." Pru thought of Grenadine Hall, where she would spend the weekend. It had been known as Cromley Manor until the 1840s, when the owner, in a fit of Victorian fancy, renamed it in honor of the popular pomegranate-based syrup.

Pru gave Davina a short treatise on primroses and cowslips, and how perhaps the beech wood had grown to cast more shade than they liked. She thought it perfectly reasonable to establish a patch in a sunnier spot, perhaps just beyond the wall of yew.

The drive had been regraveled after the house restoration, but the oval bed in front, which had been the staging area during the work, held nothing but tufts of grass and weeds. "We removed all the creepers and climbing roses from the walls, too, I'm afraid," she said. "So much work needed to be done on the house, we really couldn't go any other way."

Behind the house, a path that led out from the terrace to the yew walk once had been lined with boxwood, but left to its own devices, it had grown into a boxwood allée — as the plants had achieved small-tree status, their upper canopies leaned gracefully into one another.

"I believe we'd have a view of the Weald if the yew wasn't there," Davina said, referring to the rolling, wooded hills and sandstone outcroppings, a classic feature of the natural landscape in the Southeast.

Pru suggested reducing the yew severely to keep its fine architectural lines. "It's very forgiving, as long as it gets good drainage."

They walked across the gravel yard to the walled garden. Davina opened the wooden door for Pru and gestured widely, the countless layers of thin fabric that flowed from her arm following the movement like a wake.

Within the walls, devastation. "I should've prepared you," Davina said. "We just turned a blind eye, because we were spending all our efforts on the house, and now look what's happened."

The garden — always the last thing on the list. It was full of weeds, weedy shrubs, weedy trees, and perhaps just the remnants of a path or two, impassable with so much overgrowth. In the center, where once there might have been a large square bed, anchored at the corners by topiary yew, the yews had grown together to form one enormous green-black block.

To Pru, it was a dream come true.

They walked out of the walled garden, and Davina pointed to a small building set off on its own at the end of a short drive from the road. "There is the head gardener's accommodation — it used to be a cow shed. Now, we won't go over just at the moment, because the conversion hasn't quite started, but I did want you to see how close to the garden and to our house it is. It isn't large, but it will be cozy."

Pru tried to discern the condition of the building. Was it missing a door? There were openings in the wall, but could they be considered windows? The original advert for the post had described it as a "charming estate cottage."

"And just beyond — you can't see from here — there are a few partial walls left from another outbuilding. I suppose we should remove them," Davina said.

Pru told her about the ruins of a fifteenth-century tithe barn at Sudeley Castle near Cheltenham that had been planted up with roses and climbers and what a romantic setting it was. Davina loved the idea.

"There would be additional help, of course," Davina said. "We have old Ned a couple of days a week and the two lads that live just down the road. Special jobs, especially as the garden gets going, need extra hands, we know. I've never thought a head gardener should bother with machines and mowing; a head gardener should be for design, inspiration, planting, tending."

Pru felt herself balanced on the thin tightrope between hope and despair. They returned to the kitchen to a lunch of ribollita — a hearty Tuscan soup. The Templetons had brought back the recipe from a small Italian hill town they visited often. A perfect lunch, thought Pru.

After coffee, Pru rang the cabdriver and thanked Davina and Bryan profusely. Davina walked her to the door.

"We're very happy to meet you, Pru." She paused. "We'll let you know our choice just as soon as possible. I know you'll understand that we've talked with a few others about the post."

"Of course you have — that's the best way." Although she hadn't really wanted to hear that. "Now, you go on, I'll just wait for the cab here. Thanks again."

Davina closed the door, and Pru stroked the badger knocker's snout for luck. Her spirits soared.

"Interviewing for the gardener post, are you?" said a crusty voice behind her. She turned to find someone who matched his voice perfectly, from Wellies to cap.

"Yes, hello, I'm Pru. Are you Ned?" Pru remembered Davina mentioning "old Ned."

"I'm Ned, yes." He looked kindly at her. "I hope they didn't get your hopes up."

"No, I understand they haven't made a decision yet," Pru said.

"They made a decision all right. Rang up the fellow this morning and offered him the post. Too bad they didn't tell you about that."

Pru looked back at the closed door as if the badger knocker could verify this outrageous statement. "Someone else has taken the job?" she asked Ned, her voice suddenly high and reedy. "They've already filled the post?" She clamped her jaw tight in an effort to keep the tears away.

Ned looked left and right, and then at his Wellies. "Well now," he said, "I don't know that for sure. It's just something I might've heard."

"Why would they bring me down here if the job was filled? Who would do that — get someone's hopes up?" She hammered Ned with questions that should've been directed at the Templetons. She had a fleeting thought to knock on the door and ask them, but the thought flew out of her mind as quickly as it had flown in — she was not one for confrontation.

The cab turned into the drive, and the sound of the tires on the gravel caught their attention. Ned put his palm up as if to calm her. "I may have spoken out of turn," he said. "Don't pay me any mind. You have a safe journey. It was good to meet you."

Pru watched Ned wander off around the corner of the building. Her feet felt like lead as she dragged herself to the cab. She remembered nothing of the journey back to London.

Boxgrove Manor

Cannards Grave Road
Hornblotton Green
Somerset BA4 6SB

4 October

72 Grovehill Square
Chelsea
London SW3

Dear Ms. Parke,

I write to regretfully inform you that you have not been selected for the post of head gardener for Boxgrove Manor. Thank you for sharing with us your knowledge of the scientific, spiritual, and social history of our signature plant. We know your knowledge will help you in whatever post you do fill.

We appreciate your interest in this post and wish you well in your future endeavors.

Yours sincerely,
Gerald Charles, curator
Boxgrove Manor
GC/cjw

CHAPTER 6

After the interview at Primrose House that had begun with promise and ended with heartbreak, and the rejection from Boxgrove Manor, Pru thought perhaps she wouldn't check her email. Lydia seemed able to sense when she was at her weakest, and she didn't think she could take another plea to return to Texas. But she did look and found two messages from Lydia and one from Marcus. Would she come "home"? Marcus wrote that he couldn't put off the board much longer. His email had an even tone to it, and she was relieved that he kept his request on a strictly business level. Everyone remembered her and wanted her back, he wrote — her old crew, especially.

Pru wrote one email to both of them, politely saying no thank you. She deleted it before sending, and started again. She wrote that things were going well in London, and she had no plans to return. She deleted that one, too. She started again, writing that she was unsure of her plans, and could they wait another week for an answer? Her heart sank when she reread it. She didn't send it, but saved it as a draft.

* * *

Midmorning Friday, optimistically hoping to be well clear of commuter traffic, Jo and Cordelia collected Pru for their trip to the country. Before she walked out the door, Pru made the typical last-minute survey of rooms within view: laptop off, windows closed, breakfast dishes left in the sink. She opened the front door, and, somewhere behind her, heard a *click*. She held her breath.

Since the mouse event, as Pru described it to herself, she had heard other noises from the basement. It was as if the mice were rearranging furniture — a slight shuffling, a scraping, tiny crashes. It happened most often just after Pru arrived home — standing in the hall looking at the post or sitting quietly with a cup of tea.

It was getting on her nerves. Once, she had tried the door handle, even though she knew it was locked, and gone for a kitchen knife to see how easy it might be to spring. Just to check on things, she told herself — wouldn't any responsible renter do the same? But the second she rattled the keyhole with the knife, her phone rang as if sounding an alarm. She dropped the knife, the noises stopped, and she never tried it again.

She did broach the subject with Jo again one morning over a quick coffee at a place near Jo's flat. "Do you think we should do something about it? Tell the Clarkes there might be mice?" she had asked.

"What?" Jo looked alarmed at Pru's suggestion. "You know, I believe that your neighbors might be doing some work in their basement — that's probably what you hear. Once I thought someone was breaking into the closet in my bedroom, and it turned out to be the fellow next door hanging a painting. It's London," she said with a laugh, "you can't escape the noise."

Pru wasn't convinced. "I'm sure the Clarkes wouldn't want their possessions damaged. I looked around at the outside door, to see if there was anything out of the ordinary."

"Pru," Jo said firmly, "don't mess with that door." She ordered another coffee and changed the subject, telling Pru about Cordelia's latest doctor's appointment. Pru tried to listen, but was disappointed — and disconcerted — by Jo's lack of concern. Jo, who paid great attention to detail and who had walked Pru through the entire house upon her arrival, making sure everything worked as it should. Shouldn't this worry her?

Now, standing on her doorstep having just heard a door click shut, Pru thought carefully. She knew, just as everyone does, what sounds her house made, even one she'd been in for less than a year. She went down the list of possibilities, hoping to file the noise away in a safe category — the cracks and pops from the walls cooling in the evening, the rattle of the radiator in winter, the sound of a door out of plumb closing on its own. Yes, that's it; she let out her breath. The door into the downstairs loo clicked shut on its own. Pru dismissed it from her mind and closed the front door.

* * *

As Jo fought the traffic out of the city, Pru congratulated Cordelia on expecting and asked after Lucy, who, Cordelia said, was involved in a building project near the Olympic Park and would drive out after work.

They cleared London on the M40, cut off to the ring road around Oxford and switched to the A44, ending up on smaller and smaller roads. Pru leaned her head against the window and looked out at the emerging fields and hedgerows. Just the sight of the country cleared her mind. She would put all her cares aside for the weekend.

In May, the English hedgerows, decorated in the white flowers of hawthorn, guelder rose, and elder, looked dressed for a wedding, but early autumn held its own charms. Red haws, black berries from the elder, translucent red fruit from viburnum, and hips of the dog rose warmed up the roadside, just as a few leaves began to age to gold and red. The generous canopies of English oaks and beeches watched over fields planted with winter wheat. They drove past Blenheim

Palace in Woodstock — the palace could be seen beyond the gate and down the drive, but Capability Brown's enormous eighteenth-century landscape lay beyond . . . and beyond.

* * *

Natalie and John Bennet-Smythe — Natalie was Jo's cousin somewhere on her father's side — lived near the village of Upper Oddington and offered their field each year for the autumn fête, which raised money for the village library. The tents were full of an assortment of goods: beaded jewelry, the Women's Institute's jams and breads, a high-end jumble sale, a potter. Educational booths for Wild Britain, the National Trust, and Badger Care clustered on one side, and the tea and the beer tents anchored one end of the field. A bouncy castle and arts-and-crafts tables would keep the little ones occupied.

The competition tent — prizes given for the best autumn fruit, the biggest courgette, and the most impressive decorative use of a wheat sheaf — stood at the top of the field. Jo told her that a few years earlier, the organizers had tried a competition for the prettiest pig, but a dodgy fence led to an escape by a crafty Gloucester Old Spot named Porridge. The chase through the tea tent resulted in a table full of cream cakes upside down in the grass, and since that time, the competitions had been confined to non-ambulatory categories.

White tents with flapping edges already rose in the field when Jo pulled into the long drive and parked near the house around teatime, after a lunch stop along the way. They were met by Natalie, who gave Pru the basic layout of the house and showed them all to their rooms. Pru, in desperate need of a walk, glanced around the grounds as they passed by every window.

The Bennet-Smythes kept up Grenadine Hall, built of that fine honey-toned Cotswold stone, by a combination of family money, John's lucrative banking position, Natalie's book editing, hiring out the gardens as a wedding venue, and hosting classes for the Royal Horticultural Society. They held four open days a year for the National Garden Scheme, but the £3 admission went straight to charity, not in their own pockets — although they were able to keep some of the £2 each for tea and cake, just to help cover costs.

As it was a Grade II-listed building, they could do only so much, keeping the history deemed more important than installing a bathroom for every single one of the ten bedrooms — that would be considered a very American thing to do. The rooms that Jo, Pru, and Cordelia and Lucy occupied shared one enormous bathroom, in which they could've held a dance it was so large. It created a bit of a slumber-party atmosphere.

Pru's room overlooked the walled garden — she must remember to thank Natalie for the view — and beyond, she could see the Cotswold escarpment rising. Patches of oak woodland created dark spots against the fields, some of which displayed a light green contrast, while others a tawny autumn tone. Farther to the right, she could see the tents. Pru stood at the window and contemplated the beauty and her deep longing to stay in her new home country.

* * *

After poking around her room a bit, Pru stopped by Jo's to say she was off for a walk.

"Don't you want to see the gardens?" Jo asked, which of course Pru did. They went down together so that Jo could introduce her to the gardener, Oliver, after which Jo retreated to the house for a nap and Oliver began Pru's tour.

Tall yew hedges lined the walks, and old roses with a few flowers still coming on climbed the walls of the house. They walked down to the walled garden, where, in Victorian times, fruits and vegetables had been grown for the kitchen. A few years ago, the Bennet-Smythes had turned it from flowers back to a kitchen garden, but because it was only Natalie and John in the house, most of the food grown they gave to the food bank in Stow-on-the-Wold, keeping out just enough for themselves and guests.

The orangery had been restored, and now a modest assortment of figs and grapes occupied one wall. "We do well with the veg, but in here, we're trying pomegranates," Oliver said. "Natalie and John thought they could make grenadine syrup, bottle the stuff, and sell it." They stood looking at the four drooping shrubs in pride of place against the warmest wall. "I'm not holding out hope," Oliver said.

Pru thought of the two large pomegranate shrubs growing in the Chelsea Physic Garden and mentioned them to Oliver. "We're fair colder in winter than you are up in London," he said.

"Yes, but I don't believe the fruit ever ripens even there," she said. "They have an enormous olive tree, too, but it doesn't fruit either. At least the big bay tree can be harvested."

"We keep our bay trees outdoors," Oliver said, "but only for the summer and only in pots so we can slip them in here for the winter."

When they stepped outside, Pru had a view of a series of neatly clipped yew rectangles, each about ten feet high and a little longer. But they weren't quite as neatly clipped as she first thought. She stood still and squinted into the sun, which came in at an angle and cast shadows over the deep green surface. Clipped in relief on each yew block was a . . . "Oliver, do I see horses?"

He laughed. "I'm glad they're starting to show. I started shearing them two years ago. Each block has a running horse on it."

"They're delightful," Pru said. "How ever did you come up with that idea?"

"I visited a garden in Wiltshire once that had yew arches that were sheared to look like elephants," Oliver said. "But the head gardener had done it without permission, and when the owners finally noticed, they made him smooth the surfaces out."

"You'd think we could have a little fun in the garden," Pru said.

"These yews have been here for ages, and so I had a ready canvas," he said. "But I made sure to ask Natalie and John before I started. Fortunately, they have a sense of humor."

"In the States," Pru said, "there's a garden with an entire hunt scene clipped out of box."

"And I thought we were fanatics."

Pru thought about the overgrown yew hedge at Primrose House and wished she'd had the chance to suggest it be clipped into a series of rolling waves or perhaps as busts of famous Romans.

Romans on her mind, Pru asked Oliver about finding artifacts in the garden.

"I suppose there could be something a few feet down like at Chedworth," Oliver said. "But here, we just turn up Victorian refuse — the fields are full of broken crockery and the like. If they were finished with it, they just chucked it off the edge of the garden. Makes you wonder if everything we throw out will be important artifacts in a few hundred years. Imagine the fun they'll have excavating our rubbish tips."

* * *

Pru returned to the house to find Jo drinking tea in the kitchen with Natalie. Jo suggested it might be time to switch to wine, so they took a bottle out to the terrace where Cordelia joined them with a glass of water. They caught the last of the light, just as Lucy arrived. She went immediately to Cordelia, asking how she felt and insisting she drink a glass of milk.

Over dinner, an enormous chicken-and-pasta casserole with a salad and roasted aubergines — that is, eggplants — on the side, they mostly avoided talk of the London murder, which the Bennet-Smythes had heard about from Jo. Instead Natalie and John entertained them with stories of the early years of their marriage, which they spent on a foreign-service posting on the island of Corfu, not a bad spot to be assigned, everyone agreed.

At a lull in the conversation, Jo said in a careful voice, as if afraid of disturbing the room's equilibrium, "Pru, I spoke to the Clarkes, and they don't want you to worry a bit. They won't be coming back early — you've still got another month in the house." She turned to the others. "They are both quite chatty people," she said, "especially Pippa — the stories she can tell. I told them your business was really picking up, Pru, and they were quite interested, asking all sorts of questions about the Roman tiles. I did have to tell them about the murder, though — they were shocked."

"I don't see how a month will make a difference in my prospects," Pru said, "but thanks. Have they been buying antiques?"

"Antiques?" Jo echoed. "Wouldn't we all like to be in Italy buying antiques?" she asked, as if it was a good joke. She seemed about to go on, but Natalie, who had left for the kitchen, came back with sticky toffee pudding, which distracted everyone.

Later, as they all pitched in to clear the table, Jo said, "Lucy, you might know the fellow Pru's sublet from. He's a history professor at University College and took a sabbatical year." She set dishes down in the sink. "Clarke, Archie Clarke."

Lucy's architectural knowledge spanned the centuries — she designed modern buildings, but occasionally taught the history of architecture at University College London where her book, *Porticos, Verandahs, and Loggias: The Architectural History of Outdoor Ceilings*, was a text. "Archie Clarke," Lucy thought for a moment. "Yes, I might have heard the name."

Pru set aside any worry about the Clarkes returning, at least for the moment. "We're off to Chedworth on Sunday. I know they don't have any gardens there, but will we see mosaics in the rooms?"

As they gathered up the scattered knives, forks, and spoons, Lucy began to explain the general arrangement of a Roman Britain villa. "See here," she said, taking a few left-over knives and arranging them on the almost-empty table. "The house was usually situated around the atrium, and then outside that was another area called the peristylium — both were outdoor, inner courtyards." She added a few extra spoons at each end. "And there might have been wings of rooms along the sides."

"I'm sure there were gardens at Chedworth," Pru said. "It's too bad the National Trust wouldn't hire me to recreate what they might have been." She couldn't help it. She longed for a place to actually put to work what grew in her head.

* * *

The next morning, after a late breakfast — light fare in anticipation of all the fine treats at the Women's Institute booth and in the tea tent — Pru, Jo, and Natalie wandered out to the fête. Cordelia was experiencing just a touch of morning sickness, and Lucy, dutiful partner, stayed by her side ready with a small plate of cream crackers.

Beginning on one side of the field, they made their way counterclockwise around the booths, straggling along and calling to one another to look at this cup or that knitted hat. Jo had backtracked to walk with Cordelia and Lucy, who had just emerged from the house, when Natalie came up beside Pru and casually examined a quilted tea cozy. "Pru, I don't want to alarm you, but there's a fellow at a tent across the way who has been watching your every move since we got here."

Pru froze. Had someone followed her here from London? The bag snatcher? Malcolm? Saxsby? That exhausted her suspect list, so she asked, "Which booth? What does he look like?"

Natalie casually turned and surveyed the tents as if she was looking for someone.

"Straight behind you. He's tall, dark hair. He looks harmless, but rather intense. He's at the Badger Care booth."

Pru turned around, and across the field she saw DCI Pearse standing under a banner that read: "Badgers — our companions in the country."

"Oh God."

"Do you know him?" asked Natalie, who looked back to see Pearse talking with a couple of people at the booth.

113

"Yes, I guess I do know him," Pru said. She couldn't quite identify her reaction to seeing him — it was part surprise, part annoyance, and part . . . she wasn't sure what that other part was. He'd seen her, and so she couldn't ignore him. "I suppose I'll go and just say hello."

Pru made what seemed like an excruciatingly long walk across the grass to the Badger Care booth, cutting off not only the tea tent, but also the jumble sale, to which she intended to get back. Pearse watched her walk halfway — Pru gave him a tiny wave of acknowledgement — and then he turned to offer a brochure to someone who approached the table. By the time Pru walked up, Pearse was saying, "You might see that they've dug into the side of a small hill. The opening will be hidden with shrubs, to protect the cubs and give them a place to play." He glanced at her and gave a small smile while she perused the table of leaflets, which had a drawing of a badger head on them as a logo. It reminded her of the knocker at Primrose House.

"Hello." A girl, eight or nine years old stood holding a thick pile of leaflets. She wore denims and two sweaters and had strawberry-blond hair pulled back in a ponytail and green Wellington boots up to her knees.

"Hi," Pru said.

"Are you interested in the badgers?" the girl asked.

"Well," said Pru, "yes, I am interested in badgers."

The girl's eyes grew large. "Are you American?"

"Yes, I am. I'm from Texas."

"Do you have badgers in Texas?" she asked.

"I believe we do," Pru said, "although I've never seen one. But we do have possums, and I see those. Possums have long noses, they hang in trees by their tails, and carry their babies on their backs." The girl lifted her eyebrows. "I'd love to see a badger, though."

"Badgers can live quite close to your house, you know, and they won't bother you at all," the girl replied, launching into what sounded like a school report. "My class has adopted a badger sett near here, to help teach people about them. You can even go and watch the badgers at night, but you must be very quiet about it."

"Right, Becky, thanks for helping out here," Pearse said, now freed up from his earlier exchange. "Did your dad send you over?"

"Yes. Mum and Dad are just coming, and when they get here, I can go to the crafts tent. We're building a house for toads."

"You go get started on the house," Pearse said. "I'll be fine until your dad arrives."

"Right," she said, "bye," and she ducked under the table and headed off to the crafts tent. Pearse turned his attention to Pru.

"Ms. Parke, what brings you to the country?" he asked.

"I'm visiting for the weekend with my friend, Jo. She's related to the Bennet-Smythes." It occurred to her that this might be a problem. "Was I not supposed to leave London?"

"You're free to move about. After all, we do have your passport information. And your fingerprints."

Pru chose to ignore that. "Did the badgers bring you here?" asked Pru.

"I lived near here for many years, and I still like to get out of London when I can, although that's not often. I don't mind helping out with the group."

"Helping out? He started the whole organization," said a tall, elegantly dressed blonde walking up to the table.

Pearse's demeanor stiffened slightly. "Hello, Phyl, were you looking for me?"

The woman stretched her hand out to Pru. "Hello, I'm Phyllida Tinsdale, the ex. Are you a friend of Christopher's?"

Pru took her hand with a firm grip and replied, "Hello, I'm Pru Parke. I was a witness to a . . . I found the . . ."

"Ms. Parke is helping with an investigation," Pearse said smoothly.

"Lovely to meet you, Pru," Phyl said, and turned back to Pearse. "Have you phoned Graham? He wanted you to go for parents day if you could."

A stocky man with a shaven head came up behind the table and held out a brochure to Pru, who, grateful to be taken out of the spotlight, began asking anything she could think of about badgers, while trying to keep one ear on the other conversation.

She heard only snatches. Pearse saying, "Phyl, I talk to Graham every week — you don't have to remind me," and Phyl replying, "Yes, but do you ever take any time off work to go visit?" and something about the Lake District. Pru's mind flipped through all the possibilities at hand — ex-wife obviously, Graham, probably son, at school somewhere. Divorced for how long?

". . . And I'm glad you can come out with us this evening, it isn't far, and it's quite interesting to see them in their habitat." Pru was brought back to the moment at hand when she realized that she'd just volunteered to go that evening to see a badger sett.

"It's a fascinating look at wildlife, if you're interested," Pearse said, now free of Phyl, who was heading toward the car park.

The man, whose name Pru didn't think she got, started up a conversation with an elderly woman who lingered a second too long in front of the table, leaving Pru and Pearse on their own. "I'm not quite sure what I volunteered for. Is it tonight? Where do we go?"

"I'm sorry if Phyl distracted you. We don't see much of each other, but when I'm out here, she does stop by."

Pru felt her cheeks grow warm. "I wasn't distracted. I just didn't quite get all the information that . . ." Pru faltered at the man's name, knowing that wasn't a good sign.

Pearse handed a brochure to a woman with a baby in a front-pack, after which a young girl came over to ask for one of the badger coloring booklets. As Pru took a step back and turned to leave, Pearse said to her, "Ms. Parke, I'm finished here in another hour. Fancy a pint down the road at the Horse & Groom?"

Caught slightly off guard, she regained her composure quickly. "Yes, sure. I'll meet you there."

* * *

Pru walked to the pub, about a mile down the road, on a public footpath through a field, and then a short bit down another road, following directions given to her by Natalie. At the house, she'd left a note for Jo, whom she'd lost track of — Pru thought she might be going over the treasures in the jumble sale tent — that said she'd run into DCI Pearse, who wanted a word with her. She knew that sounded too official, but she felt it was better to keep it that way. After all, as far as she knew, it was official.

She arrived just two minutes before him, and had time to dash in the loo, coming out as he walked in the door. They ordered and collected their pints, choosing a settle opposite the bar. Pru thought badgers would be neutral ground.

"Did you really start the Badger Care group?" she asked.

"I was just one of several people. We wanted people in the country and the city to know that badgers are a vital part of our British life."

"Along with Ratty, Mole, and Toad."

Pearse smiled.

"My mother read *The Wind in the Willows* to me," Pru said, "and I still remember wishing I could get an armadillo to talk to me the way Badger and the rest of them talked."

"They are quite taciturn in real life," Pearse said.

Like some police officers. "Do you volunteer for the group often, Inspector?"

He sighed and carefully rearranged the extra beer mats on the table. "Ms. Parke . . . Pru, please call me Christopher."

"Yes. Of course. Christopher."

"I enjoy the country, and I like to help keep it. And when I get out of London and just past Oxford, I feel like I can breathe again."

"It shows," she said.

117

"I don't take much time off work, and so I suppose I keep up my official demeanor a little too fiercely."

"No," Pru said, "I didn't mean that — it's just that, it's nice to see you, as, not the detective chief inspector. For a while."

Christopher watched her and smiled. She'd seen little of that smile during their encounters in London. He had a direct way about him, she thought, and intense brown eyes that seemed to see through her. It disconcerted her when he questioned them at the Wilsons'. It disconcerted her now, too, but in a different way.

"You said your mother was British," he said. "Where was she from?"

"She was from Imber."

"Imber? Was she now?" he asked with amazement in his voice. "And where did she end up?"

She was pleased he knew about Imber, a village on the Salisbury Plain that was closed in 1943 — all the residents evacuated — so that the American soldiers could practice and prepare to invade Europe. The village remained closed, and the British army continued to use the area for military maneuvers.

"My mother and her mother moved in with some cousins in Ibsley, near the RAF base. Her father was killed in the war. I know that Imber — or, what's left of it — is open occasionally to former residents and families. I haven't looked into it, but I might be able to visit." One more reason to stay, she thought.

Thinking about her mother's early life always reminded Pru of the small box — too small a box, she thought — stored at Lydia's when she moved to London. It held a few pieces of her mother's life in England — some faded photos of Pru's grandmother, her grandfather in uniform, her mother as a child. Really, her mother was still just a child when she had met her future husband. Some old letters, including several that her mother herself had written but never sent, tied with a faded blue ribbon. After her mother died, Pru opened the letters, but had them found them too personal to read so soon, and she had carefully retied them and put them away.

"She met my father in Ibsley, when the Americans came over and he was stationed there. She was barely sixteen at the end of the war, but he waited another two years and came back from Texas for her. I grew up listening to stories of England. My father died about fifteen years ago, and my mother died two years ago, and I realized that what I needed to do, what I'd been waiting to do my whole life, was live here." Pru startled herself with how much she told him.

"England is quite a change from Texas," Christopher said.

"And Texas was quite a change for my mother. It isn't easy to plant an English cottage garden in that climate," she said, "but my mother always tried. She learned that, in order to grow sweet peas, she had to plant them in the fall, and they would bloom in April. It sort of threw off the summer garden look."

"And the English weather doesn't bother you?"

"I adapted quickly. Although I'm not sure this will all work out. My friend Lydia in Dallas has already started pushing for my return. I had a plan — I gave myself a year to find a permanent head gardener position — that seemed like enough time. But so far all I can find are bits of maintenance work, and my year is almost up."

"Is there ever any room for compromise in your plans?"

She glanced up at him and away again. *Must be those keen investigative skills.* "No," she said with a half smile, "not very often. Of course, the Wilsons' garden is more than just maintenance work. It's a whole project, and that will help. When," she emphasized, "I can get started. And so, has there been any progress in the investigation?"

"We'll try to get out of your way as soon as possible," Christopher said, "but in the meantime, you will be careful about what you do. You don't need to get involved in the investigation."

Pru watched him quietly for a moment, not wanting to argue, but knowing that she couldn't let this go. Involved was just what she need to be, and not just because she wanted to know what was going on, but also because she needed to hold on to that garden job, to say nothing of standing up for Mr. Wilson, who couldn't possibly have murdered his friend over a mosaic in the shed.

That line of thinking brought to mind the conversation between Malcolm and Saxsby that she overheard, and she was about to tell Christopher when she saw Jo walk in. Jo saw Pru, but because of the high back on the settle, she did not see anyone sitting across from her. Jo strode across the room, saying, as she walked, "Can you believe that he would start interrogating you here when all you are trying to do is have a weekend . . ." She reached the table, saw Christopher, and stopped short. "Oh. Hello."

"Jo, this is Christopher Pearse. Christopher, this is my friend Jo Howard."

"Ms. Howard. Will you join us?"

Jo became graciousness personified. "No, thank you so much, Mr. Pearse. Pru mentioned she might be at the pub, and as I was on my way back from picking up a few things in Stow, I thought I'd just stop by and see if she needed a lift."

"I'd be happy to drive you back," Christopher said.

"No, thanks, Christopher," Pru felt as if she might be overcome with giggles. "I'll go with Jo. Thanks for the drink."

"I'll call for you this evening at six. Is that all right?"

"Yes, that's fine."

"Be sure to wear quiet clothes."

As soon as they were outside, Jo burst into laughter, and Pru let the giggles out. "Quiet clothes?" Jo asked. "What kind of a date is this?"

"It isn't a date." Pru sobered up. "We're going to watch badgers." She needed to raise her voice to be heard over Jo's howls of laughter. "Other people will be there."

* * *

Pru layered her clothes for the evening trek — the weather may be mild, but sitting or standing still for she didn't know how long would surely chill her. She read through the badger brochure and learned that quiet clothing — that is, clothes that didn't rustle — decreased the possibility of startling the badgers and increased the chance of watching them do whatever badgers do when they come out at night.

She waited outside the front door, and Christopher pulled up with two other people — the other man at the booth and his wife, little Becky's parents, Michael and Susan. "Becky wanted to come along, especially when she learned the American woman would be here, but it's really much too late an evening for an eight-year-old, so she's home with her older brother."

As they drove down the country lanes, Pru turned halfway round so that she could see Susan, who talked about the fête and how more people lately seem to really care what happened in the country. Then Susan said, "Becky told us about you first, that you're from Texas. And then Christopher told us about you, and your work and how much you know about gardens. And that your mother was English." Pru had no idea she had made such an impression on Becky. Or Christopher. She looked over at him, but he kept his eyes on the road.

"Here we are now," he said, pulling off the road. "Our shelter is quite close, but we shouldn't make any noise, and there's no talking once we're settled in there."

"I'll try to keep quiet," Pru said.

They walked to a small wooden shed, like a duck blind. Susan took a cloth bag out and tossed peanuts and raisins around the clearing. Pru had read that would keep the badgers around for a while after they emerged. They stood quietly watching through the opening as dusk settled.

At first, Pru felt disconcerted to be among people she didn't know well without being able to talk, but the silence, instead of growing in size and weight, actually became companionable. Looking out onto the edge of woodland brought her a sense of peace, and she found her mind quieted. As they waited, she realized she should have been closer to the opening for a better view, and tried to stand on her toes to peer out. Christopher, standing near the edge of the window, beckoned her over with a nod of his head, and she moved as quietly as she could to stand beside him. He put his hand on her back, and they waited. Pru tried to keep her mind on badgers.

And then they came. The badgers, their long, sleek faces accentuated by the black-and-white stripes that ran from their noses straight back over their ears and into salt-and-pepper fur, snuffled about, finding the treats left for them. They were stocky animals, and bigger in person than she imagined. She could hear them make small sounds, sort of like chuckling. It was magical — much better than a Disney movie, Pru thought.

The food kept them around for a while, but eventually, as it grew dark, they trundled off on their nightly routines. When they were well and gone, the four humans returned to the car as the moon rose.

"We thought we'd stop for a meal, Pru," Susan said. "Is that all right?"

"Yes, perfect."

The Horse & Groom held a comfortable contingent of locals, most of them standing with their pints, but a few at tables where, in the evenings, they could order food — lunch orders were taken strictly at the bar.

"They do a lovely curry," Susan said. Pru thought she'd go along with her suggestion, as it would take her far too long to read through every item on the menu — especially without any reading glasses — until she noticed that the soup of the day was roasted tomato bisque. She did so love soup and ordered a large bowl.

"Is that it, then?" asked the waitress.

"Yes, that's it."

"We've got wholemeal bread, baked this morning. Would you like some of that?"

"I'd love some," Pru said.

After the waitress left, Susan asked, "Are you a vegetarian, Pru?"

"God no," said Pru. "It's against the law to be a vegetarian in Texas." They all looked at her. "That's a joke," she said. "Sort of."

"Pru," Susan said, "you don't really sound like you're from Texas."

"You mean I don't sound like a country-western singer," Pru said.

"Might your English mother have influenced your accent?" Christopher asked.

"She might have, yes."

Christopher told Michael and Susan where Pru's mother came from and reminded them of Imber's history. "It seems that some rare plants are able to survive on the plain because it's inaccessible to the public and to grazing animals."

"I didn't know that," Pru said, thinking that really should have been her line.

Christopher gave a small shrug. "I read about it recently."

"How recently?" she asked.

He replied only with a smile. She couldn't help thinking that "recently" meant some online research between their drink that afternoon and the badger expedition that evening. She tried not to be too pleased.

* * *

Michael and Susan lived close to the small town of Stow-on-the-Wold, where Michael owned a personal-computer servicing business and Susan worked at home as a technical writer. They'd been to the States before, and so the conversation began by quizzing Pru about the business climate in Texas, of which Pru was woefully ignorant. Fortunately, the topic turned to country matters and moved from there on to Roman Britain.

"I'm going to see Chedworth tomorrow morning," Pru said. "I've never been, and I'm looking forward to seeing the mosaics there, to see if they are anything like the mosaic we found in the garden where the murder took place." She stopped and, alarmed at what she'd said, looked at Christopher beside her.

"That's all right," he said to her. "You certainly aren't giving any secrets away." To Susan and Michael he said, "That's how Pru and I met. Over a body."

Pru heard Susan sigh and whisper, "Such romance."

"There are no gardens at Chedworth," Pru said, believing the conversation needed to get back onto an even keel, "but I've read up on the kinds of plants the Romans grew. They tried to bring plants from farther south to grow here, and that didn't always work out well — Italian cypress may do all right in some places, but grapes and pomegranates aren't quite so successful."

"Ooh, pomegranates," Susan said, "I wish we could grow them. They're very dear in the shops."

"Oliver, the gardener at Grenadine Hall, is trying to grow them in the orangery, in honor of the house's name," Pru said. "He says Natalie and John hope to make their own syrup and bottle it. But glasshouses tend to be humid, and pomegranates like it on the dry side, so I'm not sure it will work."

"Well, if they like it on the dry side," Susan said, "I'll give up hope right now."

* * *

"We're very happy to meet you, Pru," Susan said as they walked to the car ahead of Michael and Christopher. "We don't see as much of Christopher as we'd like, but when he does come out, he's always on his own."

Pru felt she must correct any misconception. "No, we aren't . . . that is, it's just because of the case, and we happened to . . ." Try as she might, she couldn't quite focus her thoughts to deny Susan's amiable observations. And Susan ignored her attempts.

"We have a spring fair to start off the season. I hope you can come out for it." She glanced back over her shoulder as the men approached. "We know Christopher well enough. He keeps himself to himself, if you know what I mean. But he was different this evening — he was quite relaxed, enjoying himself."

* * *

At the house, Christopher parked and walked Pru around the corner to the kitchen door, where a light had been left on for her.

"I hope it was all right that I mentioned the mosaic at the Wilsons'," Pru said.

"That wasn't a problem — don't worry about it."

They stood outside the kitchen door. She looked up to the clear sky filled with stars, and Christopher followed her gaze. "What a gorgeous sky, we don't see this in town," she said.

From inside, they heard a chair scrape across the flagstone floor followed by a muffled giggle.

Pru raised her eyebrows. "My chaperones."

"Ah," Christopher said, "gooseberries."

"Gooseberries?"

"It's an old country name for an unwanted chaperone."

"Yes, that's what they are — they're gooseberries. Thanks for asking me along this evening," Pru said. "I really enjoyed it."

"The Horse & Groom does a Sunday carvery," he said. "Would you care to join me tomorrow?"

"Thanks, I'd like that."

"I'll call for you at half past one."

"That's fine." She glanced at the door. "Goodnight." Pru let herself into the kitchen, where she found Jo and Lucy in pajamas and sitting at the table, mugs of hot chocolate in front of them.

"Well, how were the *badgers*?" Lucy asked, winking broadly.

"There's no need for innuendo," Pru said. "We went to see badgers — with other people — and we saw badgers."

"You've been watching badgers all this time?" Jo looked up at the clock on the wall.

"And then we went for a meal," said Pru in an offhanded manner.

"Ah ha — and then?" Lucy asked.

"And then they all brought me home. That's the end of the story, girls. Goodnight."

* * *

Not wanting to miss Chedworth Roman Villa, Pru and Jo set off first thing in the morning, so that Pru could still meet Christopher for lunch. "I know the Romans are important to you, Pru," Jo said in her mother voice, "but ancient Romans don't hold a candle to a lunch date with a good-looking detective."

Although Chedworth had no restored gardens as Fishbourne in Sussex had, the extensive mosaic floors that had been uncovered were impressive. She and Jo wandered about on the raised walkways — built to help keep the remaining mosaics intact — and admired the craftsmanship of the tiles and artistry of the designs, which included representations of winter, spring and summer; only autumn was missing.

But Chedworth seemed to have little to do with the mosaic at the Wilsons'. Even though only a portion had been revealed, theirs appeared to be a mosaic sitting directly on soil — soil that got wetter the further down you dug. Entire Roman floors were often set on posts, so that the space between floor and ground, called the hypocaust, Pru read on a sign, could carry heated air from the furnace. Ingenious, but unrelated, and it left her unsatisfied.

And distracted. Chedworth had been a showy, luxurious villa until the fourth century, but it was only in 1864 that a gardener came upon the remains of a building while digging for a lost ferret. *Leave it to a gardener to uncover such an amazing find.* As they strolled around, thoughts of the lost ferret reminded Pru of the hedgehog nest in the Wilsons' garden shed. That led to thoughts of badgers and then straight to Christopher. She hated to admit it, to herself let alone to Jo, but she felt just a touch of nervousness about their afternoon lunch. *It's just a lunch*, she thought. *More than a drink, but less than dinner.*

On the drive back to Grenadine Hall, Jo sensed her preoccupation. "You know, Pru," she said, in a careful manner, "if you and Christopher begin to see more of each other, then that's just one more reason to stay even if you don't have a job at . . ."

"Oh, no," Pru stopped her. "That not the deal I made." Pru already had mentioned — just mentioned — to Jo that the end of her year drew near and that Lydia and others had already started making plans for Pru's move back to the States.

"You mean," said Jo, "the deal you made with yourself? Is that the deal you're talking about?"

"I can't wander aimlessly through life." Pru knew this explanation would make no impression on Jo. "I made a plan, and I need to stick to it. I need to set some standards."

"No matter how miserable you make yourself?" Jo asked, after which she changed her tone, as if to back off from the direct attack. "It's pleasant to spend time with someone who shares some of your interests, isn't it — nature, the country, you know?"

Pru looked at her out of the corner of her eye and said nothing.

* * *

She pulled on a nubby, rose-red cardigan, brushed off her brown corduroy trousers, took out her hair clip, combed it through, reclipped, and stood in the hall, ready to go, just before half past one. A few butterflies had taken up residence in her stomach. Jo saw her waiting and intervened.

"Go stand in the library," she shooed Pru away. "I'll answer the door."

"Jo, you're not going to tell him I have a curfew, are you?" Pru joked as she stood in the doorway from hall to library.

When Christopher knocked, Pru came out of the library just in time to hear Jo say, "Hello, Christopher, let me just go and see if Pru is ready. Oh, here you are," and she made a face at Pru as she left them.

"These gooseberries don't give up, do they?" Pru smiled at him. He wore a dark canvas field coat and olive-green trousers, looking the perfect country gentleman.

"You look very nice," he said as he held the door open for her and they walked out.

"Thanks. You don't look too bad yourself."

He had walked over from the pub to fetch her where he was staying in one of their bed-and-breakfast rooms upstairs. They set out, chatting about Rome and the countryside. He asked about any family she might have in England, and she said she had none that she knew of, but told him about the Wilsons' former gardener, Simon Parke. "I hope I can meet him. He might be some distant cousin, you never know."

The way to the pub ran through the grassy verge alongside the road, over a stile, and then across a field. As they neared an oak at the edge of the field, Christopher put his hand on her shoulder and they stopped. He nodded to a low branch and, after a moment, Pru could see a tiny bird, its orange-red breast bright against the dark trunk. They stood just a few feet away, and the robin hopped down the branch, edging closer and closer to them, eyeing them all the while, as curious about them as they were about him. When a car motored past, the bird flew off into the high grass.

"How did you know he was there?" Pru asked as they continued their walk.

"I could hear his *tic-tic-tic* — I knew he must be close."

"They are so cute. American robins are much bigger," she said.

"Are they bigger all over the States or just in Texas?"

She laughed. "American robins are blackbirds," she said, and added to explain, "Well, what Americans call robins are quite close to blackbirds here, only with red breasts. We don't have these little guys."

They walked single file on the narrow footpath through the wheat field, which headed off at an odd angle to meet up with the road on the other side. The ground under their feet was hard, and Pru could see bits of broken crockery embedded in it — just as Oliver had mentioned, mementos of previous generations. She had been in a hurry walking to the pub the day before, so now she slowed down to look at the different colors and patterns as she walked and almost ran into Christopher who had stopped to wait for her.

He took her hand. "Looking for Roman treasure?"

"I don't think it works to look for it on purpose," she said. "It seems all the important finds are accidents."

* * *

The mild early-autumn temperatures — warm at least at midday — continued, so they sat outside with their pints after ordering food, and the conversation turned back around to the Roman ruins at Chedworth.

"Can you believe that such a place existed and no one knew about it?" Pru asked. "Just think what else might be at the Wilsons'. What if the whole block is a villa?" She'd started to dream again, and as she started thinking about the mosaic, she remembered the soil. "Do you know about rivers in London that have been covered over? The Fleet, and maybe others?"

"Many others. I know the Fleet was covered for sanitary purposes, and there was a river that made its way through Chelsea. It comes out — what's left of it — at the Embankment."

"Do you think that there could be a tributary, some small stream, that runs along the bottom of the Wilsons' garden? That might explain the wet soil."

"Are you thinking about your new garden?"

She shrugged. "If the stream had always been there, why did someone put a mosaic floor over it? I suppose there could be all sorts of artifacts buried there, along with the mosaic and the coins. Do you think that's what the murder was about? The possibility of valuable pieces hidden in the garden?"

"It's the only connection right now," Christopher said. "Jeremy Pendergast and Harry Wilson both love archaeology, both enjoy digging for the past. Often the pieces that are found on amateur or professional digs are donated or lent to museums, but those artifacts can go for a high price at auctions — and there are many private collectors about. However, you can't take someone else's property and auction it off as your own. And if something were found there, it didn't belong to either of them."

"But," she couldn't help herself, "you know that Mr. Wilson didn't take that coin and leave it on his own desk, don't you?" The two coins — one in the dead man's hand and one on Mr. Wilson's desk — seemed entirely too easy a link.

He nodded to concede her point. "It does appear too convenient that you found it there," he said, "but that doesn't prove that Wilson didn't pick it up in the shed."

She ignored that suggestion. "So, perhaps someone was trying to steal the coins — or the mosaic?" Pru realized she was giving Mr. Wilson the motive for murder — in order to stop Jeremy from cashing in or perhaps wanting to cash in himself. "Not Mr. Wilson, of course, he wouldn't do it. What about Malcolm?"

She knew it sounded as if she were throwing Malcolm to the wolves, but she thought a broader gallery of suspects might weaken the spotlight on Mr. Wilson. "Malcolm could've come over the wall. And he's been involved in some shady dealings." Pru saw a smile flicker across Christopher's face at such a trite phrase, but then it disappeared quickly, as if he thought better of it. "He blackmailed Jeremy last year."

"Who told you that?" Christopher frowned slightly.

"The Wilsons told me," Pru said, and then regretted it, because it made Mr. Wilson guilty of something else now: withholding evidence. "But I don't think he actually carried out the blackmail. They said Jeremy called his bluff or something. It probably didn't turn out to be much."

"What else did the Wilsons tell you about Malcolm?"

"Well," she held her new theory close to her like a prize, "the Wilsons didn't tell me this, but I suppose you saw the ladder rungs on Malcolm's side of the garden wall."

"Yes, *I* saw them," he said, "when I questioned Mr. Crisp at his house. How was it that *you* saw them?"

How did you see them, Pru? She wondered if the same excuse she had been ready to give Malcolm would work for Christopher: checking on the soil. He watched her with his deep dark brown eyes. Her bravado fell apart, and, at any rate, she had always been a bad liar. "Almost every time I'm there, he pops up over the wall to chat, like a jack-in-the-box. I wanted to see what he was standing on."

"Pru . . ." she could feel the lecture starting.

"Christopher, there's something else I've been meaning to tell you. A few days ago, I overheard Malcolm talking with someone in his garden, and I think they were talking about the mosaic."

Christopher looked puzzled. "You overheard . . . where was this?"

Pru explained the circumstances and the conversation — touching only lightly on Saxsby's mention of Mr. Wilson as the murderer, because it sounded to her as if Saxsby was feeding Malcolm a line. She admitted to crossing the line of tape around the shed, but pointed out that she left no fingerprints and ventured no further into the shed than just inside the door. She didn't mention that Malcolm had seen her.

Christopher's face took on a taut look. "Why didn't you tell me this earlier?"

"I tried to phone you after it happened, but I got your voice mail. I didn't want to leave it on a message, so I thought I'd ring later. And then it slipped my mind." Now, she was the one withholding evidence. "I thought I might try and ask Malcolm about this Saxsby. And, I will admit, I was irritated at being called 'a bloody American gardener.'"

Christopher sighed. "Pru," he said with a stern tone, "you are not a police officer. It isn't up to you to conduct interviews or try to turn up more evidence."

She bristled at this treatment — it felt as if he were chastising her. She was not a disobedient child, and she shot back, "I have common sense, and I can use that. I'm not in danger from Malcolm." *But if he's involved in the murder and I'm a witness, maybe I am.* "And no one leapt over the garden wall to grab me by the throat."

"Perhaps you aren't in danger now, but you don't know what might happen if you continue to pry." Christopher's voice stayed quiet, but she sensed a growing anger.

"Pry?" Pru raised her voice. "Pry? I'm not Miss Marple. If I learn something that might help . . ."

He interrupted. "We are pursuing several lines of inquiry and do not need your help. This is a police matter, and as much as you may wish to . . ." he seemed to be searching for the least-offensive words ". . . be involved in the investigation, your actions — such as listening in on conversations — may put you at risk."

"It was broad daylight, and Sammy showed up just a few minutes later." Pru refused to be taken care of when she knew what she was doing. Oh, wait, she thought. "Sammy caught a glimpse of the guy Malcolm talked to and said he had stringy black hair."

"You have a description of someone discussing what could be the murder, and you wait days to tell the police. This won't do. You are too close to this situation and may not be able to see clearly. A police inquiry does not involve emotional ties to suspects."

Anger and confusion filled her. She chose to ignore the distinct possibility that she might be interfering on the Wilsons' behalf only because they showed her kindness. "Surely you don't look just at someone's opportunity to commit a crime. Surely you take into consideration a person's character and—"

"If you attempt to obstruct this investigation," he began, and Pru stood up abruptly. "Wait, what I mean to say—"

"Oh, I know exactly what you mean, Inspector." She began to dig in her bag. "And here's another piece of evidence I withheld — a flash drive with photos I took of the Wilsons' garden before and after the murder." She slapped the flash drive onto the table. "Here, go ahead, arrest me." She turned, almost bumping into the server with their plates of food, and walked off down the footpath. She didn't hear Christopher call after her.

* * *

Pru pouted the rest of the day, feeling as if a potentially lovely afternoon had been hijacked by official police business and — just perhaps — her own stubborn reaction to being told what to do. Jo found it impossible to get a word out of her about her lunch with Christopher. During the rest of that Sunday in the country — croquet on the lawn, tea in the garden, dinner in front of the fire — Pru kept mostly quiet, and when she did talk, her cheerful demeanor bordered on manic. The next morning, Jo and Pru drove to London together; Cordelia returned with Lucy. As they started back in the rain, Jo ventured a few questions.

"Do you want to talk about yesterday?"

"No."

"Did he stand you up?"

"No."

"Was he mean to you?"

"No."

"Do you want to see him again?"

"No."

"Well," Jo said with a sigh, "this will be a pleasant drive."

CHAPTER 7

In London, Jo started to take the left turn just before Grovehill Square, but suddenly swerved and continued straight.

"Jo, why didn't you turn?"

"What?" Jo's face was flushed. "Oh, I wasn't thinking, Pru, sorry. I thought that was a street too early. Here now, I'll just go around. We'll be there in two ticks."

It took longer than two ticks. Jo drove what seemed to Pru far out of the way before circling back, and fifteen more minutes passed before they arrived at her door. She saw Jo glance around the square, as if doing a quick reconnaissance.

"There now," she said, the relief evident in her voice, "home again."

"Right," said Pru. "Thanks, Jo, I really did have a lovely weekend."

Jo recovered her good spirits. "You don't have any appointments at the police station this week, do you?"

Pru smiled. "I'll talk to you soon."

Pru took herself and her weekend bag into the front hall. Two days' worth of post lay on the floor. She shut the door, turned on the light against the gray outside, and bent to pick up her letters. As her hand reached down, she stopped. On top of the three or four pieces of mail, which lay scattered in a small heap, was part of a large shoe print.

Pru's hand hovered over the mail. No postman inside. She stood up quickly and listened to the quiet that filled the house. She looked back at the mail. She could see something with Sarah Richard's return address, and thought it might finally be a check. For a moment, she stood looking at the floor, then she bent down and collected the letters.

Now, be sensible, she said to herself. *How could someone get in here, and why would he want to?* She walked quietly to the back door, which was securely locked. All windows closed. The locked door to the basement — for which she had no key — was still locked.

She checked every room and saw no signs of disturbance, ending up in the front room where her laptop sat on the desk, shut down but with the lid up. She held her breath and stared at it. Hadn't she closed the lid? Didn't she always close the lid? No, wait, she remembered now — she forgot to close the lid one day last week, too.

She let her breath out. Okay, no one broke in. No one is here. I'm fine. Nothing is gone. She checked the lock on the front door, and, without allowing herself a reason, pulled the kitchen table up against the back door and hoped there wasn't a fire in the middle of the night and she couldn't get out. She fixed herself a sandwich for dinner and had a glass of wine, opting for the quiet entertainment of a book instead of trying to listen for unusual sounds over the conversation on Radio 4.

Later, Pru rang the Wilsons to ask if she could stop by the following day, and — she had to admit — to hear a friendly voice. Mrs. Wilson said they would love to see her for tea in the afternoon.

Boars Hall

The Royal Corner
Billy Row, Crook
Durham
DL15 9UA

8 October

72 Grovehill Square
Chelsea
London SW3

Dear Ms. Parke,

I write to regretfully inform you that you have not been selected for the post of head gardener for Boars Hall Castle and Gardens. Thank you for sharing with us your knowledge of the gardens, mining, and history of Durham.

We appreciate your interest in this post and wish you well in your future endeavors.

Yours sincerely,
Anne Stanhope-Worthington
Boars Hall Castle and Gardens
ASW/bbr

No email from Lydia followed the rejection letter from Boars Hall, which was a relief to Pru only until her phone rang and she saw the number. It was Marcus. She left the ringing phone on the kitchen counter and walked into the front room, to get as far away from it as she could. When it stopped — with no message left to ignore — she stuck it in her pocket and left for the Wilsons'.

"Harry's joining us today, dear," said Mrs. Wilson when Pru arrived.

Mr. Wilson had decided to take some time off work. Pru remained in the dark about Mr. Wilson's employment; she'd learned he was a director in a company, but didn't know what the company did. Whatever it was, he was senior enough to do as he pleased.

"Why don't you pop downstairs, Pru, and let him know the tea is ready?"

The basement door off the front hall was open, and Pru walked down the stairs to find Mr. Wilson staring at a letter in his hand. He hadn't noticed her.

"Mr. Wilson?"

He started. "Pru, I'm sorry, I didn't hear you." He folded the letter up and stuffed it into the envelope he held in his other hand. He rolled up the envelope until he was unable to roll it any more and it resembled a fat cigar. He stuck it in his pocket. But Pru caught a glimpse of the letterhead before it disappeared in the folds: Hodges & Hodges Appraisals. She'd seen that on a letter her first visit to the Wilsons' and she remembered the announcement on the company's website about an upcoming important auction of ancient items. She told herself Mr. Wilson must be buying, not selling.

"Tea is ready," she said.

While Mrs. Wilson fussed with the tea, Pru told them the funny story of running into Christopher in the country and about watching the badgers — she left off the part about stomping away from lunch — and Mr. Wilson told her about some of the interesting finds he'd been involved with — the reason for all the awards covering the little tables in the hall.

"Our society, well, we're amateurs, so we only help the real archaeologists — we never work by ourselves. A few years ago, we were a part of a group that found a collection of Roman vessels down in Wiltshire. It never ceases to amaze me to think that we come across pieces of people's lives, the cooking pots and jewelry and stoneware from so long ago."

"Who has the pots now?" asked Pru.

"The whole collection is in the Salisbury museum, so that everyone can learn about them and enjoy them." Mr. Wilson shrugged his shoulders. "It wouldn't be any fun if what we found was just locked away in someone's cupboard. It's in the sharing that we discover more."

He was like a gardener talking about a prized collection of dahlias — you could see that light in his eye. No gardener would want to hide the fruits of her labor, that's why there were garden open days. And, for archaeologists, museums. Mr. Wilson could never be involved in the unsavory business of stealing and murder. She wished Christopher could hear Mr. Wilson talk about his activities. "Are there collectors of Roman antiquities? Like art collectors or collectors of rare books?" she asked.

"There are indeed," said Mr. Wilson. "Just a few years ago, a fellow down in Wiltshire dug up an intact Roman helmet in fine condition — very rare, an astounding discovery. There were many museums that wanted that piece, but he wanted money, and put it up for auction, where it fetched £1 million."

Mrs. Wilson seemed to pursue her own line of thought. "It would make a lovely weekend away for you and a friend, dear," she said, "if you were to go down to Salisbury. Harry could show the two of you around."

"I'd love to, but I'm not sure who I'd persuade to go along," Pru said.

"Oh, well," Mrs. Wilson said, "you never know. What about the inspector?"

Mrs. Wilson as matchmaker, Pru thought. She decided to change the subject. "You've both been so kind to me, when I haven't even been able to get started on the garden. I feel quite at home here."

"We enjoy your company, Pru, and talking about history and gardening," said Mr. Wilson as his wife set down a plate of buns. Toffee Woof-Woof raised his head. He had been napping near his tin of treats, but now moved over to sit beside Pru.

"It feels as if we've known you for ages," Mrs. Wilson said.

Some people gather up strays, thought Pru — it's part of their nature — and whether she was the latest in a long line of lost souls that the Wilsons acquired, or whether she was a rare occurrence, it didn't really matter to her. As an only child, Pru made up her own family — or many families. The Wilsons felt like some favorite aunt and uncle.

"Look," said Mrs. Wilson, nodding toward the table, "I brought something out to show you."

A fat photo album sat on the coffee table. Mrs. Wilson opened it up to the middle and began showing her photos of their garden and house, Greenoak, in Hampshire — the one Alf owned and had booted them out of, unceremoniously, saying that he was selling it. Mrs. Wilson talked about the garden and Simon Parke, their gardener, with Mr. Wilson adding a remark or question occasionally — "Vernona, what was that tree with the pink flowers by the drive?" As Pru readjusted the large book in her lap, an old, yellowed photo fell out of the front. Pru picked it up and saw a boy in his early teens with a smirk on his face, dressed in an old-fashioned school uniform. "Who is this?" she asked.

"Oh, that's Alf. What an old snapshot that is. He was a good boy growing up, but he did have a tendency to look for the easy way out of anything," Mrs. Wilson said.

"Vernona is being kind. He owned that house free and clear. We paid him a lease all the years we lived there, and he'd still ask us for money. The house should've gone to both of you," he nodded at his wife.

"Does Alf live in London?" asked Pru.

"We're never quite sure where he is. He may be here or down in Hampshire. It's part of his shifty nature," said Mr. Wilson.

Pru started to put the photo back in the album, and as she did, she flipped it over, and on the back she saw, in a child's handwriting, the name "Alf Saxsby."

Alf, Mrs. Wilson's brother. Saxsby, the man she'd heard talking with Malcolm. Mrs. Wilson began a story about Alf as a lad and some silly idea he had about making money from marketing special telephones that wouldn't need to be plugged in at home — anyone could talk anytime and anywhere. It distracted Pru for only a moment — too bad he didn't follow through on that one, she thought — but soon she found herself dwelling on Saxsby, and Mrs. Wilson's story became background chatter. Alf Saxsby. Poor Mrs. Wilson. Alf, in trouble for most of his life. Alf, who lurked around one of Mr. Wilson's digs a couple of years ago. Alf who met Malcolm last year.

Pru pushed aside concern for how Mrs. Wilson would take the fact that her brother was involved in a murder — could Alf have murdered Jeremy? — when she remembered hearing Alf cavalierly flinging accusations. He had practically said to Malcolm that Mr. Wilson committed the murder. How could he do that to his own brother-in-law?

Alf might have wanted the mosaic for himself. Pretending it was his own, he could've auctioned it. Pru didn't understand how you could move an entire mosaic floor and sell it without someone noticing. As Mrs. Wilson finished the story — "He still believes that the company owes him money for the idea" — Pru realized that she now had acquired more information on the case. Unintentionally, she pointed out to herself. She needed to talk with Christopher.

* * *

Her thoughts preoccupied her as she left the Wilsons', and she didn't notice Malcolm coming round the corner until she almost bumped into him.

"All right there, Pru? You looked a bit faraway."

"I'm fine, Malcolm, I just stopped in for a visit at the Wilsons'." She thought it was high time to take advantage of these "chance" encounters. "Do you have time for a pint? I wanted to tell you about some new rose breeding I was reading about."

She didn't want to push her luck — perhaps he would call her out on eavesdropping, but his usual friendly manner made her think that she might get away with a few pertinent questions. Malcolm jumped at the chance to talk roses.

They found a pub partway between the Wilsons' house and hers — the Queen Charlotte. It wasn't one of Pru's favorites; the pub had taken up with some consortium and now offered the same, tired, microwaved menu as dozens of others around the city. "Real English food!" the chalkboard proclaimed — but it wasn't even a real chalkboard, just painted to look like one. Pru went for a half pint of a local bitter, but Malcolm ordered a Dubonnet on ice.

He kept to the subject of roses, even though occasionally Pru tried to veer off into another area. Finally, as the topic of rose scent — tea versus fruity — came to an end, she took another go.

"Malcolm, have you known the Wilsons long?"

He answered cautiously. "Well, neighbors, you know, you're so close, you find out a great deal about them in short order."

If the police had questioned him about Saxsby, Malcolm would know she had been the one to tell them. But for now she could pretend that she had no idea "Alf" and "Saxsby" were the same person.

"Do they have family about?" Pru kept her voice light. "Mrs. Wilson said something about her brother. Alf? I believe he lives in Hampshire."

Malcolm's face went blank. "Well, I've met him, but I don't get invited to any family dinners," he said with a tinny laugh. "You seem to be getting close to them, though. Maybe they're even confiding in you, Pru. Or perhaps they've let something slip out about Jeremy or what happened in the shed. Is that what was upsetting you earlier?"

"I don't believe they have anything that could slip out, Malcolm," Pru said. "Do you suspect Mr. Wilson of . . . murdering his friend Jeremy?"

"Pru," he began in an instructional tone, "you shouldn't be taken in by people who pretend to be kind to you. They could be hiding a great deal. This could be a dangerous situation for you."

For a moment, she expected him to tell her she was not a police officer. "Malcolm, don't you think that's a bit harsh?" She thought that his warning could apply to him just as easily as anyone else.

"They're such a chummy bunch" — he stuck out his bottom lip — "with their digs and their exciting finds and their 'I have an award for this and that.' Wouldn't it just serve him right to be blamed for murder?"

Malcolm sounded as if he hadn't been picked to play on their side for kickball — or cricket — hardly a reason to accuse someone of murder.

"That isn't exactly evidence, is it?" she pointed out.

"There may be evidence, Pru," he said in a low voice, looking over his shoulder as if someone listened in. But the small crowd of males in the pub stood up at the bar watching television — a replay of a soccer game from Brazil. "I just don't want you to be hurt when it all comes out."

He was beginning to sound like a broken record, she thought, and decided to give the record player a kick. "Malcolm, I was checking on the soil near the wall the other day. That's when you saw me." He squirmed in his seat, as if the memory of the encounter made him uncomfortable.

"Pru, you shouldn't get involved in all this."

The barmaid had come round gathering up glasses from the surrounding tables, and Pru waited until she moved on, before taking a different tack. "Is the soil at the bottom of your garden very wet? When your roses died, how far down did you dig?"

With relief clearly showing on his face, Malcolm plunged into talk about his roses again. "I went down a couple of feet and it got wetter and wetter. I knew I had to abandon any hopes of putting a Zépherine Drouhin or Félicité Perpétue on the bottom wall."

"That would've been lovely," Pru commiserated, noting to herself that the soggy soil was not isolated to the Wilsons' shed. "I suppose Alf knows about the wet soil in the garden," she said and waited for a reaction.

"Alf?" asked Malcolm in surprise. "What would Alf care about soil or roses?" He thought for a moment. "I did try to show him when he visited that first time, but he just laughed. He did say that he had the same sort of boggy place in Hampshire, but he knows nothing about roses." He looked at his empty glass, with only a film of Dubonnet at the bottom. "Would you care for another half pint, Pru?"

"No thanks, Malcolm." She knew she'd get no further. "I'd better get home."

* * *

"Thanks for walking me back," Pru said as they turned the corner near her house.

"Not at all, it's on my way," Malcolm said. "There's nothing like gardening to make you feel better, Pru . . ." His voice drifted off and Pru looked up from digging in her bag for the key to see Christopher standing at her front door. He turned and saw Pru first, then Malcolm. His face became a mask.

"Ms. Parke. Mr. Crisp," he said, clipping his words.

"Inspector," Pru said quietly.

"Inspector Pearse," Malcolm said, as if greeting a favorite uncle, "have you caught Jeremy's murderer yet? Did you look into the matter of that argument between Harry and Jeremy?"

Christopher ignored Malcolm. "Ms. Parke, I stopped by to ask you a few more questions about the day of the murder." Christopher wore khaki trousers and a heather-blue sweater with a light tan jacket, more fancy-a-pint clothes than may-I-take-your-statement. Pru regretted her outburst at the country pub and wanted to explain herself, but she had nowhere to go with both of them in front of her. Be brave, Pru.

"Malcolm, again, thanks so much. Would you mind, I do have something to . . . explain to Mr. Pearse."

"Not at all," Malcolm said. "Now, Pru" — he placed a kind hand on her arm — "you mustn't worry about people's feelings when there's a murder to sort out. You must tell the truth." It seemed that Malcolm remained convinced that she knew something that she didn't know.

Pru stayed on the sidewalk, and Christopher came down to stand beside her as they watched Malcolm walk off. When she was sure he was out of earshot, Pru said, "I'm sorry I didn't tell you immediately about the conversation and the photos. And about looking over the wall. I'm sorry I got angry — I sometimes think I can do everything myself."

"Really?" The corner of Christopher's mouth twitched. "And I'm sorry if I sounded overbearing, but this is an open investigation." He softened. "I know I'm repeating myself, but it's important. If you try to act on information you come across, it could put you in danger. I wouldn't want that."

"Do you think Malcolm was involved?" She wondered if Christopher knew who Saxsby was.

He watched Malcolm's retreating figure. "Malcolm has an alibi," he said, sounding as if he wasn't sure he believed it. "He lives with his mother, and she said he didn't go out at all the night before or the morning of the murder."

"He lives with his mother? He's never said a word."

"She has limited mobility and spends her life on the ground floor of the house. During the day, she stays in the front sitting room, and at night, she sleeps in a bed at the back of the house. She's hard of hearing but says she's a light sleeper, and she swears that Malcolm did not go out."

"Oh, his 'obligation.'" Pru remembered what Mr. Wilson had said. "Lives with his mother. Sounds like Norman Bates. Are you sure she's alive?"

Christopher looked at her for a moment without answering and then asked, "Have you eaten? There's an Italian place a couple of streets over. We could stop in for a bite."

"Gasparetti's? That's my favorite place." They turned and walked up the street.

"Did you stop by to ask me about my statement?" Pru asked.

"No," he said, "I did not," and smiled.

* * *

Pru readied herself to reveal the latest bits of information she had gathered, but decided to wait until after they ordered. Christopher glanced at the menu and began patting his pockets for his reading glasses, which were in the last pocket he searched. He looked slightly sheepish as he put them on. "No glasses for you, then?" he asked.

She grinned. "Only because I have this menu memorized," she said. "Otherwise, I'd be borrowing those from you." She paused. "You never can seem to find yours."

He half smiled. "It's my own form of protest over needing them," he said. "I never put them back in the same pocket, and so I never quite know where they are."

The café owner, Riccardo, had waved to Pru from across the restaurant when they arrived, but one of his waiters took their order and poured the first glasses from a bottle of the house Chianti.

Once settled, she began. "I have more information for you, and I'm telling you immediately."

Christopher hesitated as he reached for his glass. "What is it?"

"You know who Saxsby is, don't you?" she asked.

"Alf Saxsby, Vernona Wilson's brother," Christopher said.

"Did you ask Malcolm about Saxsby? Did you tell him I was the one who overheard?"

"I would not reveal you as the source," Christopher said.

"He knows it was me — he saw me," Pru said, wondering what kind of lecture might follow this revelation.

Christopher watched her for a moment, his face unreadable. "Malcolm said he thought it was your assistant who might have overheard something, but he said it was a misunderstanding, and that they were talking in general terms about the Wilsons. He apologized for the remarks made about you. And now, how did you" — he paused for emphasis, she knew — "find out who Saxsby is?"

Pru wanted to hurry and explain, lest Christopher jump to what Pru knew to be the wrong conclusion, but their salads arrived and so she waited until the server had left before going on.

"I only found this out today when I talked with the Wilsons. Mrs. Wilson showed me a photo album so that I could see the garden they had in Hampshire. It was lovely. They had a flagstone path with sun roses coming up in the cracks and a shallow fountain at the axis of two paths, with that little Mexican fleabane growing at its base. Just enough neatly trimmed yew to anchor the whole design. It wasn't a large garden, and the borders weren't too deep. They were just the right proportion. Mrs. Wilson said Simon included lots of late color, so it wasn't the typical spring-bash display. They had a wonderful stone wall, and he had several tender vines growing on . . ."

"Pru."

"Yes?" Pru said, still seeing visions of hardy fuchsias in bloom.

"Alf Saxsby."

"Oh, sorry." She paused as the server set her plate of pasta down. "I didn't see him the other day — only Sammy did. But an old photo fell out of the front of the album I was looking at today. I picked it up, and it was of a boy in a school uniform. When I turned it over, I saw the name: Alf Saxsby."

"Did you question Mrs. Wilson?" Christopher asked.

"She had already mentioned Alf," Pru said, "when I first met her. Alf, her brother, owned their house in Hampshire, and they had to move because he sold it out from under them with no warning. Apparently he's been in trouble off and on most of his adult life."

"And were you talking with Malcolm about Alf Saxsby?" Christopher asked.

"Well," *tread lightly here*, Pru thought, *you are not a police officer.* "I ran into Malcolm this afternoon, and we decided to have a drink . . ."

Christopher's eyes began to narrow.

Pru hurried on. "And we were talking about roses and other garden topics. I thought if I could just turn the conversation in the direction of the Wilsons, then it wouldn't look as if I was interrogating him, but he might say something useful." Pru looked at Christopher. "Do I get a lecture?"

"I don't dare — we haven't finished our meal. And did you find out anything?"

"No," Pru said, acknowledging her failure. "Not even when I said that I knew he saw me in the garden. I didn't want to admit to knowing that Saxsby and Alf were the same person. I did mention Mrs. Wilson's brother, Alf, and something about the house in Hampshire, and he admitted that they had met, but then he clammed up."

"Was Malcolm asking you questions? About the Wilsons or the shed or what you have seen?"

"Trying to get information out of me the way I was out of him? Yes, I believe he was. He keeps harping on what I saw that I might not remember. I don't know what that would be."

She looked up to see him studying her face. "Pru" — he reached across the table and took her hand — "an investigation may turn dangerous at any time." He spoke with quiet concern, and she responded in kind.

The server swept in and Christopher let go of Pru's hand as salad plates were removed the salad plates and mains set down.

"I don't need protecting," Pru said when they'd been left alone. "I can take care of myself, so don't worry." He took a breath, but she kept going. "All right, here's one more thing I found out today. A couple of years ago, Alf was hanging around one of Mr. Wilson's digs down in Hampshire." She couldn't help being a bit proud of all the information she could hand over, but at the same time . . . "I didn't ask about that. It just came out in conversation."

"Right," Christopher said. "As long as you weren't using any harsh interrogation tactics."

She smiled. "I thought it would be helpful for you to know," she said in an offhanded manner. "I am not a police officer — I remember that."

Christopher laughed and went back to eating. But Pru couldn't quite leave the subject yet. She thought again about the easy access Malcolm had to the Wilsons' garden. "Do you consider Malcolm a suspect?"

"No. At least not a likely suspect."

"Why not?"

Christopher took a breath. "Do you really want to hear this?"

"Yes."

"From the angle of the blows to the head, we can tell that the person who struck had to be taller than Malcolm." Pru remembered the sight of Jeremy's bloodied corpse. She put her fork down and wished she hadn't ordered the pomodoro sauce.

"But if Jeremy had been kneeling, then he would be shorter than Malcolm," she said.

"If Jeremy had been kneeling, most likely it would have been on the far side of the mosaic, where the hole was dug — that's where the blood was on the soil — and that is almost against the back wall. There was too little room for anyone to get behind him and . . ."

Pru had taken a sip of her wine and found she needed to use both hands to put the glass back on the table. *How does anyone get used to dealing with violent death?*

"Right," Christopher said, "that's enough on that subject."

"Yes, yes, let's talk about something else."

He studied her for a moment, and she held his gaze.

"Do you really get around London to your jobs on the Tube and bus?" he asked. She accepted the lob and launched into a description of a typical day in her gardening life.

* * *

Although they arrived earlyish for dinner, they stayed well past the rush and into the late-arrivals time, and after the plates had been cleared, they continued to explore each other's lives.

Pru told Christopher about the time, early in her career at the Dallas Arboretum, when she had been assigned the task of turning the water in all the fountains green for St. Patrick's Day. She had used the wrong kind of dye, and the fountains had to be not only drained, but also the sides and bottoms scrubbed hard to get the color off — a task that was left to her alone.

Christopher told Pru of his first investigation as a uniformed officer — tracking down the culprit who stole a highly prized and quite expensive African gray parrot owned by the local magistrate in Lower Upham. As it happened, the magistrate's hunting dog had nicked the bird, but that was learned only after an unpleasant discovery on the kitchen floor.

She compared English weather with the Texas climate. "It's really hot in the summer, in the nineties — thirty-five degrees Celsius — for three months at least."

"Well, it sounds fine for holiday temperatures, but difficult day to day."

"It's dreadful," Pru said. "Funny, I never thought of it that way when I lived there. It was just the way things were. But I wouldn't want to go back to it." She caught herself off guard as, unbidden, the thought came to her that she may have to. "Were you born near Stow?" she asked to change the subject.

"No, I grew up in Kent, near Edenbridge. But I went to Oxford, and that's where Phyl and I met. We lived near Cheltenham when we were married." He reached for the wine bottle and poured them each a last glass. "But that was a long time ago. We've been divorced for fifteen years."

"When did you move to London?" Pru asked.

"About that time," he said. "I started at the Met and climbed my way up to DCI over the years. I spent all my days and many evenings working and gave up most everything else in my life." He gave a small shrug. "I've been quite successful at that."

There, Pru thought. A glimpse behind that polished police exterior.

"Getting lost in work is an easy excuse, isn't it?" she said. He regarded her with a smile.

"You have a son?" Pru asked, remembering Phyl's visit to the Badger Care booth. Christopher nodded. "Where does he go to school?"

"Graham's in Sheffield, studying environmental science."

"Does he want to work in restoration? Policy? Engineering?"

"Soil science, although beyond that I'll have to let the two of you discuss it."

Pru played with the last few strands of pasta on her plate and thought about meeting his family. *Don't get ahead of yourself.* "Edenbridge — that's near Hever Castle, Anne Boleyn's family home. When William Waldorf Astor built the gardens there, beginning in 1904 — had them built — he diverted the river to make the big lake at the end of the Italian walk. Eight hundred men stomped down the clay soil to form the bottom of the lake." She shook her head. "No head gardener has that kind of manpower at her fingertips these days."

"It's a sad state of affairs," Christopher said.

"I applied for a post at a private garden," she said, "just outside Tunbridge Wells. I had an interview last week."

"Tunbridge Wells," he said, almost to himself. "Tunbridge Wells is close."

"Yes, it is close," Pru replied, and wondered, close to what — Edenbridge or London? After that, she remembered the short conversation with Ned. "But I don't think I got it."

* * *

Riccardo stopped by their table after Christopher had excused himself when his phone rang. Pru had become a frequent enough customer that she and Riccardo were on speaking terms. "Pru, he looks very nice. I'm happy for you." She loved listening to Riccardo speak, as he had that Italian way of adding a vowel to the end of every word, whether one existed or not.

Again, Pru felt the need to correct this misconception. "Oh no, Riccardo, we're only friends."

"I know what friends look like, Pru." He dropped his smile. "I hope you won't be leaving us now that the Clarkes are back in London."

"What? No, Riccardo, they aren't . . . did you see them? Did you talk with them?" Why do people keep seeing the Clarkes? she thought. First Wilf at the pub, now Riccardo. They couldn't be back — Jo never said a word.

Riccardo looked embarrassed. "I'm sorry, Pru, I didn't mean to upset you. Maybe it wasn't them. It could've been someone else I mistook for them, only because they were walking along Grovehill Square on Sunday."

Sunday — she wasn't home Sunday. If they were back in London, why didn't they tell her? Why didn't Jo tell her?

Christopher came back to the table, and held Pru's chair for her as she stood up. Riccardo said, "Sir, I hope you and Pru enjoyed your meal."

As they headed for the door, Christopher said, "You've become well known in the neighborhood."

"It's better than eating alone every night," Pru said, and then cringed at such a pitiful statement.

"I believe I know what you mean."

* * *

When they stepped out, it was raining — more than a drizzle, less than a downpour. Definitely more than she was prepared for. "Oh dear."

Christopher reached inside his jacket pocket and brought out a collapsible umbrella. "An Englishman is always prepared," he said. He popped it open, put his arm around her, drew her close, and held the umbrella above them. "Shall we?"

Pru supposed she would've stayed drier if they had walked faster, but she didn't really care, and apparently neither did he. The rain made enough noise drumming on the umbrella to make conversation difficult, so they walked together in silence, his hand slipping from her arm up onto her shoulder, his fingers lightly touching her bare skin, which made her shiver unintentionally. When Christopher stopped walking, Pru was surprised to see that they stood on her front step.

Out of practice with this portion of the evening, she immediately looked down and started digging in her bag for the key. Christopher dropped his arm, and when she'd found the key, she turned to open the door.

Safely on her own side of the threshold, she said to him, "Thanks so much for dinner. I enjoyed the evening."

"So did I. Goodnight, Pru." He placed one hand on her arm, kissed her on the cheek, and left. She had a small frown on her face as she closed the door. Too late she realized she should've asked him in for coffee. She decided she needed a review of the rulebook.

Trispin Hall

Bampper, Truro
Cornwall
TR4 8AG

11 October

72 Grovehill Square
Chelsea
London SW3

Dear Ms. Parke,
　　This is to inform you that you have not been selected for the post of first under gardener of Trispin Hall. We appreciate your interest in the post and your knowledge concerning the history and development of ravine gardens in Cornwall. We know that your knowledge will stand you in good stead in your future employment.
　　We wish you well in your future endeavors.

　　Yours sincerely,
　　James G. Russell-Davies, Director
　　Trispin Hall Public Trust
　　JGRD/wgs

CHAPTER 8

She had precious little to distract her from the latest bad news. Her client list had dropped noticeably. The Nethercotts discovered they could wield hedge clippers as well as anyone — although Pru feared for the fate of the nascent crown and lyres, to say nothing of the peacocks — and she had encouraged the Hightowers to hire a lawn service, explaining to them that she might be leaving soon. She barely acknowledged that to herself, and so it took great effort to say it aloud to someone else.

Reluctantly, she had emailed Lydia — and Marcus — and thanked them for all their help, and the offer of her old position back. Yes, she would take it, she wrote. She would let them know the details of her return soon. After that, she made reservations for her flight to Dallas. After that, she had a good cry.

Right, she thought, *that's my quota of self-pity for today*. She had bulbs to plant at the Hetheringtons' later, and wondered if she might check in at the Wilsons' before or after.

An image of Mr. Wilson rolling up the envelope from Hodges & Hodges into a fat cigar flashed in her mind. She wondered if the police knew about Hodges & Hodges. It could be nothing — Mr. Wilson might be putting up for auction some of their furniture or family heirlooms or . . .

or he could be involved in selling off antiquities that didn't belong to him. It would take little to find out one way or another — just a word from the appraisers, a definite statement that absolved Mr. Wilson of any involvement in the upcoming auction announced on the website.

Perhaps she did have too much time on her hands, because before she realized it, she was making plans to find out herself. She would ring up, not as herself, but as some wealthy potential bidder and ask for details. Surely she could pull off that minor deception.

She would need to be someone both rich and unknown to them, a collector of fine ancient things. After thinking a moment, she hit upon a plan. Checking the company's website, which still contained the special auction announcement, she rang.

"Hodges & Hodges, how may we help you?" came a smooth female voice.

"Well, hi there, this is Duxton Stewart, and I'm calling from Houston, Texas, about that very special auction you have listed on your website. Can you tell me about it?"

"Just one moment, and one of our associates will assist you."

Pru tried to breathe normally as she waited on the line. She thought this might work: Duxton Stewart was an enormously wealthy Houston widow whose husband, about forty years her senior, had died a couple of years back. The widow collected art, Pru remembered, and her only companions these days were her dog and her pool boy. That's about as far as her knowledge went — and she knew that much only because a member of her crew at the arboretum had gotten a job as Duxton's gardener.

"Hello, this is Gabriel Collingford speaking, Ms . . . is it Ms. Duxton Stewart?" said a voice equal in smoothness to that of the receptionist's.

"Oh, no, Mr. Collingford." Pru laughed a throaty laugh. "Duxton is my first name. It was my mother's maiden name, you see — it's a very Southern thing to do. All my friends call me Dux." She put as many vowels as possible into the nickname. Pru couldn't approach a realistic British accent, but she could stretch her light Texas drawl from here to Amarillo with little trouble.

Mr. Collingford sounded slightly flustered. "Well, yes, Ms. Stewart, please let me know how I can help you."

"Well, Gabriel, I am a huge fan of antiques and art and my dear late husband and I collected pieces from all over the world, and I am just fascinated by the announcement on your website about this special auction of . . . let's see now, is it some Greek statue? Or a special Roman, oh, I don't know . . . mosaic or something?" She hoped she wasn't pushing her luck there.

"Ms. Stewart, I'm delighted you've contacted us about this unique opportunity, and I want to assure you that I will be able to give you the full details of the auction just as soon as they become available."

Pru heard a light tapping in the background and thought for sure that Collingford was searching "Duxton Stewart" online. "Well, shoot, Gabriel," she said in a pouty tone, "I sure was hoping to find out just what this exciting thing is. Can't you tell me anything about it? Who owns it? Where it was found? Just some little thing to keep me interested."

The slight pause worried Pru.

"Ms. Stewart," Collingford said, "isn't it terribly early in Texas?"

Crap. Although she had remembered to block her phone ID, she'd forgotten the time difference. A quick glance at the clock on her computer screen showed that it was 9:30 a.m., local London time, which made it . . . 3:30 a.m. in Houston. Oops.

"Oh Gabriel, you are so right. It's terribly early here. I confess to you that I just haven't slept well at all these last two years since my dear" — Pru couldn't remember her husband's name — "husband died. It's just a curse."

He sounded marginally satisfied with the explanation and went on. "Ms. Stewart, I will be happy to let you know more just as soon as I possibly can. Would you like to leave your contact information?"

"I tell you what, Gabriel, why don't I give you a call back in a few days? How does that sound? I really must run now. I hear my little dog Cha-Cha waking up. Bye-bye!"

Perhaps she wouldn't make a good undercover investigator after all. She felt a small thrill at the attempt, but really, what had she gained?

* * *

The Hetheringtons lived near Carlyle Square, which wasn't all that far from Chartsworth Square, and so, after she'd finished the bulb planting, Pru thought she could just nip over to the Wilsons'. As she walked out onto Old Church Street and past the Cadogan Arms, she heard a voice calling from across the road, "Pru! Hello, Pru!" It was Romilda, wiggling the cherry-red tips of her stubby fingers in the air.

"Hello, Romilda, this is a surprise," she said. "Are you still looking for a flat?"

A look of mock exasperation came over Romilda's face. "I know, you thought I'd be looking for a flat forever," she said with a titter. "But I found one."

"Congratulations, that's great."

Romilda caught Pru's arm, as if to stop her from escaping. "How are you? How's the gardening?"

"It's fine, just fine." The conversation appeared to stall. "Well, good luck with your new place."

"Oh, Pru, let's have a drink, shall we? Don't you have a few minutes? I'd love to hear more about your work. And what about that murder — you must tell me more."

Pru hadn't heard from Jo since they returned from the country, even after leaving a couple of messages, and that cast-off feeling had crept in again. Romilda was chirpy and chatty and a drink might just take Pru's mind off everything else. "Yes, let's."

They walked into the Cadogan Arms, and Romilda immediately headed for a dark corner. "I'll have a gin and tonic," she said to Pru over her shoulder.

"Oh, sure." She's very good at that, Pru thought. But then, Romilda was new in town. Perhaps she hadn't started her job yet and was short on cash.

Pru took the gin and tonic and her own half pint of bitter over to the dark corner, and Romilda began a long story about her new job, which involved being a personal assistant to the owner of a high-end modeling agency.

"Romilda," Pru said — she was learning it wasn't easy to follow everything that Romilda said, but she felt sure that this was an entirely different job from what she'd heard about before. "Weren't you going to work for a social-services agency?"

The cherry-red lips pursed slightly. "That didn't work out." Her eyes widened. "Speaking of not working out, I tried a new pub the other day — the Queen's Head, over by King's Road."

"The Queen's Head," Pru said. "Isn't that a gay pub?"

"Ha-ha-ha-ha-ha." Romilda's machine-gun laugh went off. "How was I to know? I stuck my head in, and there were all these good-looking men. Well, I had to take my chances, didn't I?" She carried on with a tale of trying to chat up a particularly buff hunk at the bar, until he kindly told her the score. "'No, darling,' he said to me, 'but thanks for the offer. You wouldn't have a younger brother at home, would you?'"

She snorted into her G&T, and Pru laughed along with her. "Although," Romilda paused, "he didn't have to say 'younger' now, did he? Oh, but here's something that did work out — my flat." She proceeded to describe in great detail her new place, which was on the second floor above a Caffè Nero near Waterloo station. "But I desperately need your help, Pru." She reached across the table to grab Pru's arm.

"You mean, moving in?" Pru could see herself carrying boxes up two long flights of stairs, remembering that the ground floor in Britain wasn't numbered.

"No, no, not at all." Romilda laughed. "No, I want you to help me with my little garden. It's just a small balcony, but I want you to help me decorate it with flowers and vines and trees and . . . everything for a garden."

Pru had seen the tiny balconies accompanying some flats in London, and there didn't appear to be room for much of anything, but she thought it couldn't hurt to give Romilda a bit of advice. "I can take a look. I hope it'll be quiet for you there. I've had problems in the house I've sublet — noises in the locked basement. I think it might be mice."

Romilda found that hilarious. She laughed and laughed until Pru started giggling, too. "I guess that does sound a little silly, doesn't it? It sounds as if the mice are rearranging the furniture."

Pru continued to giggle, but Romilda stopped dead. "Are they that noisy?" And then she dismissed the subject, "Oh really, Pru, don't begrudge a little mouse a home. Here now." She reached into her bag and pulled out a scrap of paper. "Here's where my flat is. You'll come, won't you?"

"Yes, I'd love to see it. How about one day next week?"

"No, no, we don't want to wait that long . . . now do we? Tomorrow evening, I'll meet you there at eight. Right? Tomorrow?"

"Yes, sure, tomorrow."

* * *

Christopher had phoned twice since their dinner. The first time, her last visit to the Nethercotts, she had the electric shears going and couldn't hear the ring, and the other time she had been at the Wilsons' for lunch — she saw who it was but didn't think that was the place to talk. The police had informed the Wilsons they were looking into their financial affairs and had asked the whereabouts of Mrs. Wilson's brother. No one knew, although when they told Pru about it, Mr. Wilson had muttered, "I'd like to get hold of him myself."

At the lunch — a hearty autumn salad with orange segments and roasted beets, assembled by Mary, Mrs. Wilson's cook and housekeeper — Pru thought she'd ask about the mysterious Mrs. Crisp. "Have you ever even seen her?"

"Yes, she and Malcolm invited us over for coffee just after we'd moved in," Mrs. Wilson said. "She seemed pleasant enough, and, of course, that was before we knew much about Malcolm."

"Alf was still here," Mr. Wilson said, "and he went, too. He and Malcolm became quite chummy after that."

"But when we returned the invitation," Mrs. Wilson continued, "Malcolm said his mother wasn't well enough. We tried two or three more times — afternoon tea, lunch, I offered to do some shopping for her — but Malcolm said she didn't need the help, she had him, and that social occasions wore her out. After that we dropped it, and we never heard from her again."

* * *

Christopher had left a brief message each time he phoned, no more than "Hello Pru, it's Christopher." A second of silence. "Hope to talk with you soon." Perhaps these were official calls, she told herself. He wanted to question her about the Wilsons or Malcolm or Saxsby. He had, after all, phoned during the day, and that made it sound like business. Why didn't he phone in the evening and remove all doubt? She returned both calls, once leaving the same sort of message, but the second time she rang off before the beep.

That didn't stop her from talking with Jo about her dinner with Christopher. The day after she met Romilda, they sat in Jo's tiny flat over a glass of wine in the late afternoon. She'd been happy to hear from Jo and hoped that whatever had come between them — she still couldn't even guess — had been resolved.

Pru explained about the argument at the country pub, and Jo offered her own interpretation. "He must care about you, Pru," she said, "to be so concerned about you doing your own investigating."

Pru scoffed at that, but couldn't help the tiny warm feeling growing in her heart. "Really, Jo, he's the police. It's his job to tell me to mind my own business."

"And did you talk about the murder at dinner?" Jo asked.

"Yes, we did," Pru said. "At least, at first we did."

"Tell me how it went." She listened to every word as Pru described the evening, asking pertinent questions — "Did he pull your chair out for you?" — and making a comment when it was needed — "He chose your favorite restaurant without knowing it. Don't you find that interesting?" But when she asked, "Did he kiss you goodnight?" Pru felt herself go scarlet.

"I don't think I gave him the chance," she admitted and shook her head. "It's been too long. I don't even know how to go out on a date anymore."

* * *

She left Jo's for home still in that rosy glow of having shared details of her dinner with Christopher. Just about to board the bus, he rang, and she made a quick about-face, so she could answer without a crowd listening.

"Are you gardening?" he asked.

"I am not gardening," she said. "I just had a good chat with Jo, and now I'm off home."

"I'd like to see you this evening. How about dinner?"

"Oh," she said, her heart sinking, "I can't — I'm sorry. I'm going to look at a new flat and try to think up something to grow on the balcony."

"Your new flat?"

"No, not mine," she said, "some woman I hardly know. I've run into her a couple of times on the street, and we've had coffee together. She's new in town and doesn't know anyone, and, well, I know how that feels. Still, I'm not sure how I got roped into going to look at her new flat."

"What's her name?"

"Romilda . . ." Had Romilda said her surname? Pru didn't remember.

"Where does she work?" He asked it in an offhand manner. Pru wondered if the police officer in him always needed details.

"I don't know. She told me about one job the first time we met, and yesterday, she told me about another. She's a chatty thing, and a lot of fun to talk with, although it can be sort of hard to keep up with her. Anyway, I'm very sorry I promised her, because I'd much rather see you."

He paused. She wished she could see him right now. "What time are you meeting her?" he asked.

"At eight. Maybe we could meet for a drink after?"

"Good, yes, let's do that. You ring me when you're finished. Where did you say this flat is?"

Pru laughed as she dug out the paper from her bag. "Is this an interrogation?"

"Certainly not, just casual curiosity."

She read Romilda's address to him, they rang off, and she was caught up in a minor daydream about meeting him for a late drink in a quiet pub so that she didn't even notice when the next bus stopped until someone asked, "Are you boarding?"

* * *

The Victorian brick building contained a row of shops on street level, including the Caffè Nero. The coffee shop had taken in its sidewalk tables and chairs for the night, and, as this was mostly a business district, all the other shops were closed, too. The door to the small lobby was unlocked. Pru saw no lift when she passed through to the stairs. Yes, boxes and boxes to hand-carry up all the long flights of stairs made necessary by those high ceilings.

It was a building of flats in sore need of refurbishment, but maybe that's why Romilda could afford it. The wood fixtures all showed the wear of decades and decades of use. The handrail on the stairs was shiny with the millions of hands that had skimmed its surface. The floor dipped here and there, and the doors to all the flats were nicked with keys missing their mark. Several doors looked chewed at the base. The stairs were carpeted, but the carpet had worn through in the center where every foot had fallen and now, bits of wiry carpet padding stuck out as if tiny land mines had exploded.

The door to 219 stood slightly open. "Romilda?" Pru asked before stepping in. The place was dark, but lights shone from the street.

"Pru, here it is!" Romilda emerged from a corner, held out her arms, and spun around the empty room. Her hands appeared pale, and Pru couldn't see any cherry-red tips. Maybe she's between polishes, she thought. "What do you think?"

Pru thought it was a good thing it was dark. She set her bag down against the wall and looked round. Even in the poor lighting, she could see the peeling wallpaper and the pitted bare floor. Around the room all along the baseboard was a necklace of grime from years of pushing a mop back and forth and never really cleaning.

One large window, at least four feet wide and six feet high, faced out to the street, the bottom of the window only about a foot above the floor. In addition to the narrow stone ledge that ran around the building, there was a small . . . Pru didn't think she could call it a balcony. It was, perhaps two feet deep and a bit wider than the window, and had a wrought-iron decorative bib about a foot high ran around the edge. She could see cigarette butts strewn about. Ah, she thought, the smoking section.

She must think of something nice to say. "Wow, Romilda, won't it be great to have your own place?"

"Now, give me your expert opinion, Pru," Romilda said as she walked over to the window, which stood wide open. "I want to know exactly what I can grow. Come over and take a look at my little garden spot."

Pru walked over to the window, put her hand on the inside frame and leaned out slightly. Around the edges of the extended ledge, she could see the ground far below — it shifted slightly and she felt dizzy. She leaned back in.

"Well, I'm sure you could put out some pots, and they would be easy to tend," she said.

Romilda stood behind her. "No, Pru, we need to see the whole thing. You'll be surprised at how much room I have. Come on, let's get out there." She put her hand on Pru's back, pushing her gently toward the window. Pru pushed back.

"No, Romilda, really, I don't need to go out there. I can see from here." She never found it easy to explain her fear of heights — completely avoiding dicey situations worked best.

Romilda hustled her closer to the window. "Pru, let's take a good look." Her voice got louder as she pushed Pru forward. Pru was surprised at Romilda's strength. She wasn't tall, but she had the distinct advantage over Pru of not being affected by the dizzying view of the ground below.

As Romilda pushed, Pru tried to get loose and back away from the window, grabbing at Romilda for some security. Instead, Romilda shoved her hard and Pru lurched partway through the window, landing with both hands on the tiny balcony and catching another glimpse of the ground below. Her head began spinning and that old, sick feeling came over her. Suddenly, she wasn't sure where her feet were.

"Get out!" Romilda shoved her backside with great force, and Pru toppled out onto the smoking section, scrambling for something to hold on to.

"Romilda!" she shouted, and she heard the window slam behind her. "Romilda, let me back in, please." She couldn't look back; she couldn't turn her head at all. She plastered herself against as much of the window and frame as she could. From inside, she heard a door slam, followed by a *crack*, and the little balcony beneath her shuddered.

She screamed, but not loudly, because that might make her fall. "Oh God, oh God." She slowly stood and eased herself onto the ledge and away from the cracking balcony, trying to find something to hold on to. She kept her eyes on the window in the building across the street, like someone who is seasick tries to focus on the horizon, but below her, she knew the ground was rolling, just like the ocean.

Her right hand grabbed hold of some metal protrusion in the wall of the building — a big eyebolt, a flagpole holder, she didn't know. All she knew was that it didn't move. Her left hand held the frame of the window that Romilda had slammed shut. Her right foot was on the narrow building ledge, her left still on the balcony. She heard another crack and felt another shudder. Moaning slightly, she edged her left foot over to the stone ledge, which wasn't deep enough to stand with her toes straight out, and so her feet pointed in different directions, like a ballet dancer's first position.

And now what? she thought. The street was deserted; Romilda — whoever Romilda was — had disappeared. Pru's bag and phone were inside the flat, if they hadn't been stolen, but that made no difference. Her phone could have been two inches away, and she never would have been able to move a hand to make a call. Could she stay up here until someone noticed? How many hours would that be? Out of the corner of her eye, she saw the ground shift and tilt.

CHAPTER 9

She heard him, quietly at first, and then shouting from the street below. "Pru? Pru?"

"Christopher?" Her voice sounded reedy in her own ears. She knew she needed to speak louder or he wouldn't hear her, but feared the effort would send her over the edge. *Try.* "She pushed me out. I need some help."

There was no asking what happened — that was for later, if she could get to that point.

"Is the window beside you locked?" he asked. "Can you pull it up?"

"I don't know if it's locked. I can't get to it."

"Your hand is on the frame. It's just a few inches away. Can you reach over and—"

"No, I can't. I can't move. Christopher, I'm not good with heights."

He didn't speak. "Christopher?" she whispered. He hadn't gone away, had he? Then she heard him talking and realized he must be phoning for help. She pictured the fire brigade coming to her rescue as if to get a cat out of a tree. She pictured the ladder coming up close to her. She wondered how she would get on it.

"Pru, can you look at me?"

"No, I can't look down. The ground moves too much."

"Can you close your eyes?"

"If I close my eyes I feel like I'm tipping forward."

"Don't close your eyes," he said quickly. "I'm coming up there. Which flat is it?"

"It's 219. Shouldn't you go after her? I can tell you what she looks like."

"No, I'm coming after you."

"Good," she whispered.

After a minute, she heard him at the window. He lifted it slowly and said, "Pru, I'm going to come out and—"

"Don't come out here, that extension in front of the window is unstable — I think it's going to collapse. It cracked when I was on it. I don't want you to fall." She gave a little laugh. "That's pretty silly, isn't it? I'm the one that's going to fall."

"You will not fall," he said, in a commanding tone.

"Yes, right, Inspector."

"I'm going to touch your left hand," he said. "I'm not going to try to move it. I'm just going to touch it."

"Okay." His hand felt warm and comforting as it covered hers, flattened on the window frame.

"Pru, move your left foot toward me. Just slide it a few inches." She concentrated hard on the feel of his hand and slid her foot over. "Now, slide your right foot over." Once she had done that, he said, "Now, your left foot again."

"I can't go any farther, Christopher. I've got hold of something with my right hand, and if I move any more, I'll have to let go of it. I can't do that."

"Pru, turn your head and look at me."

He couldn't be more than two feet away, but he might as well have been in Dover. She knew that normal people would just take the two steps and be inside the flat again, but she wasn't normal, not when it came to this.

"Pru, look at me." She moved her head, but kept her eyes focused in the same place across the street until she could shift them directly to his face. He had his left foot propped up on the window ledge, and he was leaning far out of the window. It didn't seem to bother him. "I'm going to put my arm on your waist — not at the back, in front, to help you stay on the ledge. All right?"

"All right," she whispered, keeping her eyes on his. He reached forward and pinned her lightly against the wall. It felt good. It felt safe. She heard a siren getting closer.

"You can let go with your right hand now," he said. She loosened her grip on the metal piece. "I won't let you fall," he said. "Come closer."

If she could get her left foot inside the window, then maybe, maybe. She inched toward him, keeping herself flat against the wall, until she reached the opening, and he pulled her in, both of them tumbling together and falling to the floor. He stood and helped her up and she wrapped her arms round him, holding him as tightly as he was holding her. He had one hand on her hair, and she thought she heard him whisper, "My darling," in her ear just as the fire brigade arrived.

And the police. When they reached the flat and began talking, asking questions, looking around the flat and out the window, she opened her eyes. "I'm okay." He loosened his arms slightly, and she thought she might be able to stand alone. Then she thought again. "Maybe I'll lean against the wall, would that be all right?"

He helped her over to a wall away from the window. She leaned against it, then slid down to the floor and sat next to, she discovered, her bag. So Romilda wasn't a thief.

Christopher explained the situation to the officers, but he lacked the details and so Pru chimed in.

"She pushed me. She pushed me out the window. I can give them a description of her — I'm better now. I can stand." Although still shaky, she felt silly on the floor while everyone else bustled around.

Christopher helped her up. "We can go to the station, and you can give your statement there. There's no need to stay here. They'll look for evidence. She's long gone by now."

"Your station?"

"No, we'll go to the Kennington station." He put an arm around her. "Now, will you be all right on the stairs?"

"Of course I will," she replied, and gave him a chagrined smile, "as long as I can hold on to you."

"I'm not about to let go."

Perhaps they were letting her leave the scene on her own because she was with a DCI from another borough, but regardless of the reason, she was grateful. By the time they reached the ground floor, she was steadier. Christopher had parked one street over, and he offered to bring the car round.

"No, I can walk. I'm better, really I am."

They walked hand in hand and when they reached his car, away from the comings and goings of the police, he took her in his arms again, kissing her hair. It felt comfortable — more than comfortable — but she couldn't enjoy the comfort too much, because she felt a growing anger inside.

"I feel like such a fool," she said. "I don't even know who she was."

His voice was gentle. "Come on, let's get to the station so you can give your statement."

On the short drive, she fumed. "I should've known something wasn't right. I should've known."

"You did know," he said.

"I did?"

"I could hear it in your voice. You were uncomfortable with her or what she said. You knew it wasn't right." His hands tightened on the steering wheel. "I shouldn't have let you go there alone."

"No, you can't take responsibility for this. What do you think I would've done if you had told me not to go?"

He glanced at her and with a small smile said, "Well, there's that."

As he parked and switched off the engine, she said, "But if I knew something wasn't right, then why didn't I know that I knew?"

"You're a compassionate and trusting woman. It's just your nature. You look for the good in people." He took her hand.

For a moment, she let this lovely statement wash over her. And yet . . . "Is that a nice way of saying I'm gullible?"

He didn't reply, but asked, "Are you ready?"

She leaned over, cupped her hand behind his neck, pulled him to her, and kissed him, a long, slow kiss. Nearly breathless when they pulled apart, she whispered, "Now I'm ready."

* * *

It wasn't a quick process. Christopher sat with her in one of the questioning rooms while she filled out forms. He fetched her tea in a polystyrene cup, which she accepted with a smile. It tasted terrible, and by the look on his face, he knew it. She gave her statement, describing every minute she'd spent with Romilda, and went through, step by step, what had happened that evening.

"How much do you know about this woman?" the sergeant asked.

"Her name. Romilda."

"Do you know her surname?"

"No, she never told me."

"Where she worked?"

"She had a different story about her job every time I met her."

At one point, a uniformed officer came in and spoke to the sergeant, who then turned to her and said, "Ms. Parke, we have your fingerprints on file."

She was sure he didn't mean it to, but it sounded to her ears like an accusation — as if she were the criminal.

"Ms. Parke is assisting on a case of mine, one she was a witness to," Christopher said.

"Sir, do you think this evening had something to do with that case?"

"It may, so we will need to see what you find, of course." Christopher and the sergeant continued discussing how they would share evidence, but Pru didn't listen. She was feeling even the bigger fool now. Romilda wasn't just some con woman. This was part of a scheme to get rid of her, because she knew something. She knew something that she didn't know she knew. Was Romilda an accomplice of Alf's or Malcolm's?

Christopher turned to her and opened his mouth to speak, but he stopped and stared at her left breast. He moved his head slightly and went for his glasses. Before she could react, he asked, "What color is her hair?"

"Blond," Pru said, "she has long blond . . ." She looked down at her black sweater and saw, entwined in the wool, one long blond hair. Christopher pulled a small plastic bag out of his pocket, and the sergeant provided a pair of tweezers. Evidence, thought Pru, a piece of hard evidence.

The sergeant left the room with the bag, and they continued to wait.

"Does she know where you live?" Christopher asked.

For a moment, she felt panic rising. She thought hard about all she'd said to the woman and where they met. She breathed a sigh of relief. "No, no, I never told her. She never asked. We were always away from my neighborhood when we met." Pru stared at her tea, watching a film form on the surface.

"This wasn't your fault," he said.

Pru looked up sharply. "Are you a mind reader, as well as an inspector? Christopher, if I hadn't frozen there at the window, I might have been able to grab her, hold her, instead of letting her push me out." She could feel herself back on the ledge. "You don't know what it's like," she said. "It feels like the earth way down there is shifting, moving, and you've lost all sense of gravity. There's no place to be."

The sergeant returned. "Ms. Parke." He stood just inside the door, fingering a piece of paper, then came to the table and sat down. "Ms. Parke," he took a breath, and then another. "Would you like to . . . speak to someone?"

"You mean, besides you?"

"We have someone here that you could speak with. We know that sometimes circumstances can seem overwhelming, and you think that . . ."

Christopher interrupted. "It isn't like that," he said.

The penny dropped. "You think I was going to jump?" Pru said. "I wasn't going to jump. I was pushed."

"We have a copy of the application to let the flat," the sergeant said, as he pushed the paper across the table.

Christopher intercepted it, began patting his pockets for his reading glasses, and stopped. He gave a short laugh that sounded like relief and pushed the paper over to Pru. She didn't need glasses either. On the line that said "applicant's name," someone had written in block letters: "Prudence Parke."

"I didn't fill this out," she said, jabbing her finger at the paper. "That's not my name. My name isn't Prudence. It's Prunella."

"Are you sure?"

"Yes," she said with a smile, "I'm sure of my own name."

* * *

She could at least give a description of Romilda. She described her to the police sketch artist, who worked, not with a paper and pencil, but with a computer. Alterations could be made almost instantly. "Her bangs were a little longer, and sort of swept to either side," Pru said, and the bangs changed. She couldn't get Romilda's eyes right, though, because of the heavy black frames on the small glasses — they had done a fine job of obscuring a most important identification feature. Finally, Pru said, "Yes, I think that's right. I think that's her." The sergeant printed out a copy for her.

* * *

When finally she was free to leave, they walked to the car and stood for a moment. Pru's mind drifted back to the first time she'd met Romilda, trying to come up with some useful clue. That's why she wasn't prepared when Christopher said, "You shouldn't be alone tonight."

What did this mean? Come home with me? I'll put a guard at the front door of 72 Grovehill Square? Perhaps you could bunk here at the station? She wasn't a charity case.

He continued, "Why don't you—"

"I can stay at Jo's tonight. Would you take me there?"

His face was unreadable, but his tone was kind. "Yes, of course I'll take you there."

"Let me just ring and warn her," Pru said.

She talked with Jo briefly, giving a sketchy account of the evening. Jo wanted only to know that she was safe. Was Christopher with her? Yes, Pru replied, he would drive her over.

He wouldn't hear of dropping her at the door of Jo's building in Belgravia, but instead found a place to park not too far away, and they walked back. At the door, he put his arms around her.

"I had a lovely evening," she said, her arms about his neck. "Thank you for saving my life."

"It was my pleasure." Just before their lips met, he stopped and said, "You won't . . ."

"No," she said quickly, "I won't." *I won't try to find out who Romilda is, I won't try to try to solve the murder, I won't . . . whatever.*

He kissed her gently. And kissed her again. She quite forgot just where they were. The silent street gave her a sense of privacy, but it was a false sense. Their kisses grew more urgent, she pressed herself closer to him, and he slipped his hand under her sweater — and then a cab flew by and hit its horn. They broke apart for a stunned second, and Pru started laughing. Christopher grinned and put an arm around her shoulders in a most decorous manner as Jo opened the door, wearing a turquoise silk robe over footed pajamas. She reached out her hand to Pru.

"I've been watching for you," she said with a little smile. "Oh, Pru, this is so awful," and to Christopher, "Thank God you were there."

"He was there, and he saved me," Pru said, holding on to both of them.

"Christopher," Jo said, "will you come up for a drink?"

"No, thank you, I won't tonight." To Pru he said, "I'll see you tomorrow."

She smiled. "Yes."

Jo led her to the elevator, and as the door closed said, "That would have made an interesting headline: 'DCI saves a life and then gets arrested for indecent exposure.'" Pru smiled and leaned up against the elevator wall. She could still feel his rough end-of-the-day beard growth rubbing against her face. Jo grabbed her hand again. "You know I'm happy to have you here, Pru, but . . . why didn't you go home with him?"

Pru gave an exasperated laugh and put the heel of her hand to her forehead. "I didn't . . . he could've . . ." Bad timing, missed signals, she wasn't sure what to chalk it up to. "I don't know."

Jo had put a sheet over her sofa, and set out a large soft wool pashmina for a cover. Pru stripped to her underwear and put on an old T-shirt of Cordelia's, while Jo poured her a large measure of an eighteen-year-old Glenlivet and then Pru related the entire episode, beginning with her first meeting with Romilda.

"I was an easy mark, wasn't I?"

"No, not an easy mark, a kind person who only wanted to help."

"Christopher says I knew something was wrong with her, but that didn't help much. She seemed nice, and I was feeling . . ." her voice faded. She had finished her whisky and stretched out on the short sofa with her feet hanging off the end. A great weariness had come over her. "Oh, I'm so very tired."

"You haven't forgotten about dinner tomorrow?" Jo asked.

"I remember," Pru said as she drifted off. "Dinner at Cordelia and Lucy's. Talk about a garden for the baby."

* * *

When Pru awoke the next morning, Jo, dressed in one of her sharp business suits, stood at the kitchen counter looking

174

down at a folder and talking on the phone. Pru slipped into the loo and got dressed. When she came out, she heard Jo saying, "Your own office would be six hundred square feet with a gorgeous view. You might just be able to see the Royal Observatory from those lovely wide windows . . . Of course I can meet you there. Shall we say . . ."

Pru picked up her bag and gave Jo a small wave. "See you this evening," she mouthed, and Jo nodded and smiled.

* * *

She had little real work to do that day but could not be idle at home, and so she thought she'd stop in at the Wilsons' just to say hello. But when she arrived, her feet carried her straight past their front door and around the corner, then around the corner again. Christopher had as much as said that Malcolm was not a suspect, but she continued to dwell on Malcolm's belief in Mr. Wilson's guilt, and she wanted to pin him down about what she believed were unfair insinuations.

He had, after all, invited her for coffee, she said to herself. True, it had been a vague invitation, and she wasn't sure he meant for her to go to his house. Still, why not just drop by to say hello and meet this mysterious Mrs. Crisp?

She began to count doorways to make sure she got Malcolm's house right, but there was no mistaking it; the stone urns flanking the door held mounds of butter-yellow miniature roses still in full bloom this late in the season. Pru had never cared much for miniature roses with their dainty leaves and tiny little flowers — they seemed too cute for their own good. Give her a full, heavy Bourbon rose any day.

A young black woman answered the door.

"Hello, I'm Pru Parke. Is Malcolm at home?"

"No, I'm sorry," the woman said in a lilting voice that was heavily accented, "Mr. Crisp is out. Was he expecting you?"

"No, only I was in the neighborhood and thought I'd stop and say hello."

175

A small elderly woman in a wheelchair pushed herself into the sitting room doorway. "Are you the American gardener?" she asked with a smile. "Please come in, I'm Sophia Crisp, Malcolm's mother."

Pru stepped inside and extended her hand. "Yes, I'm Pru. I'm happy to meet you, Mrs. Crisp."

"Would you like coffee? I'm sure Malcolm will be home soon," Mrs. Crisp said. "We could make it ourselves, and Naomi" — she turned to the woman who had remained at the door — "you could take your break now."

"Yes, Mrs. Crisp. I'll be back in thirty minutes," said Naomi. She took her jacket and bag from by the door and left.

Mrs. Crisp led the way to the kitchen. "I'm happy to meet you, Pru. Malcolm talks about your gardening expertise."

"Well, he's quite a gardener himself," Pru said as she looked out the kitchen window onto Malcolm's collection of roses in the oval bed and along the side walls; only the wall at the bottom of the garden remained unplanted. Over the wall she could see the top of the Wilsons' shed and the part of the garden and terrace close to the house.

Mrs. Crisp set up the mugs, got out milk and a plate of biscuits. Pru flipped the switch on the kettle as she noticed that much of the kitchen equipment was accessible to the woman. On the other side of the room, where the Wilsons had a seating area in their house, was Mrs. Crisp's bed.

"It's instant — I hope you don't mind." She spooned a heaping amount of coffee into each mug.

"Not at all," said Pru, "as long as it's good and strong."

Pru carried the tray as they returned to the front room. She thought she might as well plunge in, albeit gingerly.

"Mrs. Crisp, it's good that Malcolm has time to be at home with you, instead of going off to a job every day."

"I don't know if it's good or not, Pru," said Mrs. Crisp. "Here he is still such a young man, and he really has no direction and no one to talk with except me. He's never made friends easily, and now that he has no place to go every day, he dwells on such odd things."

"What about his roses?" Pru asked. "Couldn't he join the rose society?"

"He did join, but then there was some problem at an exhibition — he brought it to the attention of the judges that someone was trying to slip a hybrid musk in as a centifolia. There was an accusation that he tried to attack someone with a trowel — really, how those people could ever think Malcolm capable of violence is beyond me. I think he was trying to stir up conversation, thinking that they would accept him into their inner circle."

Pru tried to sort out the two different pieces of information here. If Malcolm could attack someone with a trowel, he might be able to attack someone with a spade. That went against the details of the murder that Christopher related to Pru, but it did show a tendency for violence.

Pru thought of Malcolm's accusation that Jeremy stole an artifact from a dig, just as he had accused a member of the rose society of a misdeed. An incorrectly labeled rose may not seem like a terrible act to a layperson, but Pru knew what those rosarians were like. Malcolm sounded like a little boy who pulled a girl's pigtails just to get her attention. Did he not know how to make friends?

"Do you see much of the Wilsons, Mrs. Crisp?" Pru asked.

"Harry and Vernona seem much too busy for the neighbors, Pru. We had coffee once when they first moved in. They came over here with Vernona's brother, who, I'm afraid to say, doesn't seem the most upstanding character. After he showed up here a few more times, I told Malcolm he wasn't welcome. I got the feeling that Alf was trying to rope Malcolm into something, and Malcolm is so impressionable." Malcolm may be forty-something to the world, but he remained a twelve-year-old in Mrs. Crisp's mind. "But after that first coffee, Harry and Vernona never returned the invitation and refused our invitations that I sent over by way of Malcolm. I grew rather tired of the effort."

It seemed that the invitations from both houses stopped dead at Malcolm. And why was that? Pru wondered. Was it because Malcolm had his feelings hurt when he wasn't asked to play at archaeology? *Shame on you*, she thought. *It's one thing to have your own opinions, but to deny your mother the pleasantries of life by manipulating events was disgraceful.*

"Mrs. Crisp," Pru began, wondering if she could get Malcolm's mother to talk about the murder, "it must have been disturbing to have such a terrible crime happen so close to you — I mean, the murder of Mr. Pendergast."

"We don't know anything about what happened over there, Pru." Mrs. Crisp straightened in her chair, squaring her shoulders. "I wish the police would stop asking Malcolm questions, as if he was somehow involved. We never met that unfortunate man, and yet Harry Wilson persists in trying to accuse Malcolm of something he had no part in."

But Pru knew that wasn't right — Malcolm did know Jeremy. "Mrs. Crisp, are you sure that he hadn't met Mr. Pendergast?"

"Malcolm would not lie to his mother, Pru."

Pru heard a key in the front door followed by Malcolm's voice. "Mother? Mr. Davies had white peaches in again, but no artichokes at all . . ." His voice trailed off as he reached the door of the front room, his shopping bag in hand. "Pru?"

"Hello, Malcolm," Pru said with a smile. "Your mother and I were just having coffee."

"Malcolm," Mrs. Crisp said, "do put those things down in the kitchen, and come out and join us."

"Yes, Mother." Malcolm turned toward the kitchen.

"But you'd better take the peaches out of the bag and set them on the table, so they don't get bruised, and don't forget to put the shopping bag away instead of leaving it out on a chair." Mrs. Crisp's voice remained as sweet as when she spoke to Pru.

"Yes, Mother."

"Malcolm, you left the light on in the front hall again last night."

"I don't think I left it on, Mother . . ."

"And Malcolm, the jar of coffee was so far back on the counter, I could barely reach it." Pru looked at the floor. The jar of coffee had been near the edge of the counter, and Mrs. Crisp had had no trouble reaching it.

So that's how it is, she thought. Now her feelings toward him softened, at least slightly. Poor henpecked Malcolm. Pru thought perhaps the close quarters — both mother and son living in the same house with nothing to occupy their time — had set them on each other. They played off each other's weaknesses: Mrs. Crisp's physical limitations and Malcolm's stunted self-confidence.

When Malcolm returned, Pru said, "I'd love to see your roses, Malcolm. Is that all right with you, Mrs. Crisp?"

"Yes, of course, go right ahead," Mrs. Crisp said in a gracious tone. "Malcolm, do be careful with the latch on the back door. Close it properly so that it doesn't blow open, as it did yesterday."

Malcolm led the way into the garden, regaining a bit of his usual cockiness as he told her the story of how he planted his roses. "I'm sorry so few are in bloom now," he said.

"Oh, but I can tell it would be glorious in late June," Pru said. "I had no idea all the climbers you had." The walls were lined with neatly trained, extremely thorny stems, all pegged horizontally along the brick.

The subject of climbing roses seemed to make Malcolm uncomfortable. He changed course from walking toward the wall to walking toward the island bed that took up most of the center of the garden. "Now here are a few English roses still going," he said. "Here's Lady Emma Hamilton."

She stuck her nose into an apricot-colored, bowl-shaped rose stuffed with petals. "That's wonderful. What do you use for fertilizer?"

"I use manure every year. I wouldn't put any chemicals on my roses." Malcolm caressed the foliage of the shrub nearest him. "They're too precious."

"Just look how they respond to you," Pru said, admiring another late flower, this one an antique pink. "Is this

Heritage?" she asked, and he nodded approvingly. "You do a good job of pruning to keep the air circulating."

He looked uneasy again and glanced about the garden. "I've installed a few water butts to collect rain from the roof, but I had to put them under the windows, where they wouldn't bother Mother. I was caught out by a hosepipe ban one year, and it was devastating."

The conversation lagged, and Pru wondered how she could resurrect the subject of the Wilsons and Alf. She decided there was no easy way and opted for the direct route.

"Malcolm," she said, "Mrs. Wilson mentioned that you've become friends with her brother, Alf."

His eyes darted to Pru. "Well, you might say we're acquaintances."

"Did Alf tell you that Mr. Wilson was the one who killed Jeremy?"

"Pru," said Malcolm, once again taking on his instructional tone, "it isn't fair that you believe everything Harry and Vernona tell you. There's another side to the story, you know, and you may not want to get mixed up in all this. It could get dangerous."

It's a little late for that warning, she thought. "I got the impression that your mother thinks you don't see Alf any longer. Didn't she see him when he was here last week?"

"She was at her doctor's appointment and besides, Mother can't dictate who my friends are," Malcolm said with his chest puffed out, but then he glanced behind him to the kitchen window and lowered his voice. "I mean, I may just run into Alf occasionally when he's in town, that's all."

"Malcolm, did you actually see someone in the Wilsons' garden the morning of the murder?"

His eyes darted around, and he stuck his hands in his pockets. He took a breath, let it out, and took another breath. "Well, I might not have actually seen someone in the garden, Pru, but I think we all know who was there."

"Do we really?" she asked.

She had casually strolled the rest of the way down to the bottom wall as they talked.

"Oh, Malcolm, look," she said, as if taken by surprise at the sight of the wrought-iron rungs in the wall. "This must be how you can talk to me while I'm in the Wilsons' garden." She put a hand on one of the metal rungs and her foot on the bottom.

"Well, those have been there for ages," he said. "I didn't put them in."

Pru pulled herself up, stepped on the second rung, and looked back at Malcolm. "This is quite handy, isn't it? Why, from up here you could see all sorts of things." She popped her head over the wall and looked straight at Christopher, standing just on the other side in the Wilsons' garden.

CHAPTER 10

"Hi." She smiled at him.

"Hello." He smiled back.

"Pru," said Malcolm, "who is it?"

She looked down. "It's DCI Pearse, Malcolm."

"Oh." Malcolm looked as if he'd lost a new toy.

Pru looked back at Christopher, who was, she was thankful to see, still smiling. "Malcolm was just showing me the roses."

"Was he?"

"And I had coffee with his mother."

"Did you?"

Pru knew she needed to face up to it. "I'll just climb down and come around there, shall I?"

"If you like," he said, his eyes locked on hers. "Unless you'd prefer to leap over the wall?"

"I would," she said, "but I'm afraid you wouldn't catch me." A ghost of a smile remained around his mouth.

Pru said her thank-yous and goodbyes and walked back around the two corners. Christopher stood outside the Wilsons' talking on his phone. As she got near, he finished his conversation, and for a moment, neither of them spoke.

"How are you feeling?" he asked, looking as if he'd like to put his arms round her.

"I'm fine, really. I had a good night's sleep at Jo's. Her little sofa is quite comfortable, although I either have to hang my feet off or fold myself up."

"Pru . . ." he started.

"Is Mrs. Wilson at home?" she asked.

"She's on the phone, coordinating judges for a WI stitchery competition," he said.

"Why are you here?" Pru asked, thinking to stall his inevitable question about why she was snooping at Malcolm's.

"I was following up on the list of society members — we've talked with each of them. And then," he said with a shrug, "I asked if I could walk down to the bottom of the garden, because I had seen a hole at the base of the wall leading next door. I believe that's how the hedgehogs get in and out."

"Oh, the hedgehogs, I'd forgotten about them," she said.

"That's when I heard you in Malcolm's garden. Pru—"

She cut him off again. "Have you eaten lunch? We could get sandwiches and go back to my house. And talk."

He considered that for a moment. "Yes, let's do that," he said. "I've my car. Where shall we stop?"

"I'll phone the Cat — that's my local — and Wilf can make something up for us and have it ready to collect." They got in the car and she got out her phone. "What would you like?"

Pru phoned Wilf and ordered Christopher's beef-and-cheddar and a chicken-and-brie for herself, paid for on her account. She watched Christopher drive, smiling to herself. He glanced at her out of the corner of his eye, and when he shifted gears, he placed his hand on her knee and gave it a squeeze.

"Christopher . . ."

This time, he cut her off. "I planned on stopping to see you this afternoon. To find out how you were doing."

"Thanks again for my rescue." She made it sound lighthearted only because she didn't want to conjure up the memory of clinging to the side of a building fifty feet up in the air. He reached over and covered her hand; she put her other hand on top of his and rubbed it lightly.

"Why don't you drop me off at the pub?" she asked. "It's just before you get to the square. I'll meet you at the house. You'll probably take at least that long to find a spot to park."

* * *

At the house, Christopher took off his coat in the front sitting room while Pru made tea. They sat in the kitchen to eat, avoiding the issues at hand. "It's a nice house," he said, "but seems sparse."

"I'm the sparse one," said Pru. "The people who live here stored most of their things in the basement and locked the door. I brought over only a couple of suitcases with me. Easier to pack up," she finished, almost to herself.

He didn't speak, and she didn't look at him. Finally he said, "*Are* you packing up?"

She had trouble forming the words, facing up to approaching defeat. "Well, it doesn't look good. My year's almost up, and although I can't find a job here, there's one waiting for me in Dallas. That isn't where I want to be, but my plan failed, obviously, and I have to face the consequences." Even as she spoke, she knew how it sounded — it was her way or the highway.

She felt him watching her as she stared down into her mug. "So, you want to know why I was at Malcolm's house today," she said.

She heard him take a breath. "Yes, I'm quite keen on hearing about that."

Pru recounted the morning. Christopher didn't believe that threatening someone with a trowel meant Malcolm bludgeoned Jeremy with a spade.

She added her own interpretation. "He's socially inept. He doesn't know how to make friends, and he's jealous of the friendship that Mr. Wilson and Jeremy had. And he has an overbearing mother."

"This isn't evidence, is it?" Christopher asked.

"No," Pru admitted, remembering she had said much the same thing to Malcolm. "But it explains why he doesn't like Mr. Wilson — he's just a little kid with no social skills."

"I wanted to ask you about something Malcolm told me," Christopher said. "I showed him one of your photos, from the flash drive that shows him on his steps. I asked what he was doing." He started searching his pockets.

"Are you looking for your glasses?" she asked. "I've got a pair."

"No," he said, "not this time. I was going to bring that flash drive with me, but I seem to have left it."

"I downloaded all the photos on my laptop — we can look there." They walked into the sitting room, and Pru booted up the computer. As they waited, she remembered Malcolm watching her pull the phone out of her pocket at the bus stop. "I believe Malcolm thinks I have a photo of something important. Did you find anything?"

"Not yet, but in one photo, it looked as if he were talking with someone on the basement steps. We can just barely see the top of a person's head when we zoom in. When I asked him about it, he said the photo showed him with a fellow who was going to help him prune the climbing roses. And then he asked if I please wouldn't mention it to you, because he felt embarrassed that he hadn't hired you to do it."

"Prune his climbing roses? That's not right," Pru said.

"Why?"

"Well, you don't prune roses now, it's too early in autumn — late autumn or winter is best. Malcolm knows better than that. Do it now, and it may promote new growth that could be killed in a cold snap." She remembered how uneasy Malcolm became during the tour of his roses every time the topic of pruning came up. "Do you think it was Alf in the photo?"

"It's possible. The Wilsons didn't have a recent photo, and I haven't shown them this one yet. Not that they could tell much."

The computer up and running, Pru opened her photo library and looked for the folder, which she had labeled "Wilson Garden," but it wasn't in the program. She searched the entire hard drive and still turned up nothing.

"That's strange — I can't find them." And then she saw again, quite clearly, getting back from the country Monday, the footprint on the post, and the lid of her laptop open. Here's something she forgot to tell Christopher. She felt him standing behind her chair, and so she got up and walked to the sofa, unconsciously taking the clip from her hair, running her hand through, and reclipping. "You'd better come sit down."

His face was indiscernible, but she could well imagine what he was thinking. She held out her hand to him like a stop sign. "I didn't think there was anything to tell, and I still don't, but I will tell you this, anyway." Probably not the best way to begin, she thought.

"When Jo dropped me off Monday afternoon, and I came inside, I almost felt as if someone had been here. But," she hurried on, "no one could've been here — there was no break-in, everything was shut tight, no broken windows or busted locks, nothing missing — I would've phoned you about that. The lid on the laptop was up, and I thought I'd closed it — but the computer was shut down, and I know I've forgotten to close the lid before. Also, it looked as if there were part of a footprint." Christopher still hadn't said anything, and that made her a little nervous. "It was on the post on the floor in the front hall. One footprint," she said, shrugging her shoulders. "It had to be from the postman."

He spoke in his police-officer tone of voice. "There are people who can break in without it looking like a break-in. Do you have anything left of that post?"

With a sinking feeling, she realized she had destroyed more evidence. "There was a check — Sarah Richards finally paid me for stringing lights around her terrace — and I took it to the bank. I think I threw the envelope in the bin there." Why had she been so thoughtless? "I may still have some in the recycling here — let me look."

In the kitchen, she turned out the paper recycling bin, scattering newspapers, advertising leaflets, and post on the floor. As she picked up pieces of mail, turning each one over, Christopher walked in and got down on the floor with her.

"Pru, I wasn't scolding. But if we could find part of a footprint, it might help."

She picked up an envelope and saw about two inches of what might be a footprint on a slightly wrinkled envelope. She handed it to him.

"Was it wet or dry when you got home and found it?"

She stared at the envelope and thought. If it had been wet, it might've just happened. If it had been dry, the print was old when she arrived home.

"Wet, I think it was wet. The paper wasn't crinkled. Do you think that Romilda had something to do with this?"

He didn't reply immediately. They'd turned over every piece of mail over and found only the one partial print; he put that envelope in one of his handy plastic bags. After cleaning up the floor, they went back into the sitting room.

He looked at her, his eyebrows furrowed. "If we knew who she was, we might know that. I heard from forensics. The hair was synthetic — she was wearing a wig. They found another on the floor of the flat. But there were no fingerprints to be found."

An image popped into Pru's mind of Romilda spinning around in the dark flat with her arms held out. "She was wearing gloves. That's why I didn't see her fingernail polish — she was wearing gloves."

"The supports to the extension on the ledge had been . . . loosened."

She could almost feel the crack under her feet again. "The police don't think that I made this up, do they?"

She saw his jaw tighten. "It's been made very clear to them that they will not think that."

"I wish I could come up with something that would help the investigation. Something I could do that would . . ."

He took her hand. He appeared calm. "Pru, please . . . It's my job to be concerned about anyone who is a witness to or innocently involved in any crime," he said.

"Well, of course."

"But I am confessing to you now that I may be . . . slightly more concerned in this case, and that's why I keep repeating myself, because my warnings don't seem to be getting through."

"Christopher, I don't . . ." she stopped when she realized that it would be disingenuous of her to say that she didn't need protecting after he had literally pulled her off a ledge, but her stubborn streak wouldn't let it lie. "I'm accustomed to taking care of myself."

"Yes," he raised his eyebrows, "so I'm discovering. But if anything happened to you because of this investigation or your actions, I would feel . . ."

"Like it was your fault? Yes, I'm discovering that. Right, I won't take matters into my own hands. Well, I'll try not to take matters into my own hands. How's that?"

He took a breath and let it out. "All right, that's a start. And please, if anything happens that seems even remotely unusual, phone me. If you walk in the house and sense that someone might be in here, please walk back out immediately and phone me."

"I will," she said. They sat quite still for a moment. "I'm concerned about Mr. Wilson. Do you still suspect him?"

Christopher looked at her. "Harry Wilson certainly had the opportunity and the means, but," he said quickly over Pru's protest, "we are still looking into a possible motive. There is no evidence of him at the scene, but he's already admitted to being in the shed the night before with Jeremy. Money does not seem to be a problem for the Wilsons, and so it's unlikely he would want to steal the mosaic or the coins and try to sell them."

"He would never do that." *But then why was he corresponding with Hodges & Hodges Appraisals?*

"And so, at the moment, he is not in imminent danger of arrest."

"Good," said Pru.

"And it is not your job to try and clear him."

"Yes, I understand that."

"I believe that Harry Wilson knows more than he's telling us, and that could be a problem."

Pru chewed on her bottom lip.

"There must be something else, something that Mr. Wilson doesn't know, some other piece of information that we're missing." *Oops. I am not a police officer.* "I mean, that the police . . . I mean you . . . hmmm." She stopped so that she wouldn't dig herself in deeper.

A smile played about his lips for a quiet moment. "How is it that you are so sure about the Wilsons, after knowing them such a short time?"

Pru didn't want to admit it was because the Wilsons had made her feel like a member of the family. "I can just tell. Maybe you could hire me to vet the suspects on all your cases."

Christopher laughed softly. He still held her hand, and stroked the top with his thumb.

His phone rang.

He released her hand and stood up to answer. "Pearse . . . yes . . . bring him in. I'm on my way back now."

"Bring who in?" she said when he'd ended the call, not sure she wanted to hear the answer.

"I do have other cases," he said as they walked to the door.

"Yes, I know you do," she replied, noting that he didn't actually say that it wasn't Mr. Wilson being taken in, after which she felt guilty thinking he would deceive her that way. "Good thing we finished lunch," she said.

"I'm attending parents day at Sheffield," he said.

"Is that this weekend?"

"Well, it's tomorrow. I'm taking the train this evening, but I could wait and take an early train tomorrow . . ." he said, leaving the end of the sentence dangling.

"Jo invited me to dinner this evening at Lucy and Cordelia's. They're expecting — Cordelia's pregnant, and they're wanting to transform their tiny back garden into a child-friendly planting space. They asked me for help."

"Will you stay at Jo's tonight?"

"I'm sure she'd be happy to have me again," she said, being just as vague as he had been and hoping he would let that slip by.

"Right," said Christopher. They stood in the dim front hall. "I'll be back late tomorrow night. I could phone you Sunday, we could have a day out around the city if you're free."

"I am free on Sunday. I look forward to it."

"And tomorrow, will you see Jo tomorrow?"

"You mean, will I please not take up with strangers on the street who then try to push me out a window?"

He put his arms around her. "Yes," he said, "that's exactly what I mean."

"I'll see what I can do."

CHAPTER 11

Cordelia and Lucy owned a ground-floor flat in Islington, which came with a postage-stamp-sized back garden. Pru wasn't quite sure that the three of them — Cordelia, Lucy and baby — could fit in it and leave room for any plants at all, but she offered suggestions for pots of plants that could be grabbed and tasted by a baby or toddler without any ill effects. She warned the parents-to-be that flowers attracted bees, so perhaps floriferous plants could be grown in pots that hung from the wall, out of reach of tiny hands. When they asked about a lawn, Pru suggested they take the baby to the little park at the next corner but one.

Dinner was a communal affair. Lucy had threatened Cordelia with liver after Cordelia's doctor had suggested she needed an iron supplement, but fortunately common sense won the day and the menu consisted of grilled fish, an inordinate amount of roasted potatoes, and a spinach salad, which served as appetizer, too, as they all chopped vegetables and sampled along the way.

Pru loved dinners with Jo, Cordelia and Lucy, because they made her feel as if she had three sisters. Only children covet the thought of siblings, but Pru didn't believe for a moment that there was a problem in her pretending on these few occasions. Naturally, with the intimacy of family, came the freedom to hand out advice.

"Now Pru," Jo said, using a carrot to gesture, "I think you need to just think carefully about leaving."

"Leaving?" asked Cordelia. "You don't mean leaving London?"

"Pru thinks that because she hasn't found the job she wanted, that she has to go back to the States," Jo explained.

Pru hoped they wouldn't gang up on her, because she wasn't up to it. "I gave myself a year, and I can't just hang on making no money with no place to live. I'd end up sleeping in Hyde Park under a blanket of newspapers."

"But things have changed," Jo said, "now that you've met Christopher."

Lucy's ears perked up. "Christopher? Isn't he the policeman who was at the fête?"

Pru reached for her glass. "Now, that's not fair, Jo. We hardly know each other."

Jo scoffed. "It didn't look that way last night." Pru's face felt hot, and she busied herself getting more wine. "You can barely shut up about him," Jo continued, "there's no trying to deny it. When was the last time you felt like this about someone?"

She tried desperately to come up with the name of some man from her past, but Marcus was the only face she saw, and that had been a relationship based more on convenience than deep feelings, at least on her part. Jo saw the answer on her face.

"I told you," said Jo. "He cares about you — that's obvious. I can tell he's a very kind man, and a man who feels a great sense of duty."

Jo's description touched her, and Pru felt a bit too emotional to reply, afraid of what might come out. How did she and Christopher stumble into this? She thought of Jo's description — his great sense of duty. It did seem he took his job to heart.

Lucy leaned in. "It must be the badgers," she said. "A man who loves badgers is very sexy."

A good laugh broke the moment open, and Pru breathed a sigh of relief.

As Lucy and Cordelia went to lay the table, Jo asked in a quiet voice, "Have they found out anything about that woman?"

"No, nothing. She was wearing a wig, as it turns out," Pru said, "so even my description isn't correct." She remembered the sketch and dug it out of her bag. "They gave me a copy of what they came up with. That's what she looked like to me, but without the glasses and wig, who knows."

Jo gazed at the computer drawing for a long time, squinted, and began to frown.

"Oh Pru," Lucy said, "when we were in the country, you asked me to find out about your landlord, Archie Clarke. All that Jo cares about is that his checks clear" — Jo bent over her knife and cutting board and didn't respond — "but I'll ask around about him next week. Someone on the faculty must know him. I'll let you know if there are any skeletons in his closet."

"I'd love to find out that he wants to give me his house, free and clear, and move to Italy permanently," Pru said. "Find out if he's independently wealthy." She crushed a clove of garlic for the salad dressing. "Jo, I thought I should tell Christopher about the noises in the basement."

Jo knocked her small cutting board off the counter, and pieces of carrots clattered to the floor and rolled everywhere. Jo got down on her hands and knees and began collecting them as she said, "Oh my God, what have I done?"

Cordelia bent to help her. "Mum, it's only carrots."

Pru got the feeling Jo wasn't talking about the carrots. She didn't understand her friend's reaction, but it made her uncomfortable hiding this from Christopher — even if it was mice. "Jo, maybe the police could check, just to make sure they don't see anything amiss?" Now that she thought about it, what would she tell him? Arrest those mice!

"Oh Pru, why don't we just leave it for now?" Jo looked flushed as she stood up and began washing off the carrots.

"I'm sure it'll stop soon. I mean, what could the mice want down there, anyway?"

"A nice warm home for winter?" Pru asked. The mice were moving in just as she would be moving out. Maybe she could live in the basement with them.

* * *

Before the end of the evening, Jo reminded her that she, Cordelia, and Lucy were off the next day to visit Alan in Edinburgh. Jo quizzed her about her weekend schedule. "Will you see Christopher?" She knew that Jo didn't want her to be alone, just as Christopher hadn't, but really, she was beginning to feel badgered by all this care.

"Yes, of course I'll see him," she said, not mentioning that it wouldn't be until Sunday. She didn't need anyone Pru-sitting over the weekend.

Attention quickly shifted from her activities when Jo called for the pudding — their big indulgence, tiramisu that Cordelia made using decaf espresso to soak the cake.

When she got ready to leave, Pru glanced around for her copy of the police sketch she had pulled out to show Jo. She didn't see it anywhere and assumed she must've already stuck it back in her bag.

* * *

She spent an uneventful night alone and woke on Saturday morning thinking, *Look, now — half the weekend gone and nothing had happened.* When Jo returned from Edinburgh, Pru would point this out, as well as find out the reason for Jo's odd behavior the evening before.

By midday Saturday Pru was restless. She needed to take some kind of action, and so, after online research about the waterways of London, she decided to walk the route of the hidden Westbourne, the river that had been, like the Fleet, an open sewer until the 1850s when it was routed underground. That didn't seem to her at all a violation of the quasi-promise she'd made to Christopher — she would merely be looking into the conditions of a garden she was to build. She would like to build. She would've built except for the problem of a murder getting in the way.

She picked up the Westbourne toward the end of its journey, in Kensington and followed it to the Sloane Street Underground station, where the river passed over the platforms in a large iron pipe, and then made her way along the streets toward the Thames.

At a point where she could look west more or less straight toward the Wilsons', she paused, trying to picture some tiny tributary running underground all the way through the bottom of their garden — and Malcolm's — making the soil so wet a few feet down. She wondered why the mosaic was on soil instead of that raised area called the hypocaust that she'd seen at Chedworth. The Romans were excellent engineers, using natural waterways and making their own for everything from industry to bathing. Had they incorporated the seepage into some . . . some what? Her mind could go no further in imagining. Nothing seemed likely or possible or at all to do with a Roman mosaic.

* * *

In bed by ten o'clock Saturday evening with only a book to keep her company, the phone startled her when it rang.

"I wanted to hear your voice," Christopher said, "and to find out how your day went."

Incredibly pleased that he phoned, she still couldn't help saying, "And are you checking up on me?"

He paused. "I might be. Are you staying at Jo's?"

"As it turns out, Jo is in Edinburgh this weekend — but I didn't remember that until she reminded me last night. So I'm on my own and doing quite well." And before he could say anything, "Are you back in London?"

"I'm on a late train. I won't be back until almost midnight." His voice got quieter — she thought there must be other passengers near him. "You know I only want you safe."

"Yes, I do know that. I'll see you tomorrow, right? You can tell me all about parents day."

"I'll give you a ring in the morning."

The prospect of spending the whole day with him, wandering the sights of London, gave Pru both pleasure and pain. The pleasure was obvious, but she had to examine more closely the little stab of pain — and then she realized that the day would be a sort of farewell tour for her. Goodbye, London. Goodbye, Christopher. She knew she wouldn't be able to tell him that. Not yet. Let them have a lovely day, and she would worry about goodbye later.

* * *

She stood in front of the closet Sunday morning staring at her meager collection of clothes: two pairs of corduroy trousers, three pairs of khakis — one lined with flannel — the black suit that she used only for interviews, rarely worn during her London year and much too boring for a day out. A wider variety of tops, but mostly just what she could layer for warmth or peel off if she heated up while working or riding the Tube on a particularly stuffy day. Several sweaters had holes from getting caught by thorny roses on days she had forgotten to wear her canvas coat. She chose the same rose-red sweater she'd worn in the country and the better pair of cords.

Really there ought to be a law forcing gardeners to buy some decent outfits, so they weren't caught out when invited to do something other than dig a planting hole in the rain. At least, she thought, she wouldn't drag along her giant canvas bag, but instead got out a tiny shoulder bag and transferred a few essentials.

Just past nine, she'd made herself a second cup of tea when Christopher rang and asked if she was ready for the day.

"I thought we'd visit St. James's Park," he said, "We could watch the pelicans being fed and after that go to the organ concert at Westminster Abbey."

"I love St. James's," Pru said.

"But before that," he said, "we'll go someplace you might not have seen. How soon can you be ready?"

Pru put her cup down. "I'm ready now."

"Good, I'll be there in quarter of an hour."

When they rang off, she saw the day spread out before them in luxury. She had only one second of hesitation, the small voice of reason in her head. Reason told her she shouldn't begin something she couldn't finish, that it was better not to complicate her life at this point, that she would be wiser to stay on cool, friendly terms with Christopher. She gave reason the day off.

* * *

Ten minutes later, she perched on the edge of a chair in the kitchen, wearing her coat, waiting for his knock and when it came, she arrived at the front door in short order.

He reached for her hand and she stepped out, closing the door behind them. She looked up and kissed him softly on the cheek. "Where are we off to?"

He looked around him as if taking stock of their route. "We'll take the Circle line."

As they walked to the station, her phone rang. After the Romilda incident, as Pru had labeled it in her mind, she felt the need to hold on to Jo, however odd some of her moods had been lately, and she grabbed the phone out of her pocket, explaining to Christopher, "Jo said she would phone today — so we can arrange a time to talk tomorrow. She's been acting so weird lately, especially about the mice . . ."

"Mice?"

"In the basement — really, it's nothing." She looked at her phone. It was Lydia. *Oh no, Lydia, she thought, not now, I'm sorry, but I can't answer now.* She wanted to spend this day, just this one day, free.

"Don't you want to answer?" He had seen the caller ID, too.

She put the phone back in her pocket and said, "No." When it stopped ringing, she took a breath and said, "It didn't take you long to get to my door — you didn't sleep on my front step, did you?"

"I believe I'd be arrested for sleeping on a doorstep in this neighborhood."

Standing on the platform at the station, Pru remembered about the Westbourne. She looked up, searching for the black iron pipe. "There," she said, pointing. "That's the Westbourne, the river that runs from Hampstead Heath. It goes all the way to the Chelsea Embankment."

"Are you interested in waterworks now, in addition to gardening?" he asked.

"I did a little research, because of the wet soil under the mosaic. I wonder if there could be a tributary, some stream that runs along the bottom of the Wilsons' garden." She caught herself as this bit of reality crept in. "We shouldn't talk about the case today, should we?"

"We can try not to," he said. "Let's see how far we get."

* * *

They got off at Barbican, and as they walked, Pru asked, "Are we going to the Museum of London?"

"No," he replied. "We're headed for Postman's Park."

"I don't know it. Is it really a park for postmen?"

"It's near the General Post Office, and so they take advantage of the space. I'm happy I can show it to you," he said.

They passed the museum and turned into a gate and up a few steps. The small park, in a sort of fat cross shape, fit between two streets and was surrounded by tall buildings; the green space offered huge relief to all the concrete, brick, and stone. It was a bit of a busman's holiday, but Pru couldn't help herself as her eyes scanned the plantings and layout — Tasmanian tree ferns and other Southern Hemisphere plants stood testament to the mild London climate. She stopped when Christopher did and saw they stood in front of a wall that had a roof over it.

Large blue-and-white tiles set into the wall listed names and events. "This is the Memorial to Heroic Self Sacrifice," Christopher said. "It was started in 1900. The tiles commemorate people who died while trying to save someone else's life."

Drowning, fire, bombs — terrible deaths were recorded for people who had thought not of themselves in a time of crisis, but of others. "It's beautiful," Pru said, "and sad."

"It reminds me of my dad," Christopher said, keeping a light tone to his voice. "I'd just gone off to Oxford when it happened. A mother and a child, who was just barely walking were on a footbridge across the river. It was after a heavy rain, and the river was high. The child tumbled in, the mother screamed, and my dad, driving down the road, didn't think twice. He jumped in, got the child, and was able to make it back to the bank. But he had a heart attack and died there."

Pru looked at him without speaking. He returned her look, smiled, and put his arm around her. She rested her head on his shoulder. "It doesn't matter how long ago it was," she said, "we can still miss them." She thought she understood where his great sense of duty came from. "What about your mother?"

"She did all right," he said. "She died just six years ago. My sister took care of her at the end."

"You have a sister? That's wonderful," Pru said, always delighted to hear about siblings and always wishing she had one of her own. "Where is she?"

"Claire lives in Plymouth. Married with three children, two boys and one girl. Almost grown themselves now."

They read many of the tiles and walked through the rest of the park. With the sun, such as it was, behind the buildings, the air felt chilled, and so back to the Tube they went, deciding for lunch at the National Gallery café, as that would be near enough to the pelicans.

* * *

At lunch, Pru asked about parents' day, and Christopher said Graham had been both slightly embarrassed and rather proud that his dad had made it. "He asked me to help him out next weekend on a soil-survey project for his studies that he's doing up in the Lake District," he said. "I thought it would be a good time for us, although we'll just miss fishing season, and that's too bad."

They were to go to the Lake District from Friday until Monday; it was a shocking turn of events, because it meant that Christopher would take two days off work, which was almost unheard of. Four fewer days she would have with him before moving back to Dallas — she banished that thought almost as quickly as it arrived. Enjoy this day, she told herself — just don't make it count too much.

"Here's your chance to learn all about his environmental science studies," she said.

"He's to take samples of river sediment and measure the amounts of cadmium and arsenic. I'm to hold the equipment."

"I once wrote a paper on the effect that the temperature in a compost pile had on the number of sow bugs present. Every night for a month, I put my headlamp on and dug out a cubic foot of compost and counted them."

"Sowbugs?"

No, that wasn't what they were called in Britain, she thought. "Pill bugs? Roly-poly bugs?" She laughed at his expression. "Oh, wait — wood lice."

"Ah, wood lice, yes. And that was your major study?"

"My master's thesis was a discussion on the influence that English landscape design had on the literature of the Arts-and-Crafts and post-Raphaelite movements." She smiled at the presumption. "We're so full of ourselves at that age, aren't we?"

"I read English literature at Oxford," he said. "Quite useful in police work, as you can imagine."

"And what did you study?"

"I wrote a paper discussing the eighteenth-century naturalists' writings as literature. Do you know who Gilbert White was?"

"*The Natural History of Selborne* — 1780s? It's still in print, isn't it?"

"I rather fancied myself a modern-day Gilbert White there for a while," he said, and she could see a light color on his cheeks.

"Did you keep a journal?"

"Yes, I did."

"May I read it?"

"No, you may not," he said with a smile. He picked up his glass and put it down again. "It's been a very long time since I told anyone about that."

It was a still, quiet moment. She wanted to reach her hand across the table to him, but reason interfered and told her to back off before she got too close.

* * *

In St. James's Park, they sat on a bench to watch the afternoon event at Duck Island: feeding the pelicans — with herons, geese, and ducks also in attendance. Christopher told her that pelicans had been in residence since 1664.

"And sometimes they eat more than fish," he said.

"They don't capture little children, do they?"

"No, just the occasional pigeon."

Pru's hand went to her throat. "I'm glad I don't have to swallow my meals whole."

"So, you've been to St. James's before?" Christopher asked.

"I have walked through before, but I've never spent time watching the pelicans. I've walked through every royal park in the city in the last year — I had to do something on my days off." She dropped her face in her hands. "I didn't mean for that to sound so pathetic."

He put his arm around her. "I would've walked through them all with you," he said.

She looked up and saw him watching her. "How about a cup of tea?" she asked.

As they sat with their tea from the park's kiosk, taken outdoors where it steamed in the air, Pru's phone rang. They looked at each other before she pulled it out. It was Lydia again.

Christopher saw it, too. "Go ahead."

Pru turned the phone over as it continued to ring, so that she couldn't see the name. "No."

"Is she phoning about . . . your plans to go back to Texas?"

How could the world turn from bright and kind and romantic to bleak and desolate and lonely with the ring of a phone? She must change the subject. "What do badgers eat besides raisins and peanuts?"

They looked into each other's eyes, and she silently pleaded for him to leave the topic of Texas alone and let them move back to a happier place. After a moment, he took her hand across the table, and said, "They have a varied diet — they eat earthworms and ground beetles, and in late summer and autumn, a great deal of fallen fruit along with acorns and mast — you know mast?"

"Yes." She smiled. "Beechmast."

"And small animals," he continued, "occasionally even a hedgehog."

"No," she gasped in dismay, "not the hedgehogs."

He laughed. She squeezed his hand and said, "Thank you."

* * *

Walking across Westminster Bridge to the abbey, they stopped on the west end by the statue of Boadicea, who drove the Romans out of Britain in A.D. 60 — but only briefly — to admire the view to the north of Jubilee Gardens and to the south, the Houses of Parliament. Christopher put his hand on the back of her neck and massaged it gently, then wrapped his arms around her from behind. This was too much. It had always been relatively easy for her to keep an emotional distance in relationships, but she felt an unfamiliar pull here. Where had her reason gone now that she needed it? She tried to breathe normally. He touched his lips to her hair and murmured something in her ear, but all she caught was "My darling," which turned her into jelly.

"Sorry," she said, "I'm sorry, how silly of me." She struggled to get hold of herself, wishing that he would say something, some bold statement that would . . . would do what? His face was full of concern for her. She sniffed. "Is it time for the concert?"

* * *

For dinner, they stopped at a Spanish restaurant in Pimlico he had found and ordered several dishes from the tapas menu, her emotions back on an even keel at last. "Is this like the food you have in Texas?" he asked.

Pru looked down at the assortment of small plates with a strong Mediterranean flair. "No, it's quite different. They have more seafood along the coast, but really, in most of Texas, we're strong on beans and rice."

"Did your mother cook English food when you were growing up?"

"Fish and chips?" she asked. "Bubble and squeak? Bangers and mash? Spotted dick?" They both laughed. "Not very often." She thought it was time for a small confession. "I'm not really much of a cook myself."

"Neither am I," he said, "although I can toss a few things together for pasta."

"There's one thing my dad made sure I knew how to do," she said with some pride, "and that's fix biscuits."

"Biscuits?" he said in a polite tone. "Shortbread, custard creams, ginger nuts?"

"No, American biscuits," she explained. "They're sort of like a savory scone. You put butter and jam or honey on them."

"Well, I'd be happy to try them out."

"I'd be happy to fix them for you."

He paused, watching her with that small smile on his lips. "Why do Americans 'fix' food? Is it broken?"

"It is if I've made it."

* * *

They took a cab back from the restaurant. A light mist swirled around as they stood quietly facing each other.

"I've had such a lovely day," Pru said.

"I enjoyed it, too."

"You enjoy showing off the city, don't you?" she asked.

"I enjoy being with you," he said, and drew her close. She began to sink into such a delicious place, but reality yanked her back when her phone rang. Without meaning to, she tensed up, and Christopher pulled back slightly. She pulled the phone out, looked down, and saw Lydia's name on the screen.

Pru stared at the screen until Christopher said, "She's persistent, and I don't believe you can let this go. Go ahead and answer. I won't come in. I'll talk to you tomorrow," and he moved to leave.

"No, come in, at least for a minute." Talk about a mood breaker, she thought. They walked inside the front hall as Pru answered. "Hello, Lydia."

"Pru, I just wanted to check with you about your flight — do you know what day you're coming home?"

Misery wicked up through Pru's entire being. "Lydia, maybe I could phone you tomorrow and we'll talk."

Lydia knew her too well. She apparently sensed some hesitancy in Pru's voice and thought she'd better close the deal. "Pru, I know you're a little sad now, but it's really better this way. You know we all look forward to you coming home. Do you have your plane ticket?"

At Lydia's use of the word "home," Pru's eyes welled up. Christopher had given her some space and stood in the doorway to the sitting room, studying the Constable print on the wall.

"Lydia, I know you need to know, but couldn't we . . ."

"Pru, *mija*, it's okay to say it out loud. Tell me the day."

"Next Tuesday." Pru stared at the floor as she replied, but out of the corner of her eye, she saw Christopher turn and look at her.

"See, now, how bad was that?"

"Lydia, please . . ."

Pru was about to beg off the conversation, when Christopher came over, put his hand on her cheek and mouthed the words, "I'll see you tomorrow." He kissed her softly, just beside her right eye, which made a tear leak out and trail down her cheek. He wiped it away, kissed her again, and walked out the door.

Lydia continued, ". . . and Yolanda's about to get braces. She wants you to see her before it happens — she thinks maybe her whole face will change or something."

"Tell her she'll still be beautiful. Give the girls my love," Pru said. The conversation ended, but too late. She went to the door, hoping that he might be standing on the other side, but her front step and the sidewalk were both empty.

She slammed the door and heard a small crash from the basement. "Be quiet down there," she bellowed at the basement door. Silence. She grabbed her bag and stomped upstairs, saying under her breath, "I wish I had known that was all it took to get those mice to shut up."

Stanborough House

Church Row
Beckwithshaw
Harrogate, North Yorkshire
HG3 1QW

15 October

72 Grovehill Square
Chelsea
London SW3

Dear Ms. Parke,

This is to inform you that you have not been selected for the post of head gardener at Stanborough House. We appreciate your interest in this post and sharing with us your vision for a restored manor garden in the Dales. We know that your knowledge will stand you in good stead in your future employment.

We wish you well in your endeavors.

Yours sincerely,
Andrew O. Beckingham
Stanborough House
AOB/tma

CHAPTER 12

Monday morning she ran late. She hadn't slept well, flopping around in the bed like a fish on a stream bank. Her muddled dreams came back in snatches; there had been a badger in one of them; he was eating something, but she didn't want to think about what it might have been.

The electric kettle boiled and switched off. Pru poured her tea but ended with time for only a few sips and half a piece of toast. She told herself she'd stop for a coffee later and maybe grab a sandwich at Pret a Manger, but in the meantime, she had the last shreds of her career as a London gardener to wrap up. She would meet a client, Ann Hordern, to conclude their association and to offer instruction on gathering berried stems in the garden without massacring the shrub. At the Craddocks' she would sweep paths and water pots; they had found cheaper help within the family — their nanny was to become the gardener. Maybe she'd drop by the Wilsons, just for a chat, just to make sure everything was all right. Just to make sure the police — she declined to name Christopher in that role — hadn't arrested Mr. Wilson.

She arrived behind a well-dressed woman with thick auburn hair in a chignon who clanged from all the jewelry she wore. She carried a large Harrods shopping bag overflowing with papers.

Pru hung back at the bottom of the steps, and when the door opened, she heard Mrs. Wilson say, "Oh, Xanthe, yes, do come in. Harry is just downstairs."

"No, Vernona, I won't come in," the woman said. "I'm just leaving all this crap for Harry — it's what he asked for. I certainly don't need it, and I still have so much to clean out of Jeremy's flat. I'll be back at it today. Sorry for the bag, but really, he had an enormous amount of useless possessions to go through. At least he kept one filing-cabinet drawer labeled for the society. Otherwise, I wouldn't have known where to look. I got all this out just ahead of the police — as if they would care about it — and it's been in the boot of my car for days. They took his computer, but I suppose you know that. And they wanted the extra set of keys for this house. Jeremy always kept them on a hook in the closet, but they weren't there. I'm sure the police will ask you about that. Oh, and Vernona, I won't be at the dinner Wednesday."

She didn't wait for Mrs. Wilson to respond, but turned to leave, treating Pru as if she were a bollard in the road. Mrs. Wilson saw Pru for the first time.

"Pru, dear, what a lovely surprise, come in." She looked down at the shopping bag stuffed in such a haphazard fashion. "Xanthe never did care much for Jeremy's hobby. Really, this is just a lot of meeting minutes and the like, but I'm sure Harry will appreciate receiving them."

And then, like switching off a lamp, her entire demeanor changed, her face turned red, and she stumbled over her words. "Oh dear. You must want coffee," she said in a halting voice. "I'll just drop this bag off with Harry," and without another word, she turned and went down the basement stairs, leaving Pru standing at the open front door.

It was such an odd invitation that Pru stuck her head in the door first and looked around, in case they had company and didn't really want her to stay. But there was no one, and so Pru went back to the kitchen as usual. Mrs. Wilson returned and stayed silent while she made coffee. For the first time, Pru felt uncomfortable in her presence, uncomfortable enough to keep her canvas bag around her shoulder, as if she weren't invited to stay long.

Mrs. Wilson served her a slice of currant cake without speaking and returned to stand by the counter. Pru had taken only a bite when her hostess said, as if making an announcement, "Pru, we would like to thank you for all the work you've done here, and we want you to know that we understand that you need to move back to the States, and that you . . . you need to prepare for that move, and so we believe that it's best for you and . . . and for us that we end our acquaintance now and we wish you well, it's been . . ."

She had started to wring her hands as she spoke, and she didn't seem able to continue. Pru wasn't sure what was happening — it sounded as if Mrs. Wilson were breaking up with her.

"Mrs. Wilson, is something the matter?"

She had turned her back on Pru, and the cafetière fell out of her hand into the sink, where it shattered. Pru jumped up to help her, but was stopped by Mrs. Wilson's firm refusal. "No," she said with alarm. She did not meet Pru's eye. "Nothing is wrong. It's been lovely knowing you, and now I believe you should go. And leave for Texas. I'm sure you are looking forward to that. Now."

In her stunned silence, Pru added up each small disappointment of the past year — letter after letter of rejection, bits of garden work all over town that amounted to nothing. She had tried to make the best of it and had been comforted that here, near the end, she had found a place that felt like home. To have Mrs. Wilson, who had treated her as a member of the family since that first day, tell her to go away gave her a dull, hollow ache in her heart.

"Have I done something wrong?" she asked in a small voice.

Mr. Wilson burst into the room, banging against the doorjamb.

"It's the most remarkable thing . . . Vernona, Pru, I can hardly believe it." His face was flushed and his hair stood on end as if he'd grabbed hold of it with one hand and molded it into place. He paced back and forth, stopping and starting. "The letter. Jeremy told me, but I didn't have any idea that . . . I don't know what to do. This is . . . we can't let it be lost . . ."

"Harry, sit down, you're not making sense."

"You must see, Vernona. Pru, you must see it."

"I'll look at it, Mr. Wilson. Where is it? What am I looking for?" Pru, startled at Mr. Wilson's incoherence, wondered if he were ill.

"Downstairs, on my desk, Pru. Go and look. Yes, Vernona," he said as if to appease his wife. "Yes, I'll sit down right here. I'm fine."

Pru went to the basement as Mrs. Wilson insisted her husband stay seated until he calmed down. Downstairs, Pru saw that he had started to go through the papers that Xanthe delivered. Some were still in the bag — she had taken no great care to pack them — and some he had piled up on his makeshift desk. Sitting on top of the desk stack was a yellowed paper held rigid against a stiff backing and slipped into a clear plastic bag. A handwritten note on Jeremy Pendergast's printed stationery was taped on the plastic.

The note read:

H—
Forgive me for not showing this to you when you first moved into the house. I found this letter in a trunk left there in the attic, long ago forgotten. I thought it would be best to research the letter writer first, and then consider what should be done. Now that the mosaic has been uncovered, there is no turning back. I don't want you to try to stop me from following what is the only practical course. When you read this letter, you'll understand the importance of the find.
J
Remember Vindolanda.

She lifted the note and saw an old-fashioned script on yellowed paper.

28 June 1841

    I take pen in trembling hand to write an account of the occurrences of the previous five days. Our small piece of Chelsea brings great acclaim on itself, as the holder of an incredible discovery. The discovery now carefully covered over awaits re-awakening as soon as the proper authorities are notified and scholars gathered.

    For behind the house, so very near to our own lives, while digging to plant our garden, the spade went down too far and brought up wet soil. Our gardens need nourishing water, but the extent of water in this place brought to mind an underground stream or tributary. Before abandoning the land and our hopes of growing a few cabbages, we looked closely at the wet soil and found a coin, recorded here as closely as I can with my poor artistic skills. Could this be the head of the Emperor? On reflection, we believed this coin and two others located nearby to be markers and took our decision to continue exploring the oozing mass.

    We widened our exploration and found that a portion of mosaic floor had been placed near the coins, perhaps as a broader marker for the remarkable find beneath.

    We came upon what appears to be thin slivers of wood with writing, wrapped well in layers of what look to be linen, but sunk into the mire. We examined only a few, and carefully restored those we had retrieved back to the ground whence they came, as it appears that the waterlogged environment may have aided in their longevity. We replaced the three coins in the layer of soil above, to act as markers when we return to retrieve the treasure. I record here the writing found on one such thin wood. It will remain to be seen if this be here the work of the Emperor Hadrian or some copy to trick our minds.

    Thomas Gaskell

Pru glanced through the letter, although the dated handwriting style and the fact she wasn't wearing reading glasses made it difficult to decipher. She tried to assemble all the facts in her head: the mosaic marked the burial of something important. Whatever it was, she thought, could probably make someone a lot of money at an auction — if it had been found on private property, not a garden owned by the Earl of Cadogan. This involved Jeremy and Mr. Wilson, certainly, but most likely Alf, too. Her faith in Mr. Wilson still wouldn't allow her to classify him as a real suspect. Perhaps he had opportunity, but where was his motive? Still the presence of this letter with Jeremy's note attached here in Mr. Wilson's house didn't look good.

She looked again at Jeremy's note: "Remember Vindolanda." Was it a code?

Thoughts and suppositions tumbled about in her mind, as she heard the knock at the front door. Mrs. Wilson answered.

"Mrs. Wilson, may I speak to your husband?" asked Christopher. Pru looked down at the letter in her hand and felt dread creep over her.

"Yes, Inspector?" Mr. Wilson said. Pru heard him come out into the hall from the kitchen.

"Mr. Wilson, we have recovered from Mr. Pendergast's computer an email he sent to you that Thursday evening, the evening before he was murdered. It indicates that you know about a letter he found that has something to do with the mosaic, or what is buried under the mosaic in your shed."

Pru tried to will Christopher to stop talking.

"Inspector . . ." Mr. Wilson began.

"Mr. Wilson, why didn't you inform us about the email? Do you have this letter?"

Mr. Wilson did have the letter — it lay on the desk in front of Pru. First the coin, now the letter. Christopher would come down and find this additional piece of . . . He would come down and see the letter and mistake it for evidence against Mr. Wilson. This, this letter and the accompanying note would look as if Mr. Wilson had tried to stop

Jeremy and it went too far. But Pru thought it only appeared to be damning evidence. There must be more to the story.

"Mr. Wilson, the email indicates that you were putting up some resistance to Mr. Pendergast's plans, that you might try to stop him."

To Pru, it sounded as if Christopher was about to slap the cuffs on Mr. Wilson, and she couldn't let that happen.

"Mr. Wilson," Christopher continued, "it would be easier if you handed over what you have. We could get a warrant to search your . . ."

She heard nothing else. Mrs. Wilson may have abandoned her, but she would not abandon them. She needed time to help prove Mr. Wilson's innocence. Pru took the plastic-wrapped letter with Jeremy's note and put it in her bag. Numb with fear, she moved quickly and quietly to the door leading outside. She opened it, stepped out, and locked it behind her.

She could barely breath. What had she done? She had taken evidence in a murder case — but for a good reason, she told herself. She trusted Christopher, but he needed to stop and think, not immediately arrest Mr. Wilson for a murder that he didn't commit. Is that what he was about to do? Suddenly, she wasn't sure. Had she jumped too hastily to a conclusion?

Her mind started filling with "what if" and "how could he." She needed to think. Clutching her bag carefully so as not to bend the letter, she walked up the steps and quickly down the sidewalk, opposite of her usual direction. Five doors down, she heard Malcolm hurrying up behind her.

"Pru, were you just in to see Vernona and Harry? Has there been any progress in the case?"

She stopped. Fed up with his incessant questions and innuendos, she jabbed at the only soft spot she thought he might have. "Malcolm, how's your mother?"

His cockiness evaporated. "Mother is . . . doing well, thank you," he said in a small voice. As if a crack had opened up in his veneer, he added, "Pru, I hope you don't think that I would ever do anything to harm you."

"Then just what are you doing, Malcolm?"

"You don't know what Harry . . ."

"I have to go." She left him standing, getting away as much from him as from the chance that Christopher would emerge from the Wilsons'.

* * *

She walked. Taking with her an important piece of evidence in a murder case, needing to get away and consider not just what she had done, but also what might be happening back at the Wilsons', she headed down to the Embankment, across the Albert Bridge and along Battersea Park Road, back across the Queenstown Road Bridge and alongside the Royal Hospital. She kept walking and eventually realized she had walked to her own house. She stood on the far corner of the square, in the dim shade of one of the plane trees, its leaves beginning to turn gold, and watched her front door for a while. Everything seemed quiet. She approached and made a dash across the street for the door.

Inside, she paced around the house, still holding her bag, thinking about what she should do. Finally, she set the bag down and got out the letter, lifting it from the plastic carefully so that she could open and see the second page. It appeared to be in Latin, but instead of filling her with wonder, it made her sick to her stomach to think of what she'd done. She slipped the letter back in its plastic. Her eyes darted around the room and landed on a stack of oversized books on the shelf. Pulling *Beautiful Italy* down, she placed the letter inside the front cover and then stuck the book under one of the cushions on the sofa.

There, she thought, there, it'll be safe there. Her phone rang and she jumped. When she pulled it out, she saw Christopher's number. She couldn't answer. She'd betrayed him. She pressed fingers into her temples, which had begun to throb. Be logical, she thought. Sit down and think about what to do, what's the best thing to do. Xanthe,

Jeremy's widow — ex-widow? — had delivered the letter to the Wilsons. Perhaps she would have some information about the letter or the society. Xanthe had told Mrs. Wilson she would be working at Jeremy's flat today. Pru retrieved the letter and copied down the address from the stationery, then returned the letter and book to the safe spot under the cushion.

* * *

Jeremy's flat wasn't far from the Wilsons', so Pru made sure to avoid their door completely and approach from the opposite direction. She knocked and then paced back and forth on the small front step, unable to keep still.

Xanthe answered, her jewelry clanging. "Yes?"

"Ms. Pendergast? I'm . . ."

"Pendergast? The name is Thomas, Xanthe Thomas. Who the hell are you?"

"I'm sorry." Off to a fine start, Pru thought. "I'm Pru Parke, the Wilsons' gardener" — that was pushing it, she realized, but how else would she identify herself?

"Gardener?" She seemed about to laugh, but she stopped. "Oh, yes, you're the one who found Jeremy."

She saw his body again, slumped in the corner, the blood running down onto his shirt. "Yes," she said, then cleared her throat. "I'm sorry about your husband—"

"Ex-husband." Xanthe raised an eyebrow.

"Ex-husband, yes." Pru plunged in with both feet. "Do you know if Mr. Pendergast had any dealings with Alf Saxby before he died?"

"Alf Saxsby? I've never heard of him."

"Do you think that anyone in the society might have known about the mosaic — the one in the Wilsons' shed? Did your ex-husband say anything to you about the mosaic? Do you know Malcolm Crisp?" If she could ask every question that came in her mind, perhaps one of them would jog Xanthe's memory.

Xanthe crossed her arms and stared at Pru. "It isn't a subject that I find very interesting," she said, "although it seemed to have occupied every second of Jeremy's waking life when we were married. That is only one of many reasons we were no longer together."

I'm not helping, Pru thought. *I'm no help at all. What did I think I would accomplish?* "Thank you, anyway," she said, and turned to leave.

"Are you the American in Archie and Pippa's place?" Xanthe asked as Pru walked away.

"What?" Distracted by disappointment, she had trouble focusing on the question. "Yes, yes," she mumbled as she turned to go, "that's me. I suppose you've seen them, too."

She didn't wait for an answer, but continued walking. It came to her that she must tell Christopher what she'd done. Yes, that's what she'd do. She would explain it to him, and he would understand.

But first, she would talk with Mr. Wilson. Why hadn't she thought of that before? She believed in his innocence, but she needed to hear it from him, and then she could tell Christopher what happened. "You are not a police officer," she kept repeating to herself, sometimes aloud, sometimes whispered, sometimes in her mind.

* * *

Too nervous to sit on a bus, she walked, going far out of the way, walking across Hyde Park and circling the Italian Gardens and then walking as far as Hyde Park Corner before she realized she was walking in the direction of St. James's Park, where she and Christopher had spent such a wonderful afternoon. Was it just yesterday?

She turned back and eventually made it to Chartsworth Square. There, too, she stood at the far corner of the square, watching. Evening approached. Hours had passed since she'd first taken the letter and left the Wilsons', maybe more — she couldn't quite tell. She walked up and rang the bell, but there was no answer. She let herself in through the basement, closing and locking the door behind her. The papers, emptied from the Harrods bag, lay scattered over the plywood-topped desk. They had looked for the letter. Pru let out a little sob, wanting to phone Christopher and explain. Her phone rang, and she saw it was he. She felt lightheaded.

She opened the door to the back garden and looked out. The sun had disappeared behind buildings, and a light shone out the cracks of the shed and the dirty windows glowed dimly. The police tape had been removed from around the shed — Pru hadn't noticed that earlier in the day. She crept forward, staying near the wall and out of the line of sight from the shed door and, she hoped, from Malcolm's upstairs window. When she got closer, she heard a metallic noise, but no talking. She peeked around the edge of the door and saw Mr. Wilson on his knees with one of the short-handled spades, digging around the edge of the mosaic.

"Mr. Wilson?" Pru said in a small voice.

He looked up. His hair was wild, his clothes filthy, his eyes wide. "Pru? Pru, did you take it?" When she didn't answer, he asked, "Did you take the letter and keep it safe?"

She slipped just inside the door. "Mr. Wilson, what are you doing?"

He stopped digging. "Did you read it, Pru? Do you know what it means?"

"Mr. Wilson, where is your wife? Where is Mrs. Wilson?" Pru felt no fear for herself, but concern and anxiety for Mr. Wilson's sanity filled her. Yet, when he stood and came toward her, she backed up until she bumped her head against a shelf on the shed wall.

"Vernona is out, Pru. She had a WI meeting in Fulham. I told her to go on — I didn't want her to worry." He looked down at the ground. The hole, not much deeper than it had been, still looked oozy with water. "I haven't found the third coin yet, Pru — Gaskell wrote that he had replaced all three as markers. I must get at least that far."

"Mr. Wilson, wouldn't it be better to wait, to show someone, one of your society friends? Or your university person, someone who could help you find it . . . find the last coin?"

"Hmmm?" He had gone back to the hole, taken another shovelful or two, trying to dig out under the mosaic.

"Maybe you should wait, Mr. Wilson," Pru said, her voice trembling. "Because you should share this find, shouldn't you? You always want to share your discoveries."

Harry stopped and stared at the shovel in his hand. He looked up and around the shed, his gaze finally falling on Pru. "I shouldn't do this now. I should tell the others . . . Jeremy . . . no, not Jeremy. Archie, I should tell Archie. He'll want to return immediately."

"Yes, Mr. Wilson, that's what you should do. Why don't you wait until tomorrow, when you feel better, and then you can tell them all." Pru could see some sense return to his face.

"Oh, Pru, forgive me, I was just so caught up in the excitement." He stood and tried to brush the mud off his knees. "You do have the letter, don't you?"

"Yes, I took it, but I really shouldn't have. I need to tell the inspector about it." But would she? Could she? Mr. Wilson's temporary insanity aside, he could still be arrested. Temporary insanity, Pru assured herself. Do they have a temporary-insanity plea in Britain?

"But don't give it to him, Pru, not yet. Bring it by tomorrow. We'll want to see it."

"Yes, Mr. Wilson, tomorrow. But for now, why don't you go inside and wait for your wife?"

They stepped out of the shed, and Mr. Wilson realized he still carried the spade. He turned and chucked it back in.

"Mr. Wilson, I'll go now. Will you be all right?"

"Won't you stay? Vernona won't be too much longer."

The anxiety and fear began to grow again in Pru. She still had to hand damning evidence in to the police against Mr. Wilson and didn't know how she could or how she couldn't. "No, thank you, I'll see you soon."

"We're holding a memorial dinner for Jeremy Wednesday evening," Mr. Wilson said. He sounded weary, but calm. "It's at a place in Soho that he always loved. Almost the whole group will be there, wives, too."

"That'll be a good way to remember him," Pru said. It was too easy to forget that Jeremy Pendergast had friends that cared about him.

Dusk had deepened. As they went back to the house, Pru glanced over her shoulder and saw a curtain flickered upstairs at Malcolm's.

* * *

When Pru left Mr. Wilson, she began walking again. She knew she must turn the letter over to Christopher, but could not gather up the will to do so. She was such a failure — she failed at saving Mr. Wilson just as surely as she had failed to find a job, failed to start a new life, failed Christopher.

She stopped for a coffee somewhere, letting it grow cold on the table while she stared out the window at all the people passing, laughing, holding hands. She walked again, down to the Embankment and along the Thames path up to Westminster. A sharp wind came off the river and cut through her sweater. Her phone rang, but this time she didn't even look. A few minutes after it stopped, she sent Christopher a text that said, "at Jo's this evening." Sick with the deception, she had to sit down, and found herself at the base of the statue of Boadicea, where she and Christopher had stopped only the day before. She started walking again.

* * *

Fatigue overcame her, but she couldn't keep still and waited until almost midnight before going home. She stopped again at the far corner of the square, this time in dark shadows, and watched her front door. Christopher stood on the front step, and she shrunk back against the wrought-iron railing lest he look her way. Eventually, he left, walking down the sidewalk away from her. She covered her mouth to keep from crying out as she watched him leave. She waited an eternity before she went inside.

She pulled the book out from under the cushion, took out the letter, and tried to read it again, but now none of the words made sense, and so she put it back in its safe place. She needed to rest. All this would make sense tomorrow.

Neither a shower nor a glass of wine made her sleepy, though. She got in bed and stared at the ceiling, her head a jumble of images — Jeremy's body, the letter, Mrs. Wilson telling her to go away, Christopher kissing her goodbye. The night seemed interminable.

She must have slept, if only briefly, because she had a nightmare. She dreamed she was back at work in Dallas. Marcus was handing her a bloody spade and a wide-brimmed hat to wear against the sun. He told her she needed to prune the roses. Then Malcolm rose out of a pelican's beak, took the shovel from her, and raised it above his head. She woke up with a shout, sweating. She heard the *click* of a door closing downstairs.

Afraid even to breathe, she crept out of bed and stood, slightly unsteady, in the doorway listening. Silence. After a few minutes, she reached for her clothes and, still standing in the doorway, put them on as quietly as possible. Quiet clothes, she thought. Maybe there are badgers downstairs. She shook her head to clear it and thought, no, that's not right. There are no badgers in Chelsea. She listened again. Silence still.

Not a creak came from the stairs as she made her way down to the kitchen. Nothing seemed disturbed. She checked all the doors and windows, just as she had the day she got back from the country. Everything was locked up tight. She put her hand on the basement doorknob and found that, too, remained locked. Her uneasiness subsided but only a fraction.

It was just growing light, and she wondered if it were too early to phone Christopher. She made a cup of tea, and it sat cooling as she stared at her phone. Seven messages. Pru didn't listen to them.

She needed action. Grabbing her bag and phone, she headed for the door, dialing Christopher's number while she walked down the front steps. Looking up for a second, she saw Malcolm walking across the road toward her. Surprised, her bag slipped out of her hand. She bent down to pick it up and, when she stood up again, Malcolm approached her with his hands stretched out. Then, lights flashed in front of her eyes, and everything went dark.

CHAPTER 13

When she opened her eyes, the world appeared in a mist of amorphous shapes. One of the shapes slowly formed itself into Christopher, who held her hand, peered into her face, and said, "Pru? How do you feel?"

In a flash, she remembered the letter, placed carefully between the pages of *Beautiful Italy* and stuffed under the cushion of the chintz sofa in her townhouse, and knew she must not keep this from him any longer, even if it meant giving up evidence against Mr. Wilson. *Christopher, I have the letter, the one that Jeremy emailed Mr. Wilson about. It's what's buried under the mosaic that's the important part. I'll explain why I did it, but first, you must get the letter. It's under the sofa.*

"Sofa."

Christopher peered at her more closely. "Sofa, Pru? No, you are not at home — you're in hospital. Do you remember what happened?"

Of course I remember what happened — I hid the letter under the sofa cushion, and I've been so worried about telling you and what you might think about Mr. Wilson, I didn't eat or sleep. This morning I left. I tried to phone you on my way out the door. I saw Malcolm across the road, watching me. Then . . . then I don't remember what happened, and I woke up here. But I'm okay, and you need to go to my house and look under the cushion of the sofa to find the letter.

"Sofa."

Her vision began to clear, and she saw Christopher glance over at a nurse on the other side of the bed. "She thinks she's on a sofa. Do you think her mind was affected by the fall? Will she be all right?"

"She doesn't have a concussion. She's just waking up from a light sedative," the nurse replied as she walked out. "Give her a few minutes, and she'll be fine."

Christopher looked back into Pru's face, and then she saw, over his shoulder, Malcolm appear with a smile of concern that made Pru break out into a cold sweat.

"Pru, you had quite a fall on your step," Malcolm said. "Good thing I was just across the road and saw you. I rang for an ambulance, and they brought you here. Do you remember that?"

Christopher, I don't know how much Malcolm knows, and I don't know why he was at my house this morning. If he didn't do it, then I think he might know who did. It could've been Alf, but it couldn't have been Mr. Wilson. Please don't think he could murder Jeremy. But Malcolm knows more than he's saying.

"Malcolm."

"Yes," Christopher said, looking relieved. "Malcolm is here, he saw you faint on your front steps, and he rang 999 and then me. Good thing your head hit your bag and not the pavement." He reached up and touched her hair.

"I just wanted to make sure you were all right," Malcolm said. "I'll be off now. I'll see you soon."

As soon as he left, Pru got her mouth in working order. "I have to get out of here," she said. She started to push the hospital blanket off her and saw the IV in her right arm. "Please find a doctor or nurse. I'm fine, I just fainted because I hadn't eaten in . . . a day or so."

"Why be in such a hurry?" he asked. "Shouldn't you rest?"

"No, Christopher, I can't. There's something . . . I could rest better at home." She thought that sounded like a logical argument and tried to stand up.

"All right, all right, stay here. I'll go find someone, and we'll see if they'll send you home." He got up and started for the door, but Pru reached out her left hand.

"No, don't leave me."

He came to her, taking her hand and lacing his fingers through hers. "I'll never leave you." When Pru giggled, he said, "Oh, not what you meant, is it?"

She giggled some more. "No. Yes — I mean, thank you, that's very sweet. But I have to tell you something, show you something." She began to feel nervous. "You have to understand. Can we leave now?"

"Wait, let me find someone," he said. Giving her hand a squeeze, he walked into the hall, leaving Pru to think through what she must say to him.

He returned in a few minutes with a doctor in tow, and Pru presented her case for release.

"Ms. Parke, you were dehydrated when you arrived here. And when was the last time you ate?" the doctor asked.

"That's why I fainted — how silly of me — I hadn't had very much to eat since breakfast yesterday." Nothing, that is, since half a piece of toast and one bite of currant cake. "But the detective chief inspector will make sure I eat when I go home, won't you?" she asked Christopher, desperate for him to use whatever weight his office could throw around.

"If she is well enough to leave hospital, then I will certainly make sure she's looked after," he said.

The doctor agreed there was no need for Pru to remain if she would go home, drink plenty of fluids, eat something, and rest. Christopher waited out in the hall — on his phone — while the nurse took out the IV and helped her dress. It took awhile to get her discharged, and while they waited, Pru stretched out on the bed and dozed off. She awoke to Christopher holding her hand up to his lips, watching her.

She smiled, remembered what she needed to tell him, and the smile left her face.

Finally, paperwork finished, they made their way down to the street. Pru was surprised to see it was almost evening. They took a cab from the hospital; Christopher had left his car at the station, as it had been quicker to dash to the hospital in a patrol car with lights when he'd heard from Malcolm.

As they got closer to her house, her anxiety and fear returned. She kept trying to think of a good way to explain to him why she took the letter and how she believed that Harry Wilson did not kill Jeremy. Although she'd found Mr. Wilson in a state of mild hysteria yesterday, digging in the shed, it was with the fervor of an archaeologist who wanted to learn, not profit — and he had come to his senses. Christopher took her hand while a jumbled mess of an explanations clogged up her mind.

* * *

Once inside, he tried to get her to settle down on the sofa, but the second she sat down, she jumped up again — it was the cushion with the letter underneath. He put his hands on her arms to try to hold her still. "All right Pru, now we're here, and you can tell me what happened yesterday. I tried to phone you. I came by — I didn't know where you were."

"I saw you," she said, staring over his shoulder, remembering the image from the night before. "I was standing at the far corner of the square, and I saw you walking away from the door. It was late."

"I came by three times looking for you, the last time near midnight. Come, sit down and tell me."

Pru reached under the cushion and drew out the book with the letter inside, but didn't sit down. Instead, she held the book close, tried to steady her breathing, and began. "I was in the basement at the Wilsons' when you arrived yesterday." Christopher remained still, but she felt herself trembling all over and couldn't stop. "I heard you ask Mr. Wilson about an email and a letter from Jeremy."

"Go on."

"I wasn't thinking straight," she could only whisper, her breathing becoming irregular. "I thought that it would look as if . . . I trust you, Christopher," she pleaded with him to believe her. "But I thought maybe if things went a little slower, if you didn't find the letter right away, I might be able to help get some information, and then . . ." She felt a rising hysteria and tried to take big breaths, hoping to retain some control, but the breaths turned into sobs. "I took the letter — it's here," she opened the book to show the letter safely tucked inside and handed it all to him.

"I know it looks bad," she continued between sobs, "but I know you will be fair about this. I can't believe that Harry Wilson would murder his friend. You said that they don't need the money. He's not greedy. He would want to share whatever the discovery is with the world."

Christopher set the book and letter down on the sofa and wrapped his arms around her, trying to calm her down. "All right, all right, I know you're afraid for them."

"They don't need the money," she repeated. "You said that money is usually a good motive for murder," she said, her face buried in his shoulder.

"Yes," he stroked her hair, "money is a fine motive for murder."

Pru laughed and sobbed again before her breathing began to steady. Calmer now that her terrible secret was out, she said, "You don't believe he did it, do you?"

Christopher watched her closely. "Harry rang me this morning to tell me what happened last night."

Pru looked at him with alarm. "You mean, that I stopped by and . . . talked with him?"

"He said that he wanted to confess" — Pru began to protest, but Christopher went on — "to knowing about the letter. And that he got carried away when he found out what might be under the mosaic, and that you stopped him before he went too far. He tried to stall yesterday when I first asked about the letter."

Still guilt-ridden, Pru couldn't quite meet his gaze. "He knew I was downstairs."

"That's what he told me. He said you would tell me what happened, but as I was at that moment sitting beside you in hospital while you slept, I knew I'd have to wait awhile."

"Were you there the whole time?" she asked.

"I had to leave briefly. You were asleep when I left and asleep when I arrived back, so I hoped I hadn't missed much."

"You don't need to watch over me every minute," she said, grateful that he had.

"I want to keep you safe," he said, emphasizing every word, "and, I want to do my job. It's becoming a little difficult to do both."

"I'm more trouble than I'm worth?" she said, half serious, half in jest.

He gave a little laugh and pulled her close. "Not quite. But you are making my life interesting."

"I'll take that as a compliment," she said. She breathed deeply and settled her head back against his chest. They were quiet for a moment.

"Better?"

"Yes," she whispered. "Thank you."

"Now, we'll sit down and you can explain everything to me. Is that all right?"

"Yes."

"But first, I promised the doctor that you would eat. Does Gasparetti's do take-away? I could phone him."

"I don't know if he does take-away, but he has a lovely minestrone." Pru firmly believed in the restorative properties of soup. "I'll just go splash some cold water on my face. Could you pour us some wine?" He cocked his head at her. "I'll just sip a little until the food gets here. I'm feeling much better."

Christopher pulled out his phone as he walked into the kitchen. Pru dashed to the loo.

It was worse than she thought. She stared in the mirror at her swollen eyes and blotchy face. She blew her nose furiously, and said aloud, "Oh God, Pru, could you look any worse?" Cold water felt good on her face, but did little for her looks. She rinsed her mouth with a tiny squirt of toothpaste and dabbed a bit of pink gloss on her lips. She reached in a drawer for an extra hair clip — her usual clip lost in the chaos of the past two days — combed it through her hair, twisted, and reclipped. She looked in the mirror again. Little had changed. "Yes, now, didn't that just do the trick?"

When she came out, she found Christopher on the sofa. On the coffee table in front of him sat one large glass of water and two glasses of wine.

When she sat down, he kissed her softly on the cheek and rubbed her back. She blushed and said, "Crying is such an attractive activity, don't you think?" He kissed her again. "Is the water for me?" she asked.

"Yes, it is."

She picked up the water glass. "Cheers," she said and drank half of it. "There now, that went down a treat."

He smiled. "How much Latin do you know?" he asked.

"I know loads of Latin," she replied. "Ask me the name of any plant, go ahead."

He gave her an odd look. "Prunella — your name is Latin. It's a plant, isn't it?"

"Yes." She laughed. "I'm named after a medicinal herb called selfheal. My mother always told me I could do for myself just fine."

"Could you read this?"

"Not a word. Except for picking out Hadrian's name."

He had found his reading glasses and removed the letter from its plastic sleeve, opening it to the second page, the one written in Latin:

Imperator Caesar Hadrianus Augustus carissimo Antonio suo salutem. Non improvisam, nec inique, neque miserabiliter aut ingenio viribusque comminutis, nec ante tempus mihi

idoneum, solutam corpore animam meam maxime velim
scias. Paene videor, autem, ut comperi, iniuriam facere in
eos qui mihi succurrunt quandocumque laborem, me solantes
et ad quietum hortantes. Ex tantis rationibus, tibi talem
epistulam scribo, non, mehercle, ut longiorum excogitator
fabularum sed gestarum rerum simplex et subtilis relator
. . . ille qui me genuit pater, hic privatus aegravit et mortuus
est in anno quadrigesimo, mihi ergo est dimidium aetatis
paterni, etiamsi tam longe quam mea mater fere vixi.

"I expect Jeremy knew what it said," Christopher said,
"and Harry probably knows, too." Pru felt another twinge
of guilt. "We'll show it to him tomorrow and talk about it
then," Christopher said, putting the letter back in its plastic
sleeve. "In the meantime, I have something to show you."

He pulled two folded pieces of paper out of the inside
breast pocket of his jacket. That action brought Pru's attention to his jacket lapel, which looked rather damp.

"Oh God, look what I've done to your suit," she said.
"We should sponge it off, or you'll have salt deposits crusting on the fabric." Slightly embarrassed to remember her
outburst, which already seemed long ago, she said, "I'm not
really much of a crier, but when I do cry, I'm a mess."

He stood, took off the jacket, walked back in the kitchen,
and hung it on the back of one of the chairs. While he was
at it, he took off his tie. "There," he said, coming back to sit
down next to her, "enough about the suit. Read this."

Pru took the paper. It was a printout of an email.

H—

The mosaic we saw this evening in the garden is not
new to me. But I tell you this, that it is the beginning of
what could be the most remarkable find in our time, there
is no other way to say it. I have an old letter for you, one
that you must read carefully and consider thoughtfully before
we go any further. We have many decisions ahead of us. I
realize that you don't believe we should take advantage of

this opportunity. I beg you to put aside your concerns and do not try to block me in this endeavor. Please consider A——, his knowledge and connections. He could be of great help. I'll bring the letter around this evening.

J

Pru finished the email and sat still, afraid once more to look at Christopher. "I know this makes Mr. Wilson look bad, but you know there must be some explanation." She found a tiny ray of hope. "He didn't have the old letter. He didn't get it until yesterday, when Jeremy's wife — ex-wife — dropped it off. I was there. I'm a witness."

Her hand shook and the paper rattled. Christopher placed his hand on hers firmly but gently. "Read the next one," he said.

The second message, sent a couple of hours after the first, was shorter:

H——

I was terribly mistaken and I may have put the whole project in danger. You were right to object to my proposal. You are firm in your conviction that the public good, the educational worth far outweighs monetary gain. Before I give you the old letter, let me explain.

I must see you before anything else happens. Forgive me. I will phone you soon.

J

Pru searched Christopher's face. "That's what Mr. Wilson said," she exclaimed, "that Jeremy had reconsidered, that he didn't want to take the artifacts. This proves they weren't arguing any longer, and that Jeremy didn't want to try to sell the artifacts. Doesn't it?" she asked, hopeful that he could see this.

"We checked Jeremy's phone records and the Wilsons'. He never rang," Christopher said. Pru waited. "So this may work in Harry Wilson's favor." She began to smile. "But," Christopher said with some gravity, "why didn't Harry tell us about the emails to begin with?"

The answer was obvious to Pru. "He didn't want to paint Jeremy in a bad light. He hadn't seen the old letter and the note that Jeremy wrote to go with it — that helps Mr. Wilson's case, doesn't it? They were friends, and Mr. Wilson believed in Jeremy's integrity. He would never want his memory tainted with accusations of possible theft. He thought if he showed you the emails that it would look as if Jeremy had tried to steal the mosaic or whatever is there — that's the opposite of everything they'd always done and everything they stood for in their society."

"All right, Ms. Parke, you may stand down."

Pru looked at the first email again. "Who is 'A'? Do you think he means Alf?"

"From all we've heard about Alf Saxsby," Christopher said, "I find it difficult to imagine that anyone would rely on his 'knowledge and connections.' His speciality is breaking and entering."

Breaking and entering . . . the phrase jogged Pru's memory. "Christopher, there's something else." She looked up nervously and kept hold of his hand. "I didn't sleep last night, but early this morning, I drifted off and I had a bad dream. I woke up with a shout and I thought I heard something down here."

His hold on her hand tightened. "What did you hear?"

"It sounded like a door closing — maybe the front door." She thought hard. "I could've imagined it. I wasn't thinking clearly. I didn't hear anything else, and I looked around down here and didn't see anything different."

"Pru . . ."

"And then I left, and I was phoning you when I fainted. So I didn't wait — it's just that I didn't remember until now." Again, she caused another delay in getting information to him. "I'm sorry."

He stood up and rang the police station before she could say anything else, demanding the fingerprint crew get there immediately. When he rang off, she grabbed his arm in alarm. The trauma of the previous day lingered, and her thought process hadn't returned to normal. "But they'll find my fingerprints, mine."

He took both her hands in his. "Look at me. Yes, they'll find yours, and that's fine. We know you. They'll find mine, too. And then we'll know if anyone else has been here."

She felt on the verge of tears again and angry with herself. She said, "I'm not much help, am I?"

"Your involvement in this case has been invaluable — at least, I think so." Her laughter squeezed the tears out of her eyes and they tumbled down her cheeks.

* * *

A knock at the door heralded the arrival of both the fingerprint technicians and a surprised waiter from Gasparetti's with dinner, which consisted of minestrone, a crusty loaf of bread, and a small plate of antipasto, the last complements of Riccardo, who normally did neither take-away nor deliveries, but had made an exception when he heard that Pru was feeling under the weather.

She tried to stay out of the fray as the police dusted all the doorknobs and latches in the house. During the dusting, Christopher's phone rang. He walked into the kitchen as he talked. When the crew packed up and left, Pru followed Christopher into the kitchen just as he rang off.

As they sat down to dinner, he said, "That was Harry Wilson on the phone."

"Are they all right? Did something happen?"

"They are fine," he said. "I told him we'll need to talk with him tomorrow. But he wanted to tell me that this evening, when he told his wife about your visit last evening, Vernona broke down in tears and said that you must stay away from them, because Alf rang on Sunday and as much as threatened to harm you if you didn't."

"Alf? Do you think that Alf sent Romilda?" Alf had seemed like a clown to her until now, a harmless bungler. But he had told Mrs. Wilson . . . Her fear shifted to sympathy. "Poor Mrs. Wilson."

He picked up her hand and kissed it. "She was upset, she said, because of the way she treated you. When was that?"

Pru remembered how she'd felt when Mrs. Wilson dismissed her from their lives. "Yesterday."

"She thought she would be saving you if you stayed away from them, and the only way she could think of to accomplish that was to pretend they didn't want you around."

Her emotions still ragged, Pru's eyes filled with tears. "She said those things to protect me" — Pru put her hand over her heart and clutched at her sweater — "but it hurt when it happened."

* * *

Pru believed that Christopher believed in Harry's innocence, and it lifted a huge weight off Pru's mind. They said little while they ate. The soup and wine worked their magic. Comfortable and sleepy, she had to fight to remain alert.

"What was Malcolm doing across the street from my front door so early this morning?" she asked, returning to the events of the day.

"Out for his morning walk was what he told me when I asked," Christopher said in a skeptical tone. "Do you remember seeing him?"

"Yes," she said, thinking back to the last image she had of that morning. "He was coming toward me." She frowned.

Christopher set down his glass. "Do you think he pushed you down the front step?"

"No, I'm not saying that. It's just that the last thing I remember is Malcolm coming toward me with his hands out." She looked up at him, still frowning.

"I will talk with him again tomorrow. He said he saw you faint. And he did phone for help."

"Yes, yes," she said, "that's probably what it was. He did help." She thought about the terrible day and night she'd spent. She smiled at Christopher as she noticed the dark circles under his eyes. "You didn't sleep well last night, either."

"I almost came back over here about three this morning," he said. "If I hadn't heard from Malcolm so early, I'd have been here knocking the door down."

"That would've been . . . quite a . . . scene," she said.

Pru found it difficult to concentrate. She'd finished her glass of wine — her first or second, she couldn't quite remember — and her eyelids were heavy. She rested her chin on her hand and blinked, but it must have been more than a blink, because when she opened her eyes again, Christopher stood over her.

"You need to sleep," he said, "enough wine and talk."

"No, no, I'm fine," she mumbled as he took her hand, led her out into the sitting room and sat her down on the sofa. "I tell you what, let me just sit here for a minute and then I'll be fine."

"Lie down." He took her shoes off, held her head up off the throw pillow, and unclipped her hair. She stretched out.

"I tell you what, let me just lie here a minute. I'll just close my eyes for one minute and then I'll be fine, okay? You won't leave?"

"No, I won't leave." The last thing she remembered was the feel of his lips on her forehead.

CHAPTER 14

Pru opened her eyes when his phone rang. Christopher jumped up from the overstuffed chair and answered, "Pearse," as he walked into the hall. She saw him stretch out his back. A book lay open upside down on the arm of the chair.

He had covered her with a light throw. She'd slept through the night; sunlight now poured in through the windows and then disappeared with a passing cloud. She sat up and stretched, listening to his voice. Not really the first night together that she had hoped. She grabbed her hair clip from the coffee table and dashed to the loo, catching his eye as she did so.

When she came out, he'd put the kettle on and leaned over, peering into the small fridge.

"Not much to see in there, I'm afraid," she said.

He smiled. "Good morning." He stood up. "There's left-over minestrone."

"Thank you," she said, walking over and giving him a quick kiss. "Thank you for staying, for listening to me. For not arresting me. Now, I'll make us scrambled eggs. At least there are eggs. And look — Riccardo's bread for toast."

At the table, with plates clean and more tea poured, Christopher said, "No extra fingerprints, I'm afraid. Just yours and mine."

"And did they wonder why yours were here?"

"I made it perfectly clear that they would find mine. There were no questions asked."

"I could've imagined it," she said, looking down into her lap. "I was a little crazy."

"I'm sorry you had to spend a day and a night afraid and worried about what might happen."

"It certainly wasn't your fault," Pru said. "I just wasn't thinking straight."

"I should've stayed Sunday night."

Pru reached across the table and touched his hand. "Yes, you should've stayed Sunday night." She started to draw her hand away, but he caught hold of it.

"I didn't want to complicate things for you."

She looked down at their hands. "It's too late for that. But could you have stopped me from doing such a silly thing?"

"I could've at least made sure that you ate a good breakfast," he said.

Pru smiled and allowed herself two seconds to enjoy the thought of that breakfast and what might have led up to it. "Right," she said, back to the business at hand. "What were you reading last night?"

"Well, I was awake for a while, and I thought I'd find something to do besides watch you sleep."

"Oh no, please don't say that," she winced at the thought. "I'm so embarrassed."

"You didn't snore," he reassured her.

"Thank God. Now, moving on," she said as a prompt.

"Right, let me show you the book I found." They walked into the front room. "It's about the Roman Empire."

"I thought those were all travel books up there," Pru said, "like *Beautiful Italy*."

"Most of them are, but this small one has something we might find interesting." He handed the open book to her, and she looked down to see a photo of a coin that looked remarkably similar to the drawing in the letter.

"That's the coin, that's the same as the coins we've found."

"It seems it's as if a commemorative coin. Hadrian visited Britain, and they could've made some for that reason."

"Did he visit his wall while he was here?"

"I don't see how he could've missed it."

"Does it say anything about letters from Hadrian?" She handed the book back.

"I couldn't find a mention."

Pru noticed the cracked yellow binding. "When was it published?"

He looked inside the cover. "1963."

"1963? That's ancient."

"It's history," he protested.

"Yes," Pru said, "but who knows what else they've found since then. Mr. Wilson told me the Duke of Northumberland just found a whole Roman villa or settlement or something in west London. Let's look online. 'Remember Vindolanda,' Jeremy wrote. Let's see what Vindolanda has to say."

She found the website for Vindolanda — a Roman fort along Hadrian's Wall, and now a museum and site of many an archaeological dig — and began running her finger down the screen, looking for a timeline of discovery or a description of objects unearthed since the early 1960s.

Christopher leaned on the back of her chair as she read. She could feel his breath on her hair. He kissed her neck and worked his way up to just behind her ear. She turned her head, and they looked at each other as his hand moved a strand of hair away from her eyes, and his finger traced the side of face, her jawline, and continued down her throat to just inside her V-neck sweater.

His phone rang. He didn't move. "I could ignore it."

She smiled slowly. "No, you couldn't."

"Pearse." He walked into the kitchen as he answered. Pru took a deep breath and blinked at the computer screen a few times before it came back into focus.

A few minutes later, he came back in. "Pru, what did you say the name of . . ."

"Christopher, look," she cut him off in her excitement. "In 1973, archaeologists discovered wooden tablets at Vindolanda. Before then, they knew that Romans wrote on wax tablets and on papyrus, but these were wafer-thin pieces of wood they used to write letters and receipts and all sorts of things on. They were found in a waterlogged tip. It was the wet conditions that saved them. Because it was anaerobic, there wasn't enough air for decomposition to set in." She turned to him. "Wet soil, like the wet soil in the shed under the mosaic."

She stood up and started to pace, removing her hair clip, combing through and reclipping. "*Remember Vindolanda*, Jeremy wrote. Vindolanda is at Hadrian's Wall, and the letter has a drawing of a coin commemorating Hadrian's visit. If Jeremy was referring to these wooden tablets, does that mean there could be a letter written by Hadrian sunk in that ooze?"

She stopped pacing and sat down again. "A letter from Hadrian would be worth a lot of money, wouldn't it?" she asked. "Alf needed money. The deal selling the house in Hampshire didn't go through."

"We need someone to explain that old letter to us," Christopher said. "We might as well begin with Harry Wilson." He looked at her out of the corner of his eye and said casually, "I'll take the letter with me, shall I?"

Pru held up her hands in surrender. "Yes, please, you take it." She thought for a moment. "Christopher, if he doesn't already realize the amazing find that might be under the mosaic, Mr. Wilson will be astounded."

"Pru," he cautioned, "there are still many things to clear up. For example — and you must admit this is important — we still don't know who murdered Jeremy Pendergast."

She noticed his use of "we." Whether deliberate or not, she felt he was including her in the investigation. "Well, we'll just ask Mr. Wilson what he thinks, now that all this new information has been uncovered." She'd better check, just to be sure. "I get to be there, don't I?"

"Yes, of course you do," he said as they stood up. "But please remember . . ."

"I am not a police officer."

He narrowed his eyes, pulled her close, and kissed her. "That is correct."

When he put on his jacket, Pru could see a white crusting of dried tears on the dark lapel. As he headed for the door, he said, "I'm off to my flat for a shower."

"Me, too." Pru said as she followed him. Christopher stopped and turned to her. She hurried on. "Here, I mean. I'll shower here."

He smiled. "Right, well, I'll just take that image with me then. Now, shall I come round for you after I stop by the station, and we'll go to the Wilsons' together?"

"No, I'll meet you there. In two hours?"

It had begun to rain, and Christopher — for once without his umbrella — dashed for a cab, keeping the plastic-wrapped letter inside his jacket.

* * *

Pru arrived at the Wilsons' before Christopher, but he had phoned ahead and explained much of what they'd discovered and discussed. Mrs. Wilson looked as if she might start crying when she opened the door and saw Pru. She gave her a hug and, as they walked back to the kitchen, apologized profusely for her behavior.

"I was so frightened of what Alf might do to you and I'm appalled that he has become such a . . . thug," she said.

"There's no need for an apology," Pru said. "You were trying to protect me." When they walked into the kitchen, Mr. Wilson rose from the sofa in the small seating area in the kitchen. The kettle was on and a new cafetière was at the ready. A Victoria sponge had been placed on a footed cake stand. Murder or no, Mrs. Wilson would be a good hostess.

"Do you think Alf was the one who . . . killed Jeremy?" Pru asked.

"It doesn't look good, Pru," Mr. Wilson said. "The police still can't find him, and they've been back questioning

Malcolm. I'm sure he knows more than he's saying. It sounds as if Alf had his fingers in every piece of this scandal." He glanced up at his wife, who busied herself with pouring milk into the pitcher. Mr. Wilson appeared to have recovered from his bout of wild digging two nights earlier, but now Mrs. Wilson looked a bit pale.

"If Alf . . ." Pru wondered how to put this question with tact. "Could you get your house back if Alf . . ." she still couldn't quite say it aloud.

"Yes," Mr. Wilson said as he nodded toward his wife. "Yes, I know about the sale falling through. I believe we may be able to take the house again."

"If that happens, Pru," Mrs. Wilson said, "we want you to come and visit us, see the garden, and meet Simon."

"That would be lovely, thank you," Pru said, and thought it would indeed be lovely but seemed unlikely as she probably would be three thousand miles away. She tried to dispel the sadness that could creep in so quickly by asking, "Mr. Wilson, what do you think is buried out there?"

Harry Wilson began to smile. "Well, no one has seen it yet, but from the brief time I examined that old letter" — *before I snatched it away*, Pru thought — "and the Latin lines that were copied there, I believe this could be a momentous find. The writing is from a letter written by Hadrian that many scholars believe is the start of his lost autobiography. No one has ever seen it, and only a copy in Greek of this one letter has even been found. But so many of us can recite the English translation by heart." Mr. Wilson looked off into the distance and said,

> "The Emperor Hadrian Augustus to his most esteemed Antinous, greetings. Above all I want you to know that I am being released from my life neither before my time, nor unreasonably, nor piteously, nor unexpectedly, nor with faculties impaired . . ."

They were quiet for a moment, while the ancient words hung in the air. Mr. Wilson blinked, cleared his throat, and looked at his wife and Pru. "But copied in Gaskell's letter," he said, "was the Latin text of the same letter — Hadrian's own language. If it's complete, Hadrian's autobiography could be the biggest find since—" A knock at the front door interrupted him and gave Pru a start.

"It must be Christopher." She got up. "I'll let him in, shall I? This is amazing."

Christopher hung his raincoat on a hook as Pru said, "Wait till you hear what Mr. Wilson has to say. Here, in the Wilsons' back garden of all places." She gave him a quick rundown as they went back to the kitchen.

Christopher pulled out the letter while Pru and Mrs. Wilson served coffee and cake. "Everyone has always talked about his autobiography," Mr. Wilson said, "but only that one letter — possibly the beginning of his life story — was all that existed. Until, perhaps, now."

They all sat in stunned silence for a moment, and then Pru's phone rang. She dashed into the front hall to answer.

It was the Hightowers, at their wits' end because the new lawn service they'd hired were out there now, getting ready to spray. "Spray? Spray what?" The Hightowers didn't know what, but they were sure it wasn't organic, and they wanted Pru to come and do something about it. Now, before something terrible happened and all the good insects died and all the birds left.

The Hightowers had been good clients, and Pru was proud that they had listened when she talked about organic practices for lawns, so she felt obligated to see their relationship through to its end. But it meant she would miss all the good parts of the Hadrian story. She went back to explain, and Christopher stood up. "Are you sure you need to go now?"

"I might as well," she said with resignation. "I told some other clients that I'd stop by—" She almost added "one last time." There it went again, reality making an appearance when she least needed it to. To the Wilsons, she said, "I'm sure everything is going to be all right now. I'll talk to you later." She took Christopher's hand and led him to the front door. "I'll phone you later. Or . . . perhaps I'll see you?"

"Pru, you should hear this, too," he said.

"Christopher, they're probably about to broadcast some totally unnecessary weed and feed all over the lawn. I can't let them. And I know everything's under control now — you'll see to it. And the Wilsons are fine." Pru felt positively lighthearted, and even though the actual murderer hadn't been identified or apprehended, she could see the situation resolving itself by the end of the day. The police would find Alf and question him; he probably would confess and be charged with murder. Malcolm would be questioned and . . . Pru decided not to dwell on details at the moment. What was important was that Christopher knew Mr. Wilson didn't kill Jeremy, and she could leave the rest in his hands.

"You'll tell me about it later," Pru said. She drew close to him and said in a quiet voice, "You can tell me this evening."

He laughed, stroked her hair, and kissed her. "Right, off you go, defend the lawn. I'll see you later."

* * *

Pru relished a good chemical-versus-organics fight. When she arrived, it had started to rain and the Hightowers stood in their front doorway, huddling under the small portico. A lorry from Green Your Lawn LLC was parked on the street, and two workers in dark coveralls and waterproofs stood near the gate to the back garden looking sullen. The rain dripped over the edge of their hoods.

"'Ere," one of them said when Pru approached them. "Are you the one we're supposed to wait for? Reg and me's got to get to work."

Pru had borrowed one of the Wilsons' large umbrellas and so stood comfortably out of the rain. She smiled at the workers and looked through the gate at the Hightowers' lawn, lush and green. "What are you fellows planning to do?" she said in a friendly voice.

"What we need to do," Reg said, "is to . . . restore . .
." — he looked down at the clipboard he held and read from
a coffee-stained, limp paper — "restore the balance of nutri-
ents to the roots and stop the bugs and weeds from taking
over." He looked back up at Pru. "There, that's what Nigel
and me's doing."

"What bugs do you suppose are out there, and what do
you think they're doing?" she asked. She walked through the
gate, bent down and ran her hand over the top of the rain-
soaked lawn. "Do you see any weeds?"

"It isn't our job to look for bugs and weeds," Nigel com-
plained. "We're to apply the remedy and go to the next stop."

"And just what were you going to apply?" she asked, still
keeping a friendly tone.

"Our product is guaranteed to make a lawn lush and
green in just two weeks." Reg puffed out his chest.

"Take a look, Reg," Pru said. "The lawn is already lush
and green."

Pru could see, over Nigel's shoulder, the large plastic
container in the back of their truck, and she knew by the
color of the bucket what they had planned to apply to her . .
. the Hightowers' precious organic lawn.

"Have you noticed it's raining?" Pru asked. "Where
do you think your 'product' will end up once you spray it?
Straight into the Thames."

Nigel and Reg exchanged looks.

"I tell you what, fellows," Pru said in a reasonable tone.
"Why don't we let the Hightowers tell your boss that you
did just what they asked you to do. No one has to tell them
exactly what that was, now do they?"

* * *

She missed Christopher's call while she helped the Hightowers
search online for a truly organic lawn-care company, and
when she phoned him back, she got his voice mail. We're not
going to start this again, are we? she thought. He had left only

a brief message in a voice on the edge of a whisper — "I'll see you later" — which caused a tingle down her spine. She listened to it three times.

One more client appointment, and with what were really her last two jobs out of the way, Pru made her way home. Lunch had consisted of a slice of Mrs. Wilson's Victoria sponge. She had one more Waitrose four-mushroom risotto in the freezer. Perhaps she would heat that up and eat just a few bites of it, in case she and Christopher went out for a meal later. Before she could dwell on the possibilities of the evening ahead, her mind circled around to the Wilsons' garden.

She wished she still had her before-and-after photos to look through — before-and-after ivy, she reminded herself, not murder. And then it came to her: She did still have another copy of the photos — on the second flash drive, the copy she had planned to give the Wilsons.

It took her a few minutes to locate it buried at the bottom of her bag, under a small notebook of planting ideas, her change purse, and brochures from the Garden Museum near Lambeth Palace and the Chelsea Physic Garden. She found a hedgehog pin she got when she dropped £1 in a collection box for the Royal Society for the Protection of Birds. She had meant to go back and get two more so she could send them to Lydia's girls but hadn't managed that yet. The accumulated detritus of her year in England, each bit precious.

* * *

Slowly, she clicked through the photos again, wondering if she had missed any clues that might seal the deal on Alf. She saw the photo Christopher had asked her about, showing Malcolm at the top of his basement steps, hands on hips, as if he were talking with someone at the bottom. The police computers could enlarge the photo enough to see the top of someone's head — possibly Alf — but she couldn't see much on her laptop.

She flipped through to the morning of the murder, with the view of the Wilsons' front door. If only she'd been able to plant the pots and add window boxes and . . . Pru looked again at the large man in his socks and no shoes. *Out for a morning stroll?* She tried enlarging the photo to get a better look at him. In his sock feet, carrying a shopping bag and walking past the Wilsons'. Her photo had caught him at the moment he passed the wrought-iron gate at the top of the stairs that led down to their basement. Or did it? It was difficult to tell, but it almost looked as if he had walked not past the stairs and down the pavement, but up the basement stairs. He even had a hand stretched behind him, as if to close the gate.

As she considered that odd possibility, her phone rang. "Pru, it's Lucy. I finally remembered to ask around about Archie Clarke. He isn't in history — he's in the archaeology department."

"Archaeology?" Pru asked, as she headed to the kitchen and pulled the risotto out of the freezer compartment.

"And you might want to tell your inspector about him. Jo said Clarke was on sabbatical, but as it turns out, he was suspended from university over some theft. He had been on a dig early last year, when a silver jug that was intended for the British Museum went missing."

Pru forgot about the container of frozen risotto she held in midair. "He stole it?" she asked.

"Yes," Lucy said. "Well, at least someone phoned in a tip that said he did and that he was about to sell it to a private dealer. He wasn't charged, because the tip came anonymously, and they couldn't track the dealer, and Archie said it was all a misunderstanding, and he had never even seen the silver jug. There was no record of it from the dig, so nothing could be done. But even though he wasn't charged, he and university officials decided it would be best for him to take some time off. He legged it, so to speak, telling anyone who asked he was taking a sabbatical. That's probably why you got your place for a song."

"I wonder if Mr. Wilson knows him," Pru said, getting an uneasy feeling in her stomach.

"Clarke is the university adviser to a local amateur archaeology group," Lucy said.

Pru heard Xanthe's voice in her head. "Are you the American in Archie and Pippa's place?" She had been too distracted to realize how out of place that question was. To her, Archie and Pippa were landlords, not part of Mr. Wilson's group. "I must tell Archie," Mr. Wilson had said — that hadn't sunk in, either.

"The AASL, Amateur Archaeology Society of London?" Pru asked.

"Yes. He and his wife, Pippa, went on almost all their digs. My friend Tommy said that Archie had grown . . . cynical over the last few years. He seemed to resent finding all these valuable pieces of history and handing them over to someone else. Tommy had even heard him muttering, 'And what do you think that would fetch?' when he was examining some artifact."

Pru needed to sit down. In her head, she heard again Mrs. Wilson's voice on the phone that first day. It seemed so long ago, but Mrs. Wilson had told the caller they didn't know anything about a letter or what Jeremy might've said about it.

"Thanks, Lucy, for finding this out."

"I'm sorry it took me so long," Lucy replied. "Are you going to phone Christopher?"

"Yes, yes, I'll do that now, thanks."

Archie and Pippa Clarke, whose house she lived in, knew Jeremy Pendergast and the Wilsons. Did he know Alf and Malcolm, too? Archie Clarke already had been accused once of trying to sell some antiquity that didn't belong to him. So perhaps all those random sightings of the Clarkes hadn't been mistakes after all — they were in town. But the police had questioned everyone in Mr. Wilson's group — didn't that include Archie Clarke?

* * *

Pru heard the knocker and relief flooded through her — good, she thought, Christopher. She could explain in person. But when she opened the door, there stood a tall, bald, heavyset cheerful-looking fellow wearing black gloves and dressed in a plaid jacket with patched elbows.

"Are you Pru? Pru Parke?" he asked. "I'm Archie Clarke." He smiled. "This is my house. Pleased to meet you."

Standing in front of her was the sock man — the fellow caught in her photos carrying a bag, with no shoes on and walking up the Wilsons' basement steps the morning of the murder.

CHAPTER 15

Pru felt as if she'd been punched in the stomach. The blood rushed from her head as thoughts rushed through her mind, one on top of the other. Her photo caught him walking up from a locked basement door — he must have his own key. Was he carrying muddy — or bloody — shoes in the bag? *Does he think I know? Did he think that I knew all along?*

"Mr. Clarke, I didn't realize you'd be back from Italy so soon." Pru's mind raced trying to figure out how to call Christopher and tell him.

He shook out his umbrella. "May I come in? The rain's started up again." Without waiting for an invitation, Archie stepped across the threshold and stood next to Pru, looming large. She stepped back while he dropped the umbrella in the stand, took off his raincoat and hung it on a peg.

"Yes, of course. Would you like some coffee?" she squeaked as her voice deserted her. Her phone was in her pocket; in the kitchen she could text Christopher.

"Thank you, yes."

"I'll just . . ." Pru pointed back to the kitchen, her breathing shallow. "Please make yourself at home. Ha!" She spread her fingers, palms up. "How silly of me. It's your house!"

She backed down the hall to the kitchen as her phone rang. She pulled it out and saw that it was Jo. For a second she froze, wondering what to do. She answered, out of breath.

"Lydia! Hello, how are you? How are things in Dallas?" She raised her voice so that Archie could hear it was no one of any consequence to him. She switched the kettle on.

"Pru?" Jo sounded confused and on the verge of tears. "Pru, it's Jo. Oh God, Pru, I'm so sorry. What have I done? Lucy told me about Archie Clark — Pru, they were in the basement — those were the noises you heard."

Pru forgot her pretense for a moment. "What?"

"They said they needed to retrieve something they had stored down there and they wouldn't bother you — they'd just be in and out. He told me not to mention it to you and that they wouldn't go upstairs. I was going to tell you, anyway, because I didn't think that was fair, but you were so upset when I mentioned them, thinking that you'd have to move out straight away, I just didn't have the heart. I thought they'd be gone — they promised. Then you kept hearing noises, and I wasn't sure what to do." She heard Jo sob. "Pru, I'm so sorry."

Pru heard the anguish in Jo's voice. She couldn't blame her friend for trying to protect her, and yet she couldn't help being exasperated. "Oh, Lydia" — she said the name again loudly so that Archie would hear — "I'm glad you phoned, but as it turns out, I can't talk right now." Jo, please, she thought, you've got to know something is wrong.

Jo sniffed. "Pru, is Christopher there with you?" *Dear Jo, always looking on the bright side.* She thought that Pru and Christopher were having a romantic evening and didn't want to be disturbed.

"No! No, certainly not . . . I'm happy to hear from you . . ." Pru started to panic — Jo wasn't getting it. How did people think of coded messages off the top of their heads? Not a single word came to mind that could convey to Jo what was happening.

"Look, I'll just leave you alone right now, and you ring back when you have the chance, all right?" She heard Jo blow her nose. "I want to explain, and I hope you'll forgive me."

"Oh, Lydia, please tell everyone — really *everyone* — that I am looking forward to getting back to Dallas, I really am."

A second of silence, and then Jo said quietly, "Pru, is something wrong?"

Archie appeared behind her. "Would you like some help?" Startled, she dropped her phone on the floor where it landed screen side up, showing Jo's name as the caller. Her hand shot down to cover the screen and pick it up, and his hand landed on top of hers. "Allow me," he said. His hand felt moist and soft. She shuddered.

"No, thank you, I'm fine." She stuck her phone back in her pocket. "That was my dear friend Lydia, who lives in Texas. That's where I'm from. Texas. Lydia." She felt the need to fill the air with words. "We'll . . . just let the water boil, shall we?"

"Let's forget about the coffee, Pru." He switched off the kettle. "Come with me — I want to talk with you about something."

Pru followed him to the sitting room, keeping her distance. Instead of sitting down, he stood in the middle of the room looking at her computer. There on the screen, he could see himself in his sock feet coming up out of the Wilsons' basement.

He turned to her. "You knew all along, didn't you, Pru? You knew that you had this photo of me coming out of Harry's basement that morning? Were you biding your time hoping you could turn this to your advantage somehow, try to get money out of me?"

Pru's sense of decency made an appearance a millisecond ahead of her fear. "Are you kidding me? You murder a man and then think that somehow I want to make money off it?"

He moved fast for a large man. He shoved her up against the wall and pinned his forearm against her windpipe. He had pulled a small pistol out of his pocket and she felt the cold metal of the barrel pressed to her forehead. "Don't get full of yourself, now, Pru," he said.

Pru cut her eyes over at the sound of a key in the front door, hoping not so much for a rescue as anything that would loosen Archie's arm so that she could breathe. If she lost consciousness, would he shoot?

A woman walked in. "Archie — what are you up to?" she asked with a frown. "Not here, not yet."

"I will not be ridiculed," Archie said. He backed off but kept the pistol pointed at Pru, who gasped for air and coughed.

The woman at the door had short black hair and looked several years younger than Archie. No glasses or blond wig, but her cherry-red lipstick and cherry-red nails on the ends of her stubby fingers stood out like beacons. Pru's stomach gave a lurch as she remembered being pushed out the window. "Romilda?"

"Romilda? Ha-ha-ha-ha-ha. Romilda — my God, you are thick, aren't you?" She dropped the laugh and said, "Right, Archie, let's go."

"Pippa," he said, "hold the gun on her. I want to go down and get the silver jug."

A shot of adrenalin ran through Pru's veins. Romilda — Pippa, Pru corrected herself — was smaller than Archie. Not as small as Jo, but smaller than Pru. If Archie went downstairs, perhaps Pru could do something, distract her, and grab the gun.

"We don't have time for that. We need to leave. Now."

"But Pippa, I remember where it is now, and it's valuable. We could get rid of it right away . . ."

"Archie," Pippa shouted in his face, "*focus.*"

Perhaps, Pru thought, *Archie wasn't the brains behind this plan. On the other hand, he did hold the gun.*

Pippa's orders got both Pru and Archie moving. He draped his raincoat over his arm to hide the pistol, which he shoved into Pru's side. Then, he grabbed one arm, Pippa the other, and they marched her out the door, through the rain and into a waiting cab.

They were cozy in the back of the cab, just the three of them and the gun. Pru could feel it pressed hard into her flesh just below her rib cage. She wondered if Archie had his finger on the trigger. She wondered what would happen if they went over a bump. She tried not to breathe hard, but taking many short shallow breaths made her lightheaded.

The cab was silent. *The driver must already know where we're going*, Pru thought. She knew, too. The Wilsons were out — at the memorial dinner for Jeremy — and so the three of them would have the house and garden to themselves.

When they stopped in front of the house on Chartsworth Square, there were no lights on. Archie pulled her from the cab as Pippa paid. They stood in the rain and watched him drive away. Pru heard Toffee barking a hello at her from behind the upstairs window, then Archie dragged her down the stairs. He pulled out his key.

Once inside, they closed the door, and Pippa turned to Pru. Archie kept the gun in Pru's side, which was already sore, and shoved it harder for emphasis when he talked.

"Stay down here, Pippa. Look for the letter. I'll take her outside," Archie said.

"Jeremy had the letter," Pippa said to Pru as she pulled on a pair of gloves. "But Xanthe gave everything to Harry. We know he ended up with it. Where is it? Where's the letter?"

Pru thought for sure that Christopher would have taken the letter with him after talking with the Wilsons earlier, but if there was no letter to look for, they might both stay with her. If Pippa remained in the basement, she would have only Archie to contend with. Big, lumbering Archie.

"He put it away," Pru said, glancing around the room. "I think he put it over there, to hide it." She nodded toward an enormous stack of loose papers — many more than what Xanthe delivered. The pile teetered on the far edge of Mr. Wilson's desk. *That ought to keep her busy for a while.*

"Harry doesn't keep a very tidy work surface, now does he?" Archie said.

"Harry Wilson is a berk," Pippa spat out the words.

"Pippa," Archie said with reproach.

"This is all his fault," she said. "If he hadn't objected to selling this stuff, we'd never be in the position we are now. All this talk about educational opportunities, pride in our

British history, it makes me sick." She walked over to the pile and picked up a few of the papers. "He talked Jeremy out of the plan, and that makes all this his fault. He as much as forced you to kill Jeremy by being so high and mighty, and so it's just what Harry deserves to get blamed for it all." Pru stood between them, and for a fleeting moment forgot the danger she was in. Instead, she felt a rush of emotion at the thought of Mr. Wilson's altruism. *I knew he had no part in this*, she thought. *I knew it in my heart.*

"Well, you don't need me any longer, do you?" Pru asked as if she'd just given them directions to Westminster Abbey.

"I'll say we don't," Pippa said, a gleam in her dark eyes. "But we couldn't leave you be, Pru, now could we? That's why we went to find you — we couldn't be sure you hadn't cottoned on to what happened with Jeremy. And we can't just let you walk out of here to run to your little inspector fellow."

"Every story needs a big finale, Pru, and you're it," Archie said with a smile. "You and Harry, the two of you taken care of tonight — and we'll be free and clear."

"Go on, Archie," Pippa gestured toward the back garden. As Archie shoved Pru to the door, Pippa said, "Archie, can you do it?"

"Of course I can do it, Pippa," he snapped. "I did it before — I can do it again."

"You were sick for two days after," Pippa said. "We can't have that. We have to move fast. You come back and look for the letter, and I'll take care of her."

Archie shoved Pru out the door, saying over his shoulder, "I've got this."

Pru's mind went numb, not wanting to examine this exchange too closely, barely managing to keep her balance as Archie pushed and pulled her across the muddy garden, the rain pouring down, the pistol still stuck in her side.

He opened the door of the shed and gave her a rough push inside and then followed, pulling a torch out of his raincoat pocket and hanging it on one of the pegs, where its wide beam cast light over the mosaic.

"Start digging."

No need to ask where to dig, Pru thought. She reached for the spade on the ground — the one that Mr. Wilson had chucked back after his own bout of digging — but Archie stopped her.

"No, not that one," he said. With a gloved hand, he took the other spade off the wall and thrust it at her. "This one." He gestured to the hole. She plunged the spade in the wet soil as Archie backed off to the far corner. "We don't want to compromise the fingerprint evidence on the murder weapon," he said.

"They already took that spade," Pru said, but with a stab of fear realized Archie didn't mean Jeremy's murder. This spade, covered with Mr. Wilson's fingerprints, would soon include evidence from Pru — blood, hair, tissue — she remembered with a sickening shock Christopher's description of the first murder.

"They won't believe that for a minute. They already know it's you." Surprised to have found her voice, she lied with as much confidence as she could muster.

"By the time they can figure all that out, after all the moaning and crying about their darling American gardener, we'll be gone," he boasted. "The arrangements are all made." Pru had slowed in her digging, which prompted Archie to wave the gun at her. "Dig."

"I hope you didn't let Alf make the arrangements."

Archie dropped his smirk for a second. "What's that supposed to mean?"

"You haven't noticed he isn't the most reliable fellow?" Pru asked. "You know he broke into a constable's house while the constable was home — how smart was that? And you heard about his idea of pretending to be Scottish and trying to steal money from someone he knew? This is the man who's made your arrangements?" Pru couldn't help rubbing it in. Archie was quiet for a moment.

"Shut your mouth and dig," he said.

A thought occurred to Pru — what seemed like ages ago, she remembered Mrs. Wilson telling her that Alf asked about the "boggy place" at Greenoak in Hampshire. "You thought you could take it from this bog," she said, nodding to the seeping hole in front of her, "and rebury it in the bog at Greenoak, didn't you? You were going to take it to Greenoak and then 'find' it again on Alf's property? That way the artifacts wouldn't belong to the earl, they would belong to Alf, and he could sell it. And hand the money to you."

"He'll get his cut," Archie shouted at her. "Everybody else makes money off history — why shouldn't I?" Archie said, his anger showing again. "Why should I just give it all up to museums and universities? Is that fair? I'm sick of it."

"Mrs. Wilson said that the sale of the house fell through, but that was all a ruse, wasn't it, from the very beginning? Alf told them he was selling Greenoak because he wanted them out of the way so that you could carry out your scheme. But they're on to you now," Pru said, hoping to point out the futility of his plan. "The police, the Wilsons — everyone knows."

"Arrangements have been made," he said in a taunting voice. "We'll be away before they can ever get to us." He noticed again that Pru had slowed. "Open that hole wider!" he shouted.

"It's a poacher's spade," she shouted back, referring to the long but narrow shape of the tool. "It won't make a wide hole quickly." Her spade went down again and hit something hard.

"There now," Archie said, keeping the gun on her, while with his other hand, he popped the top on one of the big rusted tins under the bench and pulled out several large, woven plastic carrier bags from Sainsbury's. "See, I'm all prepared, and no one was the wiser that I came back to tuck these away until it was time. Now, start opening that hole."

"Don't you even care that I could damage it? The only copy in the world of Hadrian's autobiography, and all you care about is getting it into a shopping bag and selling it off?"

He advanced on her, shaking the gun as he did so, and Pru took a step back. "Listen to me, you bloody stupid woman." His anger getting the better of him. "Do you think you're doing yourself any good with this talk? It'll just make killing you all that much easier."

They both heard it. A voice called "Pru?" But because of the noise of the rain on the roof or the distance, Pru couldn't tell who it was.

Archie backed up a couple of steps to look out the door, and as he did so, Pru threw the spade at him, using both hands and aiming high, toward his face. His arms flew up to protect himself, and the gun went off, sending the bullet up through the roof.

She jumped over the exposed mosaic and lunged at him, trying to push him away from the door. She succeeded in knocking the pistol out of his hand, but he grabbed her wrist as he held onto the doorway with the other. She kneed him, and he yelled and let go. She made it out the door by three steps when he jumped her from behind. She landed face down in the mud and couldn't breathe for a moment. Archie was big and heavy, and when he tried to get up, he tripped on one of the stems of ivy she'd left looping up out of the ground and he fell on his stomach with an *oof*. It gave her enough time to crawl away through the mud a few feet.

But he was up to her before she could go far. He stood over her, swaying slightly, and as if trying to steady himself, and waved his arms in small circles like propellers. She sprang up and used the momentum to bring the heel of her hand up striking hard under his chin. He screamed, and blood squirted from his mouth as he dropped onto his backside.

Archie groaned. Pru pulled herself up, trying to catch her breath and think what to do next. Someone grabbed her from behind. She screamed and turned.

"Christopher!" She threw her arms around him. She saw police streaming into the garden.

He held her tight. "Are you all right? Did he hurt you? There was a shot."

"Christopher" — she pulled back to look at him as the words came tumbling out — "he's the sock man, it's his house, my house, and he thought I knew he was the murderer." She knew that made little sense, but all she could do was hit the high points and hope that he would fill in the blanks.

"Yes, yes, we know it's Clarke. Are you hurt?"

"I'm okay — at least I think I am." But a sob caught in her throat, and she threw her arms around him again. "I'm so glad you're here." She held him at arm's length. "Oh no, I've got mud all over your suit."

"Damn the suit, Pru, are you sure you're all right?"

"Yes, I'm just . . ." She looked back to see officers putting handcuffs on Archie. "Pippa," she said in a panic. "Pippa is Romilda. She's in the basement looking for the letter."

"We got her." Christopher stroked her cheek, smearing mud as he did so. She felt the tension begin to drain out of her body and as it did so, her ability to remain standing on her own. She leaned against Christopher and he held her tight with one arm. More help arrived, and the back garden was abuzz with officers on radios, officers on Archie, officers beginning to search the shed, and a female officer waiting nearby.

"Did you call out the whole force?" she asked.

"I did my best. Malcolm phoned me, he phoned 999, and I think he phoned the Wilsons, too. He saw Archie drag you through the garden."

"Malcolm?"

And then she noticed him, hands stuffed into his trouser pockets, standing off to the side of the garden as police moved all around him.

"Pru, are you all right?" Malcolm asked. He had no jacket, and he looked wet and miserable. "I never thought . . . I don't know who this man is." He gestured toward Archie, who still sat in the mud with four officers around him. "I only told Alf . . . well, I'm sorry I told Alf. About your photos."

"Malcolm, thank you for phoning the police," Pru said, as an officer took hold of his arm.

"Sir?"

"Yes, take him in. We'll have a few questions for you, Mr. Crisp," Christopher said without looking at Malcolm.

Pru knew Malcolm was no innocent bystander, but she couldn't help feeling a little sorry for him.

"Will your mother be all right?" she asked.

"Yes, her carer is with her now, thank you, Pru." The officer led him off.

"Sir." Another officer came up to Christopher, nodding his head toward Archie. "We'll have to take him to hospital first. It seems he's got an injury to his jaw and may have bitten through his tongue. There's a fair amount of blood."

Christopher looked at Pru, who smiled but shivered. "Right," he replied. "Post a guard and take him straight to the station after he's patched up." He tightened his grip around her shoulders and said, "Let's get you inside."

There was a commotion at the house, and both Wilsons came swimming through the sea of officers to Pru. Mr. Wilson held up a large umbrella.

"Pru, dear, are you all right?" Mrs. Wilson asked in a rush. "Malcolm rang Harry, but we really couldn't understand what he was saying. Then the police found us at Jeremy's dinner and brought us home." Mrs. Wilson turned to Christopher. "Is she all right, Inspector?"

"Yes, Mrs. Wilson, I'm fine," Pru said, grateful to see them and to know that they were safe. The rain had soaked her through; she had a coating of mud down her front, her hair hung in muddy clumps — she gave a fleeting thought to her hair clip — and it felt as if she'd applied a mudpack to her face. She looked at Christopher. She'd shared a good bit of it with him.

"You need to come inside," Mr. Wilson said. "That's all right, isn't it, Inspector?"

"Of course it is," Christopher said. He leaned close to Pru. "I need to stay out here for now, all right?" She nodded.

"Pru, we'll just get you right upstairs to the shower, shall we?" Mrs. Wilson started to lead her away.

She felt slightly giddy, a reaction to the release of the fear, and the euphoria that followed. At least, that's what she blamed it on, because as Mrs. Wilson led her away, she turned to Christopher and whispered "Wanna come?" She didn't stay to see his reaction.

* * *

Pru took off her shoes at the door, and Mrs. Wilson marched her upstairs to the shower while police swarmed through the house, basement, and garden. The female police officer had offered to stay with her, but Pru said she would be fine and asked if she could give her statement after she'd had a shower.

She left her wet, muddy, bloody clothes in a plastic bag, got in the shower and scrubbed herself hard, trying to clean away both the mud and the thought of Archie's tight grip. She examined her side; a large bruise blossomed where Archie had pushed the pistol into her.

After Pru dabbed ointment on the worst scrapes, Mrs. Wilson gave her an enormous, fluffy terry-cloth robe followed by, when she got downstairs, a large brandy. Pru sat on the sofa in the front room, and gave her statement to an officer. After he left, she stayed put, well away from the activity, alone and quiet. She could hear Mr. Wilson in his basement office on the phone.

She looked up to see Christopher standing in the doorway watching her. Her hair, slicked back and half dry, had started to frizz on the ends; her face was raw with scrubbing.

"I'm irresistible, aren't I?" she asked. "It must be the socks." She put her feet up on the coffee table. She wore a pair of Mr. Wilson's thick wool socks.

Christopher smiled. "How are you feeling?"

Pru held up the brandy, nearly gone. "Not bad. I'm glad you got here when you did. I'm not sure I knew what to do next."

"I was on my way to your place already. We'd discovered that Archie Clarke had been blind-copied on Jeremy's first email to Harry, and that Clarke was the 'A' — that was what you missed when you left here earlier today. I knew the name sounded familiar, and I started to ask you about it this morning, but we got distracted with Vindolanda, and I forgot to get back to it. This afternoon we found out what he'd been up to. Once we saw his faculty photo, we matched it to the photo you took the morning of the murder, and we realized it showed him coming out of the basement."

"Were his shoes in the bag?" she asked.

"Yes. He'd stepped in the blood and thought he'd get rid of them, but all he did was toss them in a skip at a construction site three streets over. They matched another pair of his shoes to the partial print on your post. We hadn't known Clarke was involved with Harry's society — the university adviser wasn't listed on the membership list, and Harry thought he was in Italy."

An officer stopped to say something to him; he replied, and turned back to Pru. "And then awhile ago Jo phoned, saying something was wrong, but she didn't know what. She'd phoned you to explain about letting the Clarkes get into the basement—"

"She didn't know, Christopher," Pru said. "She thought they just needed to get something out of one of their storage boxes."

"Yes, I know. But she wanted to tell me that it was an odd phone conversation, and it worried her. It took her awhile to get through to me, because she phoned the station's number and the desk sergeant . . . well, he'll be spoken to. By the time I arrived at your house, you were gone, but then Malcolm phoned to say he'd seen someone dragging you through the garden here." He frowned as he recounted his movements. "I should've gone to you straightaway. I shouldn't have left you vulnerable to . . ."

"I'm all right — well, now I am. I was afraid at first, then I was angry, then I was afraid again." She thought about her emotions pinballing around during the episode. "I was looking at that photo on my computer when Lucy phoned to tell me about him — I forgot I'd made a copy of the photos on another flash drive. Then Archie showed up at my door and . . ." Pru shuddered.

Christopher looked down at his muddy suit and shoes. She knew what he was thinking. "You stay right where you are, Inspector. Poor Mrs. Wilson, what a mess we've made. Or, I guess I should say, poor Mary — she'll have extra housecleaning duties tomorrow."

"I want to know everything that happened," he said.

"Let's go sit at the kitchen table, how about that?" She picked up her brandy and led the way. They sat across from each other, and Pru told him every detail she could think of, from the mushroom risotto, which she realized she'd left on the kitchen counter, to Archie's plan to plant the digging spade as fake evidence to implicate Mr. Wilson.

"I suppose Malcolm saw Mr. Wilson with the spade yesterday and told Alf and he told Archie. Archie had gloves on and said that way Mr. Wilson would be the suspect again when they found me . . ." Her voice drifted off. Christopher's jaw tightened, and he reached across the table to grab both her hands.

"But look," she said, brightening. "I'm all right."

He did look, one of those long looks that held her gaze. But he couldn't quite let it go.

"All right, yes, I have a few scrapes," she said, "and I've got a sizeable bruise on my side where Archie shoved the pistol." She touched the spot, tender even through the thick layer of terry cloth. Christopher watched her. "That's all."

They sat quietly with their own thoughts. "Christopher, I heard Mr. Wilson on the phone. Are they going to dig it up tomorrow?"

"Yes, it's time we see what's really there. Harry is asking his group, an archaeology firm, people from the both the British Museum and the Museum of London, and probably every academic in the city. With the earl's permission."

"Will you be here?" she asked.

"I wouldn't miss it."

Christopher was called away, and Mrs. Wilson came in. "Pru, dear, I've made up the guest room for you. It's at the back. I hope you don't mind. I've closed the curtains so you don't have to look out on all that. I'll refill your brandy and you take it upstairs and get in bed now. You must be exhausted. I'll bring you up a sandwich."

"Yes, Mrs. Wilson, thanks." Pru realized who was missing from the scene. "Mrs. Wilson, where is Toffee?"

"Toffee is safe and sound in our bedroom, Pru. He wouldn't want to be underfoot."

Upstairs, Pru pulled on the nightgown Mrs. Wilson had laid out on the bed and opened the curtains halfway. She sat on a low bench by the window in the dark room and watched the activity in the back garden. The rain had let up, although everyone looked wet enough that it didn't matter. She ate half the sandwich, used the new toothbrush left for her, closed the curtains, and crawled in bed.

CHAPTER 16

Pru woke slowly from a sound sleep, and the events of the previous evening played out in her mind. She heard a general stirring downstairs. She stretched, threw back the covers, and looked down at her flannel nightgown. She thought of the state of her clothes from last night and wondered whether she would need to wear some of Mrs. Wilson's tweeds today. There was a quiet knock on her bedroom door, followed by Jo's equally quiet voice. "Pru? Are you awake?"

"Yes, come in."

"I've brought you some clothes," Jo said, carrying in trousers and sweater, underwear, and socks and shoes, all from Pru's wardrobe. She set them down and gave her a hug. "Oh Pru, I'm so sorry for what I did. When Christopher rang . . ."

"Jo, you didn't do anything wrong. You were just trying to save me from worrying. If you had told me the Clarkes wanted back in the house to get something, I would've thought they were about to turf me out. You were only trying to help." Pru looked into Jo's face. "This isn't your fault."

"All that talk about mice in the basement," she said sheepishly. "I couldn't understand why they wouldn't leave." She pulled a crumpled paper out of her bag and handed it over. It was the police sketch of Romilda. "I took this," she said. "She looked so familiar, and yet I couldn't quite say it was Pippa. I guess I was in denial."

"When did Christopher ring? Did he tell you everything that happened?" She hoped that Jo would forgive herself and thought that a change of subject would help.

"He rang last night and said you were safe and would stay here. He told me what happened, but of course I need to hear everything from you." Jo sat on the bed with her. "That horrible, horrible man, and to think that I'm the one who arranged your digs."

"It had nothing to do with you. And my only real injury is this bruise." She pulled up the nightgown to reveal a five-inch patch of deep purple and blue on her right side. "That's where he dug the pistol in." Pru could still feel the pressure of the gun in her side. "That was the scariest part. He's an academic — what does he know about guns? I was afraid it might go off accidentally."

As Pru got dressed, she related all the details to Jo that Christopher had left out — she was well able to fill in the dramatic bits now.

"Did the police let you into my . . . the house?" Pru asked.

"When he rang last night, Christopher said Vernona wanted you to stay here, and I told him I'd stop by and get clothes for you, and he said he'd tell his officers that I would be there. Even so, I had to be escorted," Jo said, "and they looked through what I took. There were several of them when I left, mostly in the basement. They were looking for that silver jug Lucy said Archie stole."

"I'll have to get back in and start packing," Pru said, avoiding Jo's eyes.

"Pru, not now, please. Can't you wait and see what happens? You could stay with me." Jo sounded as if she had seized on the perfect solution.

"Yes," said Pru, "and where would I sleep — under the piano? In the kitchen sink?" She thought of her one night on Jo's tiny sofa.

"Well, you could . . ." Jo began.

"No!" Pru held up her finger as a caution. "Don't say it. Don't even think it." She busied herself with her socks. "What am I supposed to say? 'Hello, we barely know each other, but is it all right if I move in?'" She shook her head. "I'm not twenty-five."

"Neither is he, thank God," Jo said, and they both laughed. "Oh, dear Pru." Jo put her arm around Pru's shoulders and gave her a squeeze. "Isn't it difficult being this stubborn?"

Pru didn't reply. It wasn't the first time in her life she'd been accused of that.

She glanced at the closed curtains. "Have they started up out there yet?

"Vernona said people started arriving as soon as it was light," Jo said. "They're lovely people, Pru, Harry and Vernona . . ."

Pru knew where this was going. "I'd say they'll be packing up and moving to Hampshire once they get their house back. And they already have a gardener."

* * *

After Jo left, Pru had tea and toast in the kitchen, watching the parade of people come through and go to the shed. Only one or two police officers remained. Pru thought the rest of the people must be there for the thrill of the dig. She stood at the window and observed the scene outside. Everyone looked excited. There was a great deal of talking and periods of standing around quietly. In groups of two or three, they walked into the shed and out again.

Activity picked up when several people began measuring the shed, the back garden, the wall, the dead birch — they seemed to measure just about anything that held still. Several people made phone calls and others took photos. Occasionally, Mr. Wilson would stop and give her an update.

The sky was clear and the weak sun just warm enough. She stepped out the door and onto the wide landing to watch. The back garden had become an oozy, greasy-look-ing mess with all the rain, made worse by Pru and Archie scuffling around, after that all the police, and now a dozen or more people squishing through. There had been little enough lawn to begin with; what remained had been crushed into oblivion.

She heard Mrs. Wilson greet Christopher. He came out to her and put his hand on the small of her back. And he knew just the right spot. "You're looking cleaner," he said, so that just she could hear. "Did you sleep well?"

"I did, thank you." Pru wondered how such a perfunc-tory inquiry could feel so intimate. "I've cost you a couple of suits, haven't I?"

He smiled. "You're worth a couple of suits. And more." She wished there weren't so many people around. "And how is the dig?" he asked.

"So far," she said, "they've talked about whether or not they should remove the shed before they start digging. Some people say yes, they should, because it would give them better access to the site, while others say no, the shed is a good pro-tection for the site against the weather. Someone suggested removing the shed, but replacing it with a large tent . . ." Christopher started to gently knead the spot on her lower back, and she lost her concentration.

He had that ghost of a smile. "A tent?"

"Mmm?" She tried to refocus. "Yes, a tent. Lots of peo-ple seem to like that idea, but they haven't quite committed to it, because there were several other people who haven't yet arrived, and they need everyone's approval. And then there's the subject of how large the tent should be, who will set it up, and who will be here to monitor the whole process." She smiled at him. "I fear we won't see any letters from Hadrian today."

He drew close, but seemed to realize where they were at the last second, and instead straightened and looked out onto the landscape.

"The garden's a mess," he said.

Pru burst out laughing, shattering the quiet contemplation of the academics. Heads turned, and she clamped her hand over her mouth, but that didn't help — she couldn't stop laughing, and so she retreated to the kitchen. Christopher followed.

She regained control of herself, wiped the corner of her eye, and sighed. "I guess I won't put this job on my CV."

One of the remaining uniformed officers called Christopher into the front room as Mrs. Wilson finished pouring up a tray full of mugs for everyone in the garden.

"Let me carry that out," Pru said, and took the tray. Mrs. Wilson followed with a plate of Mary's shortbread.

"Now let's go in, sit down, and have our own," Mrs. Wilson said.

Pru took a mug in to Christopher, who stood in the front room talking on his phone, before she returned to sit with Mrs. Wilson in the kitchen.

"I'm sorry I didn't get to build a garden for you," Pru said, "but I'm so happy that you're able to go back to Greenoak."

"We'll expect a visit from you just as soon as you can get there, dear," she said. She continued talking about their house and how she'd already phoned her old Women's Institute chapter and had been put back on the competitions committee. Pru pictured herself going down for a visit — it was all too easy a dream to dream — but found that it made her eyes prick with tears. She took a breath and turned her attention to Mrs. Wilson and the subject of finding enough WI members willing to teach knitting at the local primary school.

* * *

Christopher got off the phone and sat with them at the table just as Mr. Wilson came in to give a report.

"We're moving slowly," he said, "so as not to disturb anything. But we've found the third coin, the last one that Thomas Gaskell returned to the hole as the marker."

"Mr. Wilson," Pru said, "I hit something when . . . when Archie made me start digging." Christopher reacted to this by grabbing her hand and holding it tight. She smiled at him. It was a memory of fear now, and not the fear itself. She squeezed his hand. "Do you think that I might have struck the actual wooden tablets?"

"We believe that there is a covering, perhaps another piece of mosaic or tile of some kind that covers the collection of tablets," Mr. Wilson said. "But it may take us a while to get to that part of the excavation — it's a delicate operation." Mr. Wilson glanced out the window. "And to think that Archie was going to dump it all in shopping bags. Had he lost his mind?"

"Is he talking, Inspector?" Mrs. Wilson asked Christopher. Pru suspected that she might be a fan of detective shows.

"He isn't talking very much at the moment," Christopher said, with a sideways glance at Pru, "but that may be because he has several stitches in his tongue."

Mrs. Wilson said, "You're brave, Pru, to stand up to someone like that."

"I got the feeling that it was Pippa who was in charge," Pru said, "and Archie was the muscle."

"Pippa's been running Archie ragged since they married five years ago." Mr. Wilson shook his head.

A man with silver-gray hair and wearing a black-and-white sweater put his head in the door. "Harry? We're looking at where to put the poles for the marquee. Can you come out?"

Mr. Wilson stood up and said, "Everyone, this is Dr. Timothy Morrison, Oxford. You know Vernona, of course, and this is Pru Parke . . ."

Dr. Morrison interrupted him. "Are you the young woman who saved the tablets?"

Pru laughed at the compliment. "I'm happy to have helped."

"And Detective Chief Inspector Christopher Pearse." Mr. Wilson finished the introductions and then left with

Dr. Morrison to discuss the marque. Mrs. Wilson started another round of coffees.

Christopher and Pru stayed seated, holding hands. "Oh, by the way," he said, reaching into the inside pocket of his jacket and pulling out an envelope that looked as if it had been rolled up. She saw the letterhead. "Do you know someone named Duxton Stewart? She apparently used your phone to ring Hodges & Hodges Appraisals."

He watched her face. Disguising her phone number wasn't as foolproof as she had thought. She could feel the color start to creep up her cheeks.

"It was just a phone call. I did phone and pretend to be her, but I only did it to find out if they would tell me what they were going to auction off and only because I wanted to make sure that Mr. Wilson had nothing to do with it, which I'm sure was the case. Wasn't it?"

She saw that ghost of a smile. He opened the letter for her to see.

"Collingford, the man you spoke to on the phone — that is, the man Duxton Stewart spoke to — is an old school friend of Harry's," he said. "Knowing his interest in archaeology, Collingford wrote to say he had a client — he couldn't name him — who wanted to set up a private auction of a few Roman items. Harry gave me the letter, and I spoke to Collingford yesterday to find out that it had been Archie trying to set something up. Harry had thought it was Alf."

Pru read through the letter as he spoke and looked at the closing. Between "Best," and "Gabriel Collingford" was a scribbled signature, a single name. "Is it signed . . . Stinky?"

Christopher took the letter and returned it to its envelope. "British old-school nicknames."

"Did you have a nickname at Oxford?"

"Well," he said, standing, "I believe it's time for me to leave."

Pru walked him to the door. He would leave tomorrow first thing for the weekend to help his son, Graham, with his university study in the Lake District. That cut her already precious time with him short, but she would not let that color what they had left. As they stepped outside, Mrs. Wilson came to the door, too. "Inspector," she began.

"Christopher, please," he said.

"Christopher, we're having a small dinner party this evening for Pru. We hope you'll come. We didn't think she should be alone tonight."

"Yes, thank you, I'll be here." The door closed and he said, "I didn't think you should be alone tonight, either."

Pru smiled. "The Wilsons invited me to stay here for a few days. Your sergeant told me that I can go back into my house this afternoon, as long as an officer is there. I have to start packing."

His smile faded as he watched her.

"You're very silent on this subject," Pru said as she looked down.

"I don't want to make you feel worse than you already do," he said.

"I don't believe that's possible."

His phone rang.

He didn't make a move to answer it until she kissed him lightly. "See you this evening." As she closed the door, she heard him answer, "Pearse."

Without the hope of a world-famous archaeological discovery anytime soon, Pru decided she'd get some air. She walked back to the kitchen and said, "Mrs. Wilson, I think I'll take Toffee for a walk."

* * *

The evening atmosphere in the kitchen was festive. Mr. Wilson opened the wine, Jo chopped vegetables for the salad, and Lucy and Cordelia offered to lay the table. Pru had just opened the oven door for Mrs. Wilson to take out a lasagna left by Mary when they heard the knock. Everyone looked at Pru.

"Oh," she said, looking around at their pointed stares, "let me get that."

"Hello," she said to Christopher as he stepped in, a bottle of wine in one hand. She took his other hand and slipped it around her waist. He kissed her softly.

"I'm happy you're here," she said. "I'm happy to have all of you together this evening." *My farewell dinner.* Her smile faded.

Christopher held her close with his free arm and began, "Don't you want to . . ."

"Pru, dear?" Mrs. Wilson called out from the kitchen. "Red or white?"

"Red, please, Mrs. Wilson," she called back, determined to regain her good mood. "For both of us."

As she took his hand and they walked down the hall, Christopher said, "We'll talk on Monday."

She turned back and gave him a sly smile. "Is that what we're going to do on Monday? We're going to talk?"

He had just enough time to give her bottom a pat before they walked into the kitchen.

As Jo and Lucy carried the food to the table, Pru saw Christopher take Mr. Wilson aside and talked quietly for a few minutes. She wondered if Mr. Wilson would be in any trouble for withholding evidence — the emails sent to him from Jeremy — but thought that couldn't be the case, because both men ended the conversation by shaking hands.

Over dinner Mrs. Wilson said, "Christopher, Pru says that you work for country matters. I want you to know that at Greenoak we never trap, and we have our own badger sett, just at the edge of the wood. I hope you'll come down and see it sometime." Mrs. Wilson pointedly looked at Pru, who smiled at her.

Pru listened to the talk around the dinner table and thought, *this is my family — the sum total of my life in England.* The conviviality of the company, a glass or two of wine, and Christopher sitting across the table from her made Pru almost believe that it would be possible to stay without money, without a job, without a place to live. Tomorrow it would be a different story, but for tonight, she could pretend.

They all needed to tie up loose ends. Having had little time alone with Christopher, Pru took the opportunity to ask, "What about Malcolm?"

"Malcolm is in serious trouble," Christopher said. "He may not have had direct knowledge of the murder, but he believed everything that Alf told him — that Archie told Alf — he kept back information and he followed directions. He was the one who planted the coin on Harry's desk. He really did believe that Harry killed Jeremy."

"He phoned you when he saw Archie drag me through the garden," Pru said, "and he phoned 999 when I fainted Tuesday morning. Although I suppose he was told to be there and watch me. And there's his mother."

"Those things may help his case," Christopher said, "but it's really up to the courts now."

"And Alf?" Pru asked.

Mr. Wilson supplied that information. "Alf was a stooge. He didn't really know what Archie was about. Christopher says they caught up with him this afternoon in Southampton — what did he think he was going to do, steal away on a packet to Australia?"

Mr. Wilson had apparently had a moment to fill his wife in on the details, because she didn't look surprised. "But he helped in the end, didn't he?" asked Mrs. Wilson. "He kept records and photos and even a voice recording of Archie and his scheming. That will help, won't it, Christopher?"

"It will indeed help."

Mrs. Wilson looked down in her lap. "Alf wouldn't really have hurt Pru, I'm sure of it. And Harry understands that Alf wouldn't have let him be arrested for murder."

Those claims hung in the air above the dinner table for a moment, no one wanting to dispute Mrs. Wilson's kind but misguided effort to excuse her brother's inept criminal activity. Mr. Wilson broke the silence, saying in a quiet voice, "It's all right, Vernona." And to Christopher, "They weren't the most polished criminals, I expect."

"No," Christopher said, "but that doesn't mean they weren't dangerous." He gave Pru a quick glance. She still found it difficult to believe that Malcolm — or Alf, whom she had not even met — could be dangerous. But then, she would never have thought a professor of archaeology capable of murder.

"Do you know who Archie was planning to sell the letters to — or the silver jug?" Mr. Wilson asked.

"Clarke gave us a name, but it's a fake, and that person was probably not the final buyer, just a go-between. So, we're still looking," Christopher said.

When the plates were empty and the wine glasses drained, Jo announced, "Right, everyone go sit down and get comfortable. Vernona and I will clear away and take out the coffee."

* * *

Conversation over coffee continued but grew quieter and quieter until they heard Cordelia snore. It was time to be off. Pru said goodbye to Lucy and Cordelia, making sure she didn't sound maudlin. Jo would spend the weekend helping her clear out of 72 Grovehill Square.

Mr. Wilson shook hands with Christopher, said good night to Pru, and followed his wife upstairs. Christopher stood by the fireplace examining a book while Pru turned off a few of the many lamps around the room. As Mr. Wilson's figure receded, Pru said in a loud whisper, "Oh good, Mom and Dad have gone upstairs. Now we can make out on the sofa."

Christopher smiled and met her in the middle of the room, slipping his arms around her waist. She flinched as he touched her bruise.

"I'm sorry, I forgot," he said with concern.

"It's just in an awkward place," she said, and smiled. "Aim high. Or low." He watched her with an arched eyebrow. She gave a little gasp. "Oh, that's much better."

The reminder of her injury brought a frown to his face. "I'm sorry he hurt you," he said, his lips against her forehead.

"Oh, Pru," Mrs. Wilson called from upstairs.

"Yes?"

"I'll just leave the landing light on for you, shall I, dear? You can switch it off when you come up."

"Yes, ma'am," Pru said, not letting go of Christopher.

"Goodnight, Christopher," Mrs. Wilson called down.

"Goodnight, Mrs. Wilson."

"Vernona," they heard Mr. Wilson's voice faintly pleading, "let them alone."

"Well, Harry, she's been through such an ordeal, and she's exhausted . . ." Mrs. Wilson's voice faded, and they heard a *click* as the bedroom door shut.

Things were just getting interesting when the clock began to strike midnight.

Pru pulled back and looked at him. "What time is your train in the morning?" she asked in a whisper.

"Four fifty."

"Oh, dear." She kissed him once more and said, "Go home. You won't be any use to Graham if you fall asleep on the job."

* * *

Over the weekend, she finished packing up her meager existence and said her goodbyes to the Wilsons, who had begun to box up their possessions in preparation for the removals van. Simon Parke, eager to get back into the garden at Greenoak, had already phoned them. "You'll come down to see us when you come back from Texas," Mr. Wilson said. "We'll be settled, and we've plenty of room for you." Pru admired his wishful thinking and smiled at him, but said nothing.

"I'll be back Monday," Christopher had said before he left her Thursday night. "An early-afternoon train, and we'll have the rest of the day and evening together."

But there was no rest of the day. British rail workers called a surprise, one-day strike Monday, throwing the travel plans of hundreds of thousands of commuters and travelers into chaos. By the time Christopher and Graham arrived at the bus station in Cockermouth, given a lift by the farmer who owned the remote river cottage they had rented, no chance remained of finding any kind of transport anywhere in the Lake District. Christopher phoned several times during the day, reporting on their lack of progress. Pru could hear the anger and frustration in his voice.

Their tortuous journey back began in Cockermouth at four o'clock Tuesday morning with a bus to Keswick, and then another bus to Penrith before they could get a train that took them into Euston by late morning. Christopher had to go directly to the police station.

* * *

"I came to say goodbye." Pru stood just inside the door of Christopher's office. She meant to make this short and clean — she didn't want to break down in the middle of the station. He stood behind his desk holding a file. He looked terrible, unshaven, eyes red-rimmed.

"I'm so sorry." He slammed the file down. "Bloody British rail system."

She smiled a cheerful, fake smile. "You couldn't do anything about that. I don't have much time. Jo is taking me to Heathrow."

"Are you sure you want to leave now?"

"It isn't as though I didn't try. It just didn't work out."

"If you were to stay . . ." Christopher said.

Pru pressed her lips together to keep her chin from quivering. She had tried. She had failed. She couldn't accept anyone else's terms — even if it meant forfeiting what could be . . . Pru slammed the door on those thoughts.

"I can't," she whispered, her voice deserting her. "I don't know how . . ." She meant to say she didn't know how to make that leap, but could go no further.

As he moved around the desk toward her, a uniformed officer stuck her head in the door. "Sir? Sorry to disturb you, but the chief super is waiting."

Before anything else could happen, Pru widened her fake smile and said, "Goodbye." She almost added, "I'll phone you," but couldn't bring herself to leave on such a cheap note. She slipped out the door.

* * *

Pru walked back and arrived on her front step not a moment too soon. She had trouble fitting the key in the lock, as it appeared to be floating through the sea of tears. She left the door open slightly for Jo, who would be around in fifteen minutes to take her to Heathrow. The house was clean and everything packed up or given away except for, on the kitchen counter, a box of her favorite tea, Yorkshire Gold, opened just a few days ago. Pru looked at the box for a few seconds, and then turned it upside down, dumping the tea bags into her canvas bag.

The post from Saturday caught her eye. She'd left it on the counter not wanting to pile bad news onto her already fragile emotional state. There was a letter from Primrose House. She knew it was the rejection had expected. The letter taunted her, daring her to open it.

Could she not just for once give up a tiny bit of control and step into the unknown without a plan — at least, without a plan of her own devising? She picked up and fingered the unopened envelope with a small frown on her face. She set the envelope back on the counter, then snatched it up again, ripped it open and pulled out the letter. She straightened herself, putting on her invisible armor against inevitable defeat, and scanned the contents.

"Pru?" She turned to see Christopher, out of breath, standing in the kitchen doorway. Once again, she was on the ledge, toes hanging out into midair, and he was holding out his hand. "I want you to stay. Please."

His tie was crooked, and the sight of it brought the tears back to her eyes. She looked down at the letter again, reading the few lines once more.

"Pru?"

She fairly flung herself into his arms. Catching him off guard, they both staggered a bit before finding equilibrium. She kissed him and leaned her head back so that she could see his brown eyes, that gaze that could see right through her. She laughed, and kissed him again, as she let go of the letter and it drifted to the floor.

Primrose House

Bells Yew Green Royal
Tunbridge Wells East
Sussex TN3 9BJ

20 October

72 Grovehill Square
Chelsea
London SW3

Dear Pru,

We thoroughly enjoyed meeting you last Thursday week! Your enthusiasm for and knowledge of English gardening far surpasses anyone else we have met, and it's with a great deal of pleasure that we offer you the post of head gardener at Primrose House.

Please, please phone us the moment you receive this letter (0871 951 9177), as we are eager to discuss details — including accommodations (don't worry, we feel sure that the cottage conversion will be finished quite soon!) We hope you can assume your post as head gardener just as soon as possible, so that you can begin rebuilding what we know will be a lovely and historic landscape.

Our very best,
Davina and Bryan (Templeton)

THE END

AUTHOR'S NOTE

Thanks to Mary for suggesting the Potting Shed books and for the great support of my writing group: Kara Pomeroy, Louise Creighton, Deb Slivinsky, and Joan Shott. Dear friend and editor Mary-Kate Mackey, with her keen understanding of character and plot, greatly improved that first meager draft.

Thanks to the folks at Random House and Alibi for this opportunity, editor Kate Miciak for first spotting *The Garden Plot*, and editor Dana Edwin Isaacson, whose enthusiasm and guidance are beyond worth. Copy editor Kelly Chian's sharp eye kept me from slip-ups. My first agent, the late Kit Ward, started me on this journey, and now Colleen Mohyde has graciously carried on — many thanks.

Thanks to those from the University of Washington who provided facts that I mixed with fiction: Dr. Alain Gowing and Joshua Hartman, who translated Hadrian's letter from English into the Latin of Hadrian's time.

Read more about Roman Britain in *Roman England* by John Burke (W.W. Norton & Company, 1984) and *Ancient Roman Gardens* by Linda Farrar (Stroud-Sutton, 1998).

Vindolanda, the British Museum, and the Museum of London tell the story of the wooden tablets found in the 1970s and of Hadrian.

Thanks to family, friends, and colleagues for their unfailing support.

ADDITIONAL NOTE

Many thanks to Joffe Books, publishing director Kate Lyall Grant, and to my agent Christina Hogrebe (Jane Rotrosen Agency) for re-publishing my Potting Shed series!

THE JOFFE BOOKS STORY

We began in 2014 when Jasper agreed to publish his mum's much-rejected romance novel and it became a bestseller.

Since then we've grown into the largest independent publisher in the UK. We're extremely proud to publish some of the very best writers in the world, including Joy Ellis, Faith Martin, Caro Ramsay, Helen Forrester, Simon Brett and Robert Goddard. Everyone at Joffe Books loves reading and we never forget that it all begins with the magic of an author telling a story.

We are proud to publish talented first-time authors, as well as established writers whose books we love introducing to a new generation of readers.

We have been shortlisted for Independent Publisher of the Year at the British Book Awards three times, in 2020, 2021 and 2022, and for the Diversity and Inclusivity Award at the Independent Publishing Awards in 2022.

We built this company with your help, and we love to hear from you, so please email us about absolutely anything bookish at feedback@joffebooks.com

If you want to receive free books every Friday and hear about all our new releases, join our mailing list: www.joffebooks.com/contact

And when you tell your friends about us, just remember: it's pronounced Joffe as in coffee or toffee!

Made in the USA
Las Vegas, NV
24 November 2023

81417681R00166